TRANQUEBAR
A PACK OF

Urmilla Deshpande lives in Tallahassee, Florida with her family. Modelling, photography, editing and motherhood prepared her to write. She never thought she would follow in the footsteps of her mother, Gauri Deshpande, and her grandmother, Irawati Karve. But at forty-six, this is her first book, and won't be her last.

A Pack of Lies

URMILLA DESHPANDE

TRANQUEBAR

TRANQUEBAR PRESS
An imprint of westland ltd
571, Poonamallee High Road, Kamaraj Bhavan, Aminijikarai, Chennai 600 029
No.38/10 (New No.5), Raghava Nagar, New Timber Yard Layout, Bangalore 560 026
Survey No. A - 9, II Floor, Moula Ali Industrial Area, Moula Ali, Hyderabad 500 040
Plot No 102, Marol Coop Ind Estate, Marol, Andheri East, Mumbai 400 059
47, Brij Mohan Road, Daryaganj, New Delhi 110 002

First published in TRANQUEBAR PRESS by westland ltd 2009

10 9 8 7 6 5 4 3 2 1

This is a work of fiction. Names, characters, places and incidents are either the
product of the author's imagination or are used fictitiously and any resemblance to
any actual person, living or dead, events or locales is entirely coincidental.

ISBN 9789380032832

Typeset in Palatino Linotype by SÜRYA, New Delhi
Printed at GH Prints Pvt. Ltd. New Delhi

For my mother, Gauri Deshpande,
I wish she could have read this.

And for Ashish, who I hope will read it.

Acknowledgements

My enormous thanks and, as Prita says, many loves, to my many loves:

My sisters Saheli Singh, Meithili Mitchell and Joseph Hellweg (half, full, and male) who convince me every day that life without sisters is no life at all.

My children Tissa and Sukhi.

Pat Regan who trusted me with his book, and sent love and encouragement for mine.

Nikki Bedi, who was always there, through children, cats, men and miles.

Paul Mitchell (Ralf), my very first, very patient and generous editor.

Bruce Drummond, quiet spirit and loud talent.

Will Moore who gave me unbridled criticism and insisted on getting it right.

Sheila Curran and John Corrigan, Jane Macpherson, Julianna Baggott and Dave Scott, Julia and Philip Sura, Joanna Mateo, Laurel Blackburn, Brian Tranmer, Kathy Berger, Drew Ericson and Tracy Sumner, Paul Shepherd, my beautiful friends, who make Tallahassee home.

Chanda Nimbkar and Gavan Bromilow, I cherish your delight and your oats.

Peter Susewind, an unexpected German.

Shashi Deshpande, who found me, gave me to Tranquebar, and in whom I found a friend.

The fabulous Tranquebar women:

Nilanjana Roy, who asked—no, told me to write this book— and asked the questions that demanded the hard answers.

Prita Maitra, my editor, who sent me patience and tolerance, and many, many loves.

Subhashree Krishnaswamy, who, in the summer of 2008, softly informed me that I was a writer.

Frank-Udo Tielmann, in whose presence, in his grandfather's chair in an aerie in Cologne I found it in me to finish this book.

$\mathcal{M}$y mother named me Virginia, but she never called me that. Usually she didn't call me anything. And when she did it was 'Ginny', or 'Gin'. On those occasions I heard the whole name, pronounced emphatically with an edge-of-a-knife sharpness, I knew I was in trouble. Sometimes it was the last word I heard in days.

I always wondered why Virginia, why that particular Virginia. It was hopeful in some way—either she wanted me to be a writer, or then a virgin, or she wanted me to weigh myself down with the pebbles of my thoughts, and drown myself in the ocean of life. That was an unfair, nevertheless, recurring thought about the woman who had named me, but also, had taught me to swim. Perhaps teaching me to swim, literally, absolved her of the responsibility to teach me to swim metaphorically: she had made sure I would not drown literally, then, but I would, and perhaps did almost drown in that other, most imperceptible way. This kind of drowning is not as dramatic, as immediate, as obvious as the watery death. But it is drowning, and not obvious until it is too late.

We sat on the stairwell outside the Intensive Care Unit and held each other's hands, my sister and I, waiting for the doctor to come out and tell us that our mother was dead. This doctor had been her childhood sweetheart, she had turned him down when he had asked her to marry him. This man could have been my father. He had come out twenty minutes before, and said, 'We have to try, you know. We have to do what we can to keep your Ami alive.'

And I had said to him, 'Why? And for how long? A few more hours? Days? Let her go, let her be.' And he had looked at me with those eternally sad doctor's eyes and said, 'Yes . . .' and patted my hand awkwardly and turned and gone back into those innards of the hospital that are out of bounds except in that final circumstance. Inside, where I had been, where I had left my mother, when she had left me, when her eyes no longer knew me, her hands no longer held mine holding hers, she had the look my child had when he had cried himself to sleep after the pain menacing him for hours had finally let him go. The pain had let her go, or she, after holding onto it for so long, the last touch of life, she had let it go, knowing she was letting life go. And so I let her go.

People skirted around the two of us on their way in and out, lost in their own troubles, and I thought, their memories of this time would always be, like my own, soaked in the smell of this place. No, it wasn't bleach and Lysol. It was the delicious hot homely comfortable smell of boiled rice and fried mustard and cumin. The hospital kitchen must have been near that stairwell, and the smell carried up to us, a reminder of life, of the vitality of the senses, of this mother's cooking.

She had not always been a good cook. There were times, when I was little, when she would give me slices of white bread and poisonous yellow butter for dinner, and I thought it a treat. She even put sugar on it sometimes, in a thick layer, and then it was a real treat. But sugar was probably expensive, and she didn't buy it very often, and didn't take any in her coffee. I was seven, we had just moved to Bombay, the big city, I didn't know how big, we were in a little apartment, just her and me. I didn't know why my father was not around anymore, why we weren't in the big house with the cats and the two maids to oil and comb and braid my hair, iron my uniform, give me milk and a snack when I got home from school, one young and cheerful, the other, a bitter and mostly toothless walnut, and my grandfather's dapper driver to take me wherever I needed to go, my beloved piano lessons or to St Mary's school in my bright blue ironed uniform and my polished black shoes. I never polished them, or even knew they needed to be, I just put them on where I found them, at the bottom of the stairs, waiting for me each morning, shiny Mary Janes. But I learned to polish shoes, in Bombay. When I went to my new school and the principal pointed out my scuffed shoes in the morning assembly, I came home and told my mother that I needed my shoes polished.

'You'll have to do it then,' she said. It was a week of humiliation, though, before she had enough money to buy polish. When I got it, I read the instructions on the precious little can, it had a picture of a weird bird on it—a kiwi—and I polished those shoes. They sucked in the polish that I patted on them with the edge of an old t-shirt. I went at them with the brush, the wrist's flick motion getting better with each successive stroke. Then I buffed them with the t-shirt till they were shiny crow's-wing black. The principal nodded acknowledgement at me the next morning, and life improved. I was always hungry, but my shoes were polished. I sat under a tree at lunch time and ate the three or four Glucose biscuits I had in a little box, and drank lukewarm water from my grey plastic bottle, and that would keep me going for a while. But soon enough, I was hungry again. My class teacher came by one day, and said, 'Child,' (they always called everyone 'child'. I suppose it was kind and comforting, and they didn't have to remember the names of all the self-effacing girls of my type) 'what did you have for lunch?' I was terrified, I thought I must have done something wrong. I would have burst into tears, but I didn't ever do anything that dramatic. I melted.

'Come with me,' she said, and I followed her into the giant school cafeteria, and nearly fainted from the smell. The school was a Parsi orphanage that allowed a small number of day students. The big hall smelled of hot spicy meat, boiled potatoes, rice, things I had not smelt, let alone seen or eaten, in six months. She marched into the office with me snivelling behind her, and asked the head lunch lady to see if I was on the ledger. And then she said, 'You come here tomorrow at lunch time. To eat. And every day you eat lunch here.'

My mother had signed me up for the free school lunches, but had neglected to tell me.

I found out what days without hunger could be. I went to the cafeteria, stood in line with a tin pan, received a huge dollop of whatever they were serving, ate it all, and didn't get hungry again until almost dinner time. I still think Parsi food is some of the best in the world. The way they spice the ground lamb, all the grease floating on the surface to be soaked up in gobs onto fresh rolls, their biryani made with unidentifiable parts of chicken, great hunks of potato waiting to be discovered in mounds of steaming rice fragrant with cardamom and way too many peppercorns, beans, boiled to a pulp, hardly any colour left in them, and probably no nutrition, but how I loved them. The other girls piled theirs on my plate, they would not stoop to eating those green beans. I love them to this day. They make them the same way in the school cafeterias here in the American south, and they sit there proudly next to the fried chicken in the buffet trays. I find them in my child's school and eat them with a secret longing, and they bring tears to my eyes. Yes, boiled green beans were my friend. They staunched that eternal one-sided conversation between my stomach and me.

And in Bombay I found the aggressor in me, someone who came out and fought back, someone who knew words that could hurt and shock people, someone who could fly at a boy twice her size and knock him to the ground if the situation called for it. Someone who protected me. My mother laughed when the parent of that boy came to complain that I had beaten her child. The boy was at least a foot taller than me, and certainly two feet wider. I had found him poking a stick at a kitten under a parked car, and had made the mistake of requesting him to leave it alone. He had started poking the stick at me.

Men are much larger and impossible to stop if they want to fuck you, I found out later, but this boy was only ten, and fortunately for me, didn't have any idea that I was of the female persuasion. It was a long time before anyone found that out. I wore shorts and t-shirts, had no breasts, and my mother took me to the men's barber shop where haircuts were cheap, sat me down in the chair, and had me clipped every time she could afford it. She didn't tell the barber I was not a boy, and he didn't ask. He did give me a lollipop after each haircut, which he didn't give any of the other real boys, so maybe he knew.

Sometimes my mother would send me to visit my grandparents in their town, a four-hour train ride south, and I would get a taste of that old life we had had, and it was good, to sit at a dining table, to be served real food, to be taken shopping for new shoes in a car. But I was used to being on my own by then, and I didn't want the constant supervision that came with the comforts of home that I had stopped missing a long time ago anyway. I was used to scarfing down as much as I could when I got food, like a dog, looking over my shoulder to see if there were other dogs with their eye on my lunch, like it was my last meal, or one that had to last me till my next one, whenever that would be. I was used to wearing what I wanted, coming and going as I pleased, answerable to no one as long as I was home at seven-thirty every day. At my grandparents' house there were three meals a day, like clockwork. I could depend on them. But I didn't know how not to pile up my plate and suck up all the food in minutes, I didn't know how to tell them where I was going and with whom, I didn't know how to be accountable, to be around people that cared for my practical existence. I went off for a walk in the hills behind their house one day in the summer holidays, and when I got back, my grandmother was in her bed, my grandfather was pacing the long living room with his walking stick. They had placed a phone call to my mother. A phone call. We had no phone, so they must have had to call the neighbours, and ask for my mother to be brought over there. To have to make a long-distance call because something I had done was simply unacceptable. I had caused my grandmother stress, but I didn't understand the significance of that, I didn't know what angina was. I was sent back home the next day, and my mother didn't say anything. She didn't say anything for a long time. And by that I mean, she didn't say a word. Not a single word. I learned about deafening silences. The loneliness of not being acknowledged was terrifying. I tried doing things to make her see me. First I did good things—chores— I washed the dishes, I tidied things, I threw the garbage into the chute. Then I did the big thing—I cleaned my room. She walked past me, she looked through me, she said nothing at all. I began to imagine I may not be there. That I was a creation of my own imagination. I looked in the mirror a lot. I broke a teacup that was part of a set I knew she loved. She just picked up the pieces and threw them in the trash. I ironed a nylon t-shirt so it melted and stuck onto the iron. I threw fried eggs in the kitchen sink so it clogged up and overflowed. And then, almost two weeks into this, I had a breakthrough. I slammed the door of the apartment as I walked in. And she looked up from her typewriter right into my eyes, and through a hard clenched mouth said, 'What do you want from me?'

I thought, though I didn't answer her, that I would have liked to be yelled at, to be hit even, to be acknowledged in some, any way. As a bad person, as a shitty child, as anything. I just wanted her not to look past me anymore. There wasn't anyone else in my life. I had changed schools too often to have any real friendships with classmates, or relationships, good or bad, with teachers. There wasn't another parent, or uncles, cousins, grandparents. There was, as she herself once said, just her and me. And I needed her more than she needed me. It was the indifference, I suppose, that killed me. The negation. I recognise it today, when a friend, or man in my life, is too busy to acknowledge me, I get that same feeling of the child who feels always in an adult world, afraid to take someone's time, even more afraid to ask for attention.

How far are we willing to go, to get that attention without actually asking for it? I follow the same patterns I did before. First I do the good things. I clean up, smell nice, I lay out the goods. These things didn't work with my mother, but men are not mothers. This is so easy at age thirteen, there's an aura about thirteen-year-olds that is irresistible to men. They might pretend it's affection for a niece, or love and concern for a step-daughter. But it's the smooth just-popping-up breasts, the smooth never-had-hair pubic candy, the smooth unstretched-out-by-births-and-hormones ass and belly, and best of all, the smooth never-been-into-cunt, too smooth and vanilla to be even called a cunt yet. There has to be another name for the thirteen-year-old virgin cunt. ***. We'll call her ***. I carried her between my legs, a burden, a strength, a magnet, a force for good or evil. Mostly evil. In fact, all evil. If there is such a thing as evil. To me it was just life, survival. Not in the way of my next meal or anything that dramatic. Just my next quota of attention.

I carried her around for a long time, all of two years. She was more and more of a burden, but by the time I was fifteen, it was hard for people not to notice that smell. They didn't know what it was but it drew them all, men, women, children, cats and dogs. The men for ... oh, I don't know what, the women perhaps curiosity or social work, children, because sexuality is a cheerful thing—or can be—and cats and dogs, it's natural for them to go where it smells interesting. And what smells more interesting than sex? They don't know what it is that they respond to. They just do.

I went through two years of co-ed boarding school—they surely smelt it then—the ooze, the promise, the want. They had no idea what to do with it, though. So a few gropes in the dark, behind the boys' hostel, was all I could extract from the slightly older ones, the ones who at least recognised that smell, the possibilities. But there was nothing there really, just possibilities. A sense of the possibilities. A sense of the world out there of touch, of being. Like standing on the seashore and having a sense of sharks and sardines. And I eventually had my share of sardines. And yes, a few sharks too. But you do have to jump in the ocean for those. And find out you can't swim.

My mother could swim. She was long-limbed and supple and learned to swim before she had lived long enough to learn to fear the water. She won races and got awards for the speed and grace of her breaststroke, taught to her by a coach who was himself never seen in the water. The man, she told me, patrolled the edge of the pool with a long wooden pole, jabbing at the girls when they didn't do the stroke right, pushing them underwater when they put their feet on the floor of the pool, or when they didn't breathe right. They never knew and never found out if he could swim himself, but it didn't matter. He knew how to teach, though his methods were strange if not downright abusive. My mother, whether from fear of the barge pole or the man himself, did learn to do a fine breaststroke. As for me, we had no access to a body of water, in Bombay. Yes, the Arabian Sea counts, but it is not a friendly sea, it sits there growling even when it isn't the monsoon, and there was no way I was going to do more than dip my feet in the water. Even that scared me. Even in very shallow—ankle-shallow distance—the waves would come rolling in to snap at my feet, and I would stand there in terror, feeling the falling away as they receded, still, waiting for them to come back, each time thinking, this time they would suck me in. Even my mother did not take on the Arabian Sea. There were rich cousins, and rich acquaintances, and they would take me to a pool at their club sometimes. But I could not swim. I sat a safe distance from the water and watched the girls in their bathing suits. I imagined myself in one suit in particular. It was a hideous green with bitter-gourd texture, and this cousin wore it with its matching cap that made her look like a cabbage on a stalk. But I wanted to look like that cabbage. What fascinated me most of all was the cheeks of her ass snooping outside every few minutes. She would grab the edge of the suit in her fist and pull it down. Nonchalantly, unselfconsciously. That gesture was what I really wanted to own. It came from having worn swimsuits, from having been at a pool, from having been half naked and from never having cared what anyone thought. That I wanted. It was one of my images of myself, one of the ones that you play in your head right before falling asleep. This was before I had men to dream of. I am in the green bathing suit, I have breasts, not too big, just little ones, and the nipples get lost in the bumpy texture of that suit. I have the green cap on. I had touched it once, when the girl had flung it down beside me and run off to eat french fries. It was a powdery skin that stretched when I pushed my finger against it. I had wanted to try it on, but all I did was put my fist in it. I knew how it would look on my head. And when I ran this picture through my head, I would always, and many times, grab the suit and yank it over my exposed rear. And then eat french fries. The smell of chlorine, french fries, the feel of a rubber bathing cap. The sense of rich people. The sense of being put up with.

That being my only access to water meant I didn't learn to swim when it was still instinctive. In Hong Kong, many years later, there was a pool in the building. I had owned many, many bathing suits by then. And been photographed in many stages of exposure, butt cheeks and more. I had practised the gesture and made it mine. We went shopping, my mother and I, and bought me a new suit, a white one. She warned me it would turn transparent the moment it hit the water, and that decided me. We came back home, I put on my new suit, and we went downstairs to the pool, to take on this beast.

'Get in and put your head in the water,' she said.

'I won't be able to breathe then,' I said, softly.

'Of course you won't be able to breathe. Take a breath, let it out slowly under water.'

I couldn't put my head under the water for more than a moment, and even that seemed too long to me.

'Open your eyes,' she said, when she saw that I had jammed them shut against the sting of chlorine.

I said nothing this time, just stood there in my transparent white suit, yanking it down again and again, my hair wet and unsexy, looking at her and knowing I couldn't do this. She said nothing, just walked around the pool to the deep, sliced in, and began to do her laps. I stepped out, walked over to the towels, and dried off. I left her there and went back upstairs, defeated.

She came in an hour later, slim, tall, exhausted in an elegantly athletic way. I said nothing more about swimming, at least not then. She said, 'Stay away from the water.'

Swimming came up again when we lived for a while in a compound which had a pool, when I was a lot older. She lived there too, and I would go and watch her every morning. She approached the water as a friend, not as I did, a hostile force. She would lap back and forth without stopping too often, for almost an hour. I loved watching people swim. I loved watching people drive. I love watching people do gymnastics, dance, paint, cook, ride bicycles. It was not so much that I appreciated their artistry, bravery, skill, talent. I just pretended and daydreamed I could do all those things. It was a way of pleasuring myself. A way of being slim, tall, a swimmer, a driver of cars, a maker of fine meals that I served to fine people, some of whom stayed after the meal and went to bed with me. It was a pleasure, and of course a distraction, a dodge from life as I lived it.

One of those mornings I woke up and saw a bathing suit in my pile of underclothes. It was one that my mother had brought for me on one of her trips back from Greece, Spain, Hong Kong, I don't really remember. She had bought it for herself, on her last day before she left to come back home, she hadn't had the time to try it on. It was the wrong size. It was my size. It was a swimmer's suit, not one of those flatter-suits I bought for myself. That morning I saw it there when I went to dress for the day, and without thinking, I put it on. It was black, it was unflattering to any but the most dedicated swimmer, it showed nothing it should not, and it flattened any and all curves into a sleek dolphin shape. I looked like a sea creature. I looked like I belonged in the water. I put a t-shirt over the suit, tied my hair in a tight knot, picked up a towel, and went down to the pool. There was no one there, and I put the towel and t-shirt on one of the lounge chairs and went down the three steps in the shallow end. The water was cool, but not unpleasantly so, it had been heating all the day before, and the nights were not cool enough to make much difference. When she came to the pool for her daily swim, my mother found me waist deep, hanging on the edge and floating my legs behind me. She said, 'Well, that suit fits you perfectly. Good thing I gave it to you, instead of hoping it would fit me one day!' She took off her cap and goggles and said, 'Here, *you* wear these. I hardly have any hair, and one time in the chlorine won't ruin it. Put the cap on first, before the goggles.'

I did as she instructed. Then she got in the water, and said, 'Now take a deep breath, put your head underwater, and blow all of it out.'

I took a deep breath. I filled all the air I could into my lungs, and dipped my head under the water. I closed my eyes instinctively, but then opened them, and I saw my feet in the water, and hers right in front of mine, and I saw little air bubbles sticking to my suit and hers, and I saw her face when I looked up, it melted and moved and lost form and reformed through the blue-green water. I suddenly needed to breathe, and came up gasping.

'Good,' she said. 'That's exactly how you do it. Now stand with your feet on the floor, but let's go a little deeper so I can show you how to do the arms.'

And so began a month of swimming lessons. She was impatient, of course, she spoke to me sometimes through clenched jaw and gritted teeth, but I had to trust that she was teaching me to swim, not trying to kill me for my stupidity, ineptness, fear, laziness, for being too short, for looking too much like my father, for having full lips, awful hair, or just for being alive. I didn't think about anything but doing what she was telling me to do. Four, one, two, three. Breathe. And then came the day I put all the elements together. The arms, the kick, the breath. And I swam. I swam the breadth of the pool. The shallow end, so I could stand up any time I wanted. But I didn't. I swam there, I swam back. I stood up. 'There. Now just do that to the deep end and back,' she said.

'How deep is the deep end?' I asked her.

'That is really stupid,' she said. 'You're swimming on top of the water. What difference does it make how much water is under you—whether it's eight feet or eighty-eight or eight thousand?'

I didn't swim to the deep end that day, or that week or that month. One morning, I came down to the pool, as I had done every morning since that first day. I walked over to the deep end and looked in. I could see leaves and red gulmohar flowers sitting on the bottom. They didn't seem so far away. I climbed off the metal ladder and held the edge, letting my legs float up and breathing into the water. Then I turned around and swam as fast as I could to the shallow end. I didn't run out of air or gumption. Then I got out of the pool and looked around. There was no one there but a hawk on a tree. He had seen what I had done. I was a swimmer.

I've seen people throw themselves off the diving platform into the unknown depths of Wakulla springs as gators lie silently on the opposite bank of the river. I've kayaked these North Florida rivers and looked into the clear distances between boat bottom and river bottom. There are gators that swim here, shadow-fast, figment-fast, faster than I can, surely. They would chew up my flesh, and mullets would swallow my soul. I would surely drown in these waters. But I can swim the length of a swimming pool. I'm a swimmer. I can swim. Every time I get into a pool, along with other swimmers, all better than me, I say it to myself. The sibilance of the beginning, the 'o-o' of the middle, the comfort of the 'em'. I enter the water, yank the suit, a swimmer's suit, unnecessarily, over my large ass, I yank my cap down over my hair, jammed willy-nilly under the silicone, I cup down my goggles till I feel them sucking at my eyeballs, and I say it to myself. Swim.

And then I am like a foetus in a womb, before I get too large and fill up all that space. I own it. Like the first days of love, those first days of life. You have space to gesture wildly, you don't hit anyone, you can shout without being too loud, you can cry, laugh, bite, kick, and there's enough space for it all. And then you eat and eat and grow and grow, and grow out of the space, and you have to leave, splitting the host apart, hurting everything in your path out of there. But you have no choice, what else is there to do? That's how it always was, one relationship after another. Sometimes you are the womb, sometimes the other person is. But always, comes the time for birth. (And afterbirth.)

I wonder what it was like for those foetuses that were expelled before they were ready—those that were inadvertent, and unwanted and unintentional, side-effects and by-products, but they didn't know it. I had expelled some inadvertent foetuses myself. It cost seventy rupees in those days. There were advertisements plastered in every local train, especially the women's compartment. I saw them every day I travelled: 'Pearl Centre' would solve all problems. I think they went all the way into the early part of the third trimester—not that I knew what that meant at the time. I had enough money for the abortion, but not for anaesthesia. I was a little afraid, but not as afraid as I was of being pregnant, of giving birth, and certainly not as afraid as I was of having a baby. I knew about those. I had a baby sister by then, I knew what it took. So when I missed my period, I took myself off to Pearl Centre, seventy rupees in the pocket of my jeans. I knew when I had missed it. I started at age twelve and it was deadly accurate, and I knew what it meant when I missed it. I had to take the train. Pearl Centre posters reminded me there would be no pearl growing from this grain of sand in my oyster. I had to walk through one of the largest vegetable markets in the city to get to the building. The abortion centre was on the second floor, sandwiched between a class for women who had failed the tenth grade, on the first floor, and a typing school on the fourth. I could change my life just walking up those stairs—pass tenth grade, get an abortion, learn to type. You didn't have to make an appointment. I was half hoping I would be told to come back another day, but the young woman at the reception just took my name and address and said, 'Wait. Just ten or fifteen minutes.' It wasn't even that long. I heard my name called from behind the curtain that hung in the doorway. I thought there would be a room, a gown, perhaps. There was just another young woman in her day clothes, and a very high bed. She told me to take off my pants and panties and lie down on the bed. While I undressed she briskly pulled the sheet off the bed and dropped it in a bin. She didn't bother to hide the blood from me. She put a new sheet on, and asked, 'How many months?' and I said, 'A few weeks.'

She said nothing more, and I lay there a few minutes, looking at the fan on the ceiling, there was no window. The doctor came in then, and he did have a clean green gown on, it even had ironing creases. I didn't see his face, he had a mask on, and thick glasses, and rubber gloves. He told me to hold my legs apart. I couldn't tell what he was doing, but it hurt suddenly, like a period cramp. It got more and more intense, and then when I said so, he stopped for a moment. 'Two minutes,' he said. And then it hurt again, but soon stopped. Then he took the gloves off and threw them in another bin by the bed. And left. The young girl told me to put on my pants. 'You have a sanitary napkin?' she asked. I didn't. She shrugged and gave me one. 'Pay outside,' she said. 'If you get too much bleeding, come back.'

I paid the cash, no tax, on the way out, and took the train back home.

Before my own intentional pregnancy, my mother was in the hospital. I went to visit her, and she lay in a nice room, on clean sheets. She had a white gown on, and she looked rested, if a little paler than usual. I asked her how she was. 'Fine,' she said. 'It's a little embarrassing, at this age . . .' I hadn't known what she was in for, I hadn't asked, but I suddenly understood. A nurse in a crisp dress and an elaborately pleated starched white cap held on her head by black bobby pins came in with a glass of juice and some food. 'How are you feeling, madam?' she asked. 'No bleeding?' My mother shook her head. 'If there is no bleeding for two hours, you can go home. I waited around, there was no more bleeding, we took a taxi home.

I had an odd conversation with her when we got home. She was obviously tired, she lay on a futon in the living room. 'This was a nice experience,' she said. 'Considering what I was there for. They were very nice.'

She took sips from her coffee. 'I was pregnant once before I had you,' she said. 'It was a boy. Born too soon—I lost him at about four months. It was strange: some people have abortions at that time. But the nurse, she brought me the baby in a jar. I saw him . . .'

She drank her coffee and said nothing more then, and never mentioned it again.

Pearl centre. Oysters. Grains of sand. Abortions.

Swim. My brother swimming in a jar forever. I had other pregnancies and other abortions after that. But there was something about that place that was matter-of-fact. I am still grateful for the way it all happened. There was very little talk, a mutual understanding of what I was there for, what they were there for. No sympathy, no sweet talk, but no judgement either.

On the eve of my fifteenth birthday, I knew that what I wanted was to lose my virginity, and I knew who would be the recipient of my dreadful gift. I did not think about whether or if he was strong enough for that albatross around his neck.

When I came back to live with my mother and her husband, Varun, I was fourteen years old. I had left as a small thin ten-year-old, barely aware that I was female. When I returned, I had come back with a definite, though small, set of boobs, a stay in a co-ed boarding school where inept attention was drooled, pawed, sweated on me. I was in no doubt about what I was made for. Still a virgin, but barely. This man, who might have been a father figure had I lived with him, was now a stranger to me, as I was to him, and a challenge to my 'what I was made for'.

This man, this challenge to me, this ultimate prize to the winner of that particular age-old competition, he lived without seeing me, his eyes passed over me, over my exploding virginity that I hated, that I wanted gone so bad I would have given it to the first male that asked. Especially him, especially him. I haunted him, I followed him, I touched him with my eyes, I flaunted myself, you could smell that fourteen-year-old sex like a perfume, Beaujolais nouveau, this year's fresh and saucy vintage, ready to be uncorked for an early taste on a light summer evening, it had to have been hard for him. The accidental contact, the constant physicality, must have done the intended damage. It had to happen, it had to break, and it did. I went into his room that night. I was not fifteen yet, it was before midnight, my mother was gone, somewhere, I didn't know or care where, this thing consumed me, and I wanted it done. I wanted to be free of it, the obsession with this man. I wanted this door unlocked, broken down, ripped off its hinges, gone.

There was no first-time pain, no orgasm that split my mind, no, it was just done, over with, out of my system and into my system forever. No, this was not the hard part. He was done with it, with me, and I was done with him. I was left with the relief, and hunger, of a new convert. I knew it was going to be good.

That was not the hard part, no. That came later, when she—I—realised that it was not over or done. It was not going anywhere.

I don't know why I came awake suddenly that night, not a week later, why I came out of my room on the far side of the house—as far away from their bedroom as it could be—to the kitchen for water, why I came right up to the closed door, stood in front of it, the glow from the light inside illuminating my toes, why I looked through the keyhole—the latch had been broken and my mother had unscrewed it in a fit of contempt and thrown it away one afternoon, leaving a hole large enough to see into the room—and why I stayed there, watching, nine seconds, no more, that dripped acid-etched images on my brain, my naked mother, her legs spread, her husband thrusting into her as he had done into me, the filthy green glow of the curtains behind them, the spreading burn between my thighs, the need to fuck somebody there and then, scrape that picture off my eyes. I turned away, went back to my room, aching with sex, it was all down there, in that one elegant teardrop of red coal that glowed so hot I thought it must show through my clothes. I was deliberate then: I took my bag, my keys, my single precious condom, I left quietly, turning the key to shut the door, I took the stairs because the elevator whined, I went to the back of the building to the mechanics' workshop, where two of the mechanics lived, sleeping on cotton mattresses between grease cans and carburettors. Laurie would be there. He had always had eyes on me. He would do me. He would ice my burn. He was there, sleeping in his dark blue uniform. He stank of cars and metal and workday sweat. I woke him. He saw my eyes, he knew he had his chance. He got up urgently, he dragged his mattress to the far end of the workshop, I helped him by moving screwdrivers and spanners off the floor. As he took his workpants off, I had that lifesaving thought. I would not think of what I had seen. I would be with Laurie, and there would be nobody else in this space but the two of us. And it was, just the two of us. He was delightful, this fixer of cars, this grease monkey, with his tight breath, tight muscles, tight arms around me, sensing my pain perhaps, he was delightful and gentle, and smiled and enjoyed it all so much that eventually I did too. No, there was no mind-splitting orgasm then either, but I loved him for the duration, and I didn't think of anything but axle grease and that tire iron too close to my breast.

That burn came back like burns do, as soon as you take the ice off. It fades slowly, over a long time, coming back a little diminished each time, but each time needing the ice of a kind boy or man who did me the favour of lending me time and body. I have been lucky with men, I found the sweetest ones, perhaps because I didn't want much more than love and trust for what time we had together, even if it was just one night, just one hour.

The rich cousin had a birthday party. The once skinny obnoxious girl in the green bathing suit was a young woman now, with willowy arms and legs and a Madonna-esque face framed by long willowy hair. She was tall, much taller than I was then, as my mother pointed out. There was something about her skin too, that I longed for. My mother said once, after we had been to their house for dinner, that rich people have different skin, that you could tell a person was rich by their skin. They had a lifetime of the right food, expensive creams and travel in chauffeured, air-conditioned cars, away from the grime and common air of the city that the rest of us shared. It was quite impossible for us to achieve that texture and luminescence with any amount of products slathered on from the outside, she said. I picked at my few but omnipresent zits. I already had a boyfriend, I had already lost my virginity, but I still felt uncomfortable around these people. They were not only unbearably polite, they were nice. No one commented, or even looked askance at my outlandish clothes, my gypsy skirts and silver rings on every finger and thumb. The only thing my aunt said, kindly and with a smile on her undeniably beautiful, waif-thin face was, 'How interesting that you wear different earrings on each ear—we should all do that!'

The evening wore on, for me, in a peculiar kind of mist. I felt a disgust and contempt for them, mixed with disgust and contempt for myself, compounded by my disgust and contempt for my mother and Varun, who sat next to her, and avoided looking at me. I went to the bathroom at one point, just to get away, but also to be in the guest bathroom of that house, one that I had been in so many times in my life. It had wide spaces of the palest blue luminescent tiles that gave me an unhealthy yellow tinge when I looked in the expanse of mirror. That mirror played me back quickly, it was familiar with my face, from the time I was a titless boy-girl, it had watched me grow up into this. My acne was emphasised by the light, and my messy, overloaded style stared out at me. I wished I had worn something more simple and elegant, my rings and bangles seemed too festive, too 'nautch', compared to my cousin, with her plain dark-green kurta and single gold bangle on her slender hand. And my hair, frothing like snakes from my head, dismayed me. I wetted my hands and tried to pat it down, but the humidity of the city made it even more angry and springy. I was near tears, but I peed, flushed, and went back outside. The cake was brought out, and canned peaches in a huge clear glass bowl, and vanilla ice cream. It was all too elegant and genteel for me. Peaches. That was an unthinkable luxury. My mother suddenly noticed that she had left her purse in the car. She asked if I would go out and get it for her. We had parked right at the end of the street, it was a bit of a walk. To my surprise, my other cousin, the male one, who had been lurking in his sister's shadow for all the years I had known him, said, 'I'll come with you.'

I shrugged. He was tall, very tall, and had a spindly moustache on his pale lip that he chewed incessantly. He had read everything he could lay his hands on, and in that house, he could lay his hands on a lot. He had endeared himself to my mother by being able to talk, not just about facts from various literary classics, but his opinions. He could argue with her about the intentions of the writers, and even of the characters. He read contemporary American writers, he had read Philip Roth, and Updike, and Vonnegut, and also Graham Greene, and the poems of Eliot. He had read every word Virginia Woolf had ever written. He had tried, once, to shame me into reading her.

'You would like *Orlando*,' he had said. He had given me a copy for my fourteenth birthday, hardcover, beautifully wrapped in indigo blue tissue and a huge aqua silk ribbon. I had kept the ribbon and still used it to tie my hair. The book lay unopened on my shelf. I had pushed it behind my

Superman comics and Modesty Blaises and Suddens, angry with him for giving me the task of reading it, and the opportunity. I know my mother would have liked to say, 'I named her after Virginia Woolf, and she's read every word she ever wrote.' It was more likely that she would have stopped telling everyone whom I was named after had I read every word my namesake ever wrote. But I was too lazy to actually find out.

My cousin stood up and said to me, 'Come on,' and to my mother, 'Car keys?' She smiled sweetly at him and said, 'Thanks, Sanju.'

I hated him. I even hated his abbreviated name, Sanju. It had an undeniably sweet sound, no matter who said it.

We walked down the street toward the car. I said nothing. Neither did he, but his silence was more from discomfort than petulance. I took my cigarettes out of the pocket of my skirt and lit one.

'You really shouldn't smoke,' he said, predictably.

'Why, because I'm going to die of a lung disease?' I asked him, blowing the smoke toward him.

'No, actually, I just thought they might smell it on you, and you might get in trouble.'

I was silenced for a moment. 'I don't really care if they smell it, and they won't care either. My dear mother would probably be delighted if I were to die of a lung disease. Anyway, she smokes too, so what's she going to say to me?'

We walked in silence after that, until he spoke again.

'You know, our names sound kind of the same.'

I thought that was ridiculous, and said so.

'That's just stupid. Sanju sounds like Virginia?'

'No, Ginny, Ginny, Gin.' He said the 'g' with a French twist to it, a softness. Of course, he took French classes at Alliance Francaise, I remembered, and hated him some more.

'Never mind,' he said then. And to my complete horror, he took my hand in his. We were almost at the car, and I snatched my hand away and went around to the driver's side. He had the car keys. He laughed, and took them out of his pocket. He opened the door and waited for me to get the purse. I took it out, opened it, took a twenty-rupee note and put it in my pocket. He didn't say anything. On the walk back to the house, he said nothing at all. As we were entering the front door, he said rapidly, before we were in earshot of the others, 'Do you want to go see a movie with me?'

I said, 'Call me', and walked in and threw the purse at my mother, who was deep in conversation with my beautiful cousin, his sister, about which college she was going to. I wished the evening would end soon, and it did end, but not soon enough.

The peaches were finished by the time we got back. I was disappointed to see that empty bowl with the syrup lying temptingly at the bottom. I would have liked to pick up the bowl and tip its contents into my mouth. I knew the peaches had left their essence in the juice. I didn't have the gumption to be that rude in that house in front of those people. I remembered the time when my mother and I were still just the two of us, and she had so many friends who found me fascinating. There was one man in particular who made sure there were nice things for me to eat, and something interesting for me to do, every time we went to visit him. He had an apartment right on the beach in a bohemian part of north Bombay, Juhu beach. It was on the ground floor, and the french doors opened onto sand. I loved to go there, I spent hours exploring the intricacies of shells while he and my mother were locked in his bedroom. One night, after dinner, he brought out a bowl of strawberries from the fridge and, to my dismay, they were shrouded in cream. I hated cream. He tried to convince me that the cream was not the same as the terrible skin that formed on my mug of milk when I didn't drink it quickly enough. I didn't believe him, and wouldn't try even the single strawberry he served me. He was obviously disappointed, but I wouldn't relent. While they ate, he kept asking me to try just a little bite. Finally, my mother intervened, or simply got fed up of his constant begging and pleading and wheedling and said, 'If you don't eat a bite of that goddamned strawberry, I will tie it around your stupid neck. And I won't ever bring you back here again.'

I opened my mouth tentatively and he popped the strawberry in. It was divinely juicy and the cream only enhanced its precious red taste. I looked in the bowl for more. It was the last one. I vowed to him, and to myself, that I would always, always try everything at least once.

Sanju called me the very next morning. We went to a one-time showing of *Nosferatu*. He felt it was perfect for me. I was, in spite of my determination not to like any movie we went to, moved by the slow, dark, loneliness of the film. It took hold of me, and by the time we got out, I was outside my usual self, I was willing to talk to Sanju, my distant cousin, as if he were a real person. We had had an uncomfortable cup of coffee at a small café outside the theatre though I did not really want to, and then, after the movie, he asked me if I wanted dinner.

'Only if we go where I want to go,' I said, 'and if I can pay for it'. He agreed. We walked down to the Excelsior Café, a crowded Irani restaurant which served the finest, and I mean the very finest, mutton biryani on the planet. It was very crowded, there were several movie theatres in the area, and they all had approximately the same movie times. We waited for a while on the sidewalk, and then the owner waved at me from his spot at the register.

'Come, I'll find you a place. You want to go upstairs?' I said no. Upstairs was a series of dark booths. I suspected they were for short-term business, especially at that time of night. I did not want to be sandwiched between moaning johns and impatient whores. I said we would wait. The owner came out from behind the counter and signalled to me to follow him. He walked right up to a couple of men drinking tea and asked them to leave. I was embarrassed and appalled, but he explained that they had been sharing the same cup of tea for two hours, and were bad for business. Sanju and I sat. Our waiter came up and said, 'Two mutton biryani? Extra green chillies? Two fresh lime juice?'

'Will you have the same as me?' I asked Sanju. He nodded yes, and smiled. The waiter nodded approvingly at him and left.

'Is that all they serve here?'

'No,' I said, 'he knows that that's what I want'.

'Yes, they seem to know you here. How come?'

'I come here in the afternoons and sit and read a book sometimes.'

'Did you ever read *Orlando*?' he asked me. I was hoping he would not.

'No, of course not. I won't ever read Virginia Woolf. Not ever, not ever, not ever.'

'Ginny,' he said, so kindly, so sweetly, that I had to look up at his face, 'Why ever not? Who else do you know has the privilege of being named for such a wonderful writer?'

'I hate my name, Sanju, really I do. In school the Hindus thought I was Catholic, the Catholics thought I was an idiot, no person could pronounce it, and the teachers thought I was weird for having a non-Indian name. She could have named me after some Indian writer, there's no shortage, is there?'

'Well, I think it's a wonderful name, Virginia,' he said, and put his hand on mine. I didn't move for a moment.

'I'll sleep with you if you want, Sanju. I've always thought you pretty. You don't have to take me out and do all this random romantic shit.' I said. He drew his hand back and considered me.

'I enjoy being with you. When you are not biting my head off for no fault of mine,' he said, 'but I don't really want to jump into bed with you'.

'Why, are you saving that for some special girl whom you will marry? It's just sex, you know.'

'Yes, I know. But with you it won't be.'

The waiter came with our food, and we didn't talk after that. It was truly delicious. I thought such a meal deserved dessert. I told Sanju so, and I recommended the bread pudding highly. I couldn't afford the dessert, he said he would get it. We got into an argument about the film we had seen, and though I didn't remember later what we had disagreed about, it was fun and funny, and we laughed through the dessert, which was particularly creamy and richly studded with soft raisins that burst in my mouth when I held them between my teeth. We were friends by the time we had jointly paid the bill. We walked to the bus stop, and waited there for a bus. They were infrequent after midnight, but it wasn't midnight yet. He held my hand again.

'What is exactly the point of this if it's going nowhere?' I asked him.

'It has no point, and doesn't have to go anywhere. It's fine where it is,' he said.

'Well, I don't see the point,' I said, 'I'm no virgin you know, I have a lover.'

'Really,' he said, 'and who might that be? Roy? I hardly see him as a lover!'

'No, not Roy. Someone a bit older. You know him, and you know what I'm talking about. Don't act all coy. Everyone knows it!'

'Who is everyone? And what are you talking about?'

I should have known better, but I did not. I should have changed the subject, but I could not.

'You can't be that stupid, Sanju,' I said, looking right into his pale large eyes. He looked at me for a few minutes and then his eyes narrowed.

'I don't believe you,' he said.

'Well, just because you don't want to sleep with me, doesn't mean no one else wants to! Maybe he likes me because I am older than I am. Maybe he's not afraid.'

'This is bullshit, plain and simple,' he said. He seemed angry, and I was a little afraid. We didn't speak after that. And he didn't call me again. A few months later he left the country to do a masters degree at Stanford. I never saw him alone again. We ran into each other at a family wedding many years later, he was married and had twin daughters and a wife who obviously doted on him. He smiled and said, 'How are you, Ginny?'

I smiled back and said, 'And how are you, Sanju? Are we still friends?'

He didn't say anything, but had a look on his face that I

did not know the meaning of. I did not know him well enough to understand the little nuances of his peculiar gestures. He narrowed his eyes, chewed the end of his moustache, shifted his weight, and then shook his head. It was too much of a performance to not mean anything. I wondered what my innocent question had brought on.

'Sanju?' I said, not expecting an answer, but at least a polite exchange and goodbye so we could both move on from the spot, and from whatever we did not have.

'Yes,' he said, 'we are friends, and I have always been your friend, Ginny. Even though you never knew it. I have always loved you. Since you were six years old, and I was twelve.' And then he put his drink down on the table next to him and hugged me, deliberately, and long. And then he picked up his glass up and said, 'You take care,' and moved away into the crowd. And I understood, suddenly, what he had done for me.

Things were different after my single date with Sanju. I just hadn't connected him with the shift. Our contact with that family had never been consistent, but now it was totally missing. My mother talked to me less and less, and Varun was out of town more and more. He didn't talk to me unless it was absolutely necessary, and even when he did, he would not look at me. Before, there had been some sort of ease in our small household. There were times when we ate dinner together, when we appreciated the cooking phase that my mother was going through. There were other people who appreciated it too, friends would drop by with things they wanted her to cook and feed them. A friend from her college days, a paper-thin man with inch-thick glasses, came with an odd-looking fish one morning. We laughed about the two eyes on the same side of the fish's flat body, and she told me it was a flounder. The thin man said it was a bacchus, or a John Dory. I'd never heard any of those names before. I knew 'flounder', but this was the first one I had seen. We had a moment of hysteria in the kitchen when we talked about pigeons and fish who had eyes on the sides of their heads so that when they seemed to be looking at you, they were really not, and they had to turn their noses, or beaks, away from you to see you, and then only saw you out of one eye. Then of course it struck us at this moment of high hysteria that the flounder looked quite like the man who brought it. For many reasons, some of which may have had to do with the half-empty bottle of white wine that she had been using for cooking the pale sauce polka-dotted with fresh green peppercorns that the fish would lie poshly in later that night, we found the idea funny to the point of wetting our panties, and had to rush to the bathroom. I let her go first. She said, 'Your muscles are stronger, you hold it.' We had found some equilibrium in those days, the two of us. But after my cousin's birthday party, we never went back to that particular aunt's house, and my mother really stopped talking to me. Something changed, perceptibly, and rapidly, almost from one day to the next. I thought about it, and didn't think that my behaviour that particular evening had been any worse than normal, at least in any social situation involving my mother and her friends or family.

The days took on a different tune, a different momentum, a different colour. She wrote all day, and assumed, and perhaps hoped that I was going to school. I was not. I drifted. I spent my days hanging outside the American consular residences in their neat gardens, reading, hanging with children of expats, one boy in particular, with an upturned nose and sun-bleached white blond hair, and lazy jungle-green eyes. He and I would kiss and grope entire afternoons away, and some days I helped him do his appallingly elementary school work. All the more appalling to me was that he could not circle the verbs in a sentence or accomplish the simplest of long division sums. I tried teaching him, but soon discovered that it was beyond his intellectual means, and then I just did the worksheets for him. He watched me and drank Budweiser. He wore a t-shirt with a cross on it, which he told me was the Confederate flag. 'Heritage,' he said. I didn't really know what that meant, then. The person that interested me more was a black man who brought his black Mustang screaming into the driveway. He would park, nod at us expressionlessly and disappear into his ground-level apartment. I had never seen a black man in such close proximity. Africans, yes, there were enough Kenyans and Ghanaians in the city. But an American black man was a novelty. And this one was a particularly pretty one. I was drawn to his lean darkness, his features, not African at all, more Roman, I imagined. A Roman statue soaked in dark bitter chocolate. I spent an inordinate amount of time waiting for a glimpse of him, even if it meant having my breasts mauled by a well-intentioned and permanently erect boy from the southern states of America.

My patience eventually paid off. One of those summer days I lounged outside his apartment, reading Modesty Blaise again, waiting, or pretending to wait for Bobby to come out,

he peeled into the driveway and sprang out of the car in a
smooth motion that scared me a little. He smiled and nodded
as usual, and felt for his keys in his pocket. He seemed
almost unaware of me, and worse, he seemed to be about to
disappear into his apartment. He took his key out of his
pocket, it was a single key without any ring attached to it.
And he dropped it, right at my feet. He said 'Uff' and bent
down to pick it up, and his face was a few feet from mine,
right at my level. And he looked into my eyes and smiled.
His eyes were a shiny hard black, like patent leather, like
shellac, like opaque black glass. His hair was close to his
skull, tightly wound, and to me, alien. I had never seen
anything like it. I could smell him suddenly, a hint of earth,
of herbs and spices unknown to me. And the smell of him
went straight to my cunt, like raw meat to a lioness. There
was a moment of recognition, and then our conditioning
crowded in quickly between us, quickly, like air into a
vacuum, quickly, before we both succumbed to our mutual
sighting, smelling of each other.

'Are you waiting for Bob?' he asked.

'No, I was about to leave actually. Been waiting a while.'
And then, I said under my breath, 'For you.' He may or may
not have heard me, but if he did he did not flinch.

'Want a beer?' he asked.

'I don't drink.'

'Oh sorry,' he said, 'a coke then?'

'No, but I'll come in, if that's what you're asking.'

I stood up and he opened the door. It was a gorgeous
apartment, but unremarkable, in that there were no clues to
him, it was all beiges and pastel stripes.

'Where are you from?' I asked him, following him into the
kitchen where he half filled a glass with ice cubes and then

poured coke into it from a large bottle of a kind I had never seen before.

'Boston,' he said, 'sure you don't want some?'

'I don't like drinking carbon dioxide any more than I like breathing it,' I said, and he laughed.

'Have you been there?'

'Where? To Boston? No. The only places I have been outside this country are parts of Yugoslavia and Rome.'

'Really? Yugoslavia? Why there?'

'My stepdad worked there. He and my mother lived there, I visited them. To meet my new baby half-sister. She is a whole baby, but only half a sister.'

He laughed again. 'You're funny. Are you in school?'

'School? I'm too old for school. And I'm supposed to be in college, but it's boring, I hate it, so I just don't go.'

'And your parents know this?'

'They don't give a shit what I do, as long as I don't hang around the house all day.'

He didn't say anything. We stood around his kitchen table for a while. I thought I should leave, there didn't seem to be anything more to be said. And then he started telling me about America. He told me about his life, his school, his grandmother, his passion for gospel, his church. I listened. His voice was soothing, in the same way he was graceful— a snake, reptilian, smooth, powerful. Finally, two hours and many words later, I said I had to leave. He didn't ask me to stay longer.

'Would you like to go out to dinner sometime?' he asked me at the door.

'Sure. I could take you to a place I know.'

He laughed his low and confident laugh, and said, 'No, I'll take you to a place I know. You like Chinese food?'

'How could a billion people be wrong?' I said. He laughed again, and said he would pick me up Friday night.

I paid some attention to what I wore that Friday night. I changed in and out of several things before I chose a pair of dark pants and a black shirt. I thought about leaving off the silver, but after taking it all off and trying on the single silver bangle, I put all my bangles and rings and bracelets back on. As the doorbell rang, I realised I had no nice shoes, and slipped on my Mary Janes from school, they were the cleanest ones I had. Alex Hayes stood outside the door with a small bunch of flowers, a negative rendition of all the images I had seen of such situations. He wore blue jeans and a black shirt and black shoes. He smiled, and his snake eyes slanted.

I thought the flowers were for me, but they were for my mother. He was wonderfully charming, he came in and sat down, when she asked him if he wanted a drink, even had one with her. They talked about William Faulkner and, of course, Virginia Woolf. I hadn't told him my full name, but now he knew. I felt, waiting there for them to finish talking, as if I was the child being taken out on a treat, and had to let the adults finish their adult business first.

He held the door of the black Mustang open for me to get in. I'd never been in a car like that before. It was beautiful. We went to a fancy Chinese restaurant in downtown Bombay, where I had been once. I was uncomfortable, and my shoes pinched, but I was in a heightened state, I was aware that this was something different. I was uncomfortable about the way I felt around him, squirmy and somehow out of time. He seemed to feel my discomfort.

'So what do you want to eat?' he asked me, looking at the menu. I considered the choices. I looked at the price column. I wondered how all this worked. I gave up and took the easy way out.

'I don't know,' I said to him. 'Everything is too expensive, I don't know what the food here is like, I think I like you, and my shoes . . . do you mind if I just take them off?'

He laughed, put the menu down and stood up. I was alarmed for a moment, I thought he was going to walk out. We had been sitting across from each other. He came around to my side of the booth and sat next to me. He turned me sideways toward him and pulled my legs up across his lap. Then he pulled my shoes off one by one, and rubbed my feet. I was glad I had showered before dressing.

'I get paid lots of money. We can order anything we want. So let's read this menu together and eat something perfect,' he said. 'Are you better now? Have I solved all your problems?'

It was my turn to laugh. I only wished now that I couldn't smell his strong smell so clearly.

Dinner was smooth, after that. The food was good, better than the street Chinese I was used to. Alex was apparently riveted by everything I said, or at least acted as if he was, well enough that I couldn't tell if it was an act. He liked to hear himself talk too. He was quite explicit about his dislike of the country he was in, and some of his talk involved stories of all the trouble he had because people lied about who and what they were in their visa applications. I was surprised to find myself defending my country, defending those very lying cheating people that he was complaining about. I found it strange that he would find it hard to forgive people who were trying to escape a difficult existence, to a country that claimed to accept the poor and downtrodden from the world. My own vehemence and anger was new to me. And unexpected. And naïve perhaps. I suddenly preferred Bobby from the deep south who was happy to muck about with native wenches. He was honest and straightforward and responded to me just for who I was. There was something condescending about Alex, I felt, and I was right, but I didn't get it then. I didn't know anything about the black, white, north-eastern, southern divides in America. I sensed, but didn't understand, the complexity of those intricate historical threads that I was looking at.

Alex took me out almost every week. I still hung around with Bobby. Alex saw me there one day and commented about it at our next meeting. 'That kid is up to nothing, and will probably get nowhere,' he said. 'I would find new friends if I were you.'

I thought it a presumptuous thing to say, but let it pass. It was said in an offhand way, I did not see anything serious behind it.

'Would you like to see the Ali exhibition fight?' he asked me one day after we had had dinner at his house, smiling slightly, knowing he was offering candy to a hungry child.

'You mean *the* Ali fight? You mean you have tickets? You mean you will take me?'

I was a huge Mohammad Ali fan, like everyone else on the planet. I also had a giant, Ali-sized poster by Neil Leifer in my bedroom, alongside Bruce Lee, James Caan in *Rollerball*, Al Pacino as Serpico, and on and on. To actually see any one of these men in the flesh was not something I had ever thought would happen to me. Alex laughed.

'Not only do I have tickets, I have ringside tickets. You will get to shake his hand, maybe.'

I just sat there and stared at him.

He was as good as his word. We went out to dinner, and then to the exhibition match where Mohammad Ali, in the flesh, five feet from where I was sitting, pretended to be knocked to the floor by a fat little boy. I felt sorry for the boy in some odd way. The rest of his life would never measure up to that one moment of glory. I imagined he would take up boxing as a sport and do badly at it and then kill himself at the age of twenty. I did not get to shake the greatest boxing hand in the known universe, but that might have been, in fact, my moment of glory too. After the event, I went home with Alex. 'For a drink and a snack,' he said. We sat at his dining table and talked. I couldn't imagine what he might find interesting about a not-yet-seventeen-year-old girl, but he had spent hours talking and listening to me already, so there must have been something about me that interested or intrigued him. It may have been the same thing I saw in him, a kind of fascination for the unknown, the exotic. Mingling with the natives for him, for me something else. There was an urgency of now in our collaboration, a lack of any future, a lack of any intention except the one we had both pushed aside in favour of some dating dance that brought us no closer to consummating and then ending a relationship that had no other purpose. There was a lull in the conversation that night at his dinner table. Everything else had been said. He stood up, a tall imposing dark god of a figure, and I didn't move from my chair. He walked around to my side of the table and knelt down in front of me. He turned my chair, with me on it, easily, so I was facing him. Then he pushed my silky black skirt up my legs, sliding his hands up my thighs, and pushing my legs apart. He looked up at me for a moment, and then bent down into the source of that smell that had drawn him in the first place. I was stunned into inaction by what I felt. I drew in a breath when I first felt his tongue, forked, an elegant black lizard's tongue, a live snake itself, snaking into the folds and plumpness, probing and searching deeper and deeper for something I did not know or understand. I was not part of this moment, neither for him, nor for me. I watched, I felt, but I was not there, with him or with me. I could not separate myself from the horror, and it was primarily horror I felt, enough to grasp the erotic delight of what was happening to me. It was new, and it was something I did not know could or should be done. He laughed, and I felt the vibrations in my flesh around his ears and shuddered. He mistook it for something and he laughed again, and pushed himself away from me. I had wanted to push him away, and now I was disappointed that he had stopped. But he stood up and said, 'You should go home. I'll drive you.'

In the car on the way home he put his hand on mine and said, for no apparent reason, 'You never told me when your birthday is.'

'I'll be seventeen next month,' I said. And he braked hard and parked the car on the side of the road.

'You will be seventeen? You are sixteen now?'

'Yes, why?'

He just sat there with his hands on the wheel, and I could see how hard he gripped it. I ran our conversation through my head, I wondered what I had said wrong, that made him suddenly so cold. I sensed fear, and was confused by it.

'What's wrong? Do you want to go back? I don't have a curfew, you know?'

'No,' he said. 'No, I will take you home. I will take you home.'

But he did nothing, just sat there.

'Did I say something . . . did I do something wrong?' I tried again. 'Did you want us to . . .'

'No, no, my God, no.'

'Why, is there something you did not like about me?' I whispered, afraid of the answer, but ready, willing, wanting it. He would say he did not want me. Did not like the way I looked, spoke, smelled.

'It is nothing about you. Nothing.'

And still he sat there, making no move to start the car.

'Well. Whatever you say, Alex. I don't know what is wrong, but I'm no virgin, so you don't have to worry about that. I haven't been for a long time. And it's not that I don't know what older men are like either.'

He turned toward me in the dark, momentarily out of his mood. I had intrigued him by what I had said.

'What older man?'

'Now that would be telling you too much. Besides, you're not an older man. You're twenty-eight, right?'

'That I am. But tell me what you were saying. What older man? What man?'

'I live with an older man who isn't my father, you know. Anyway, that's not the point, I'm just saying I know older men.'

There was another silence in the car. I could hear the frogs outside. He finally said, after clearing his throat several times, 'Tell me about your father.'

'Nothing, I'm just saying, he's an older man, that's all.'

'You were going to tell me something,' he said.

'No.' Some instinct kept me quiet. Something about him disturbed me, something about his response made my hackles rise, I had a sense of circling sharks. One circling shark. I wished I could swim, but I felt safe on my island. Small as it was. He took me home, and I didn't hear from him for a few days. I thought that was over and done with, I didn't think I would hear from him again, and I felt little regret. I came home one evening from loitering all day with my confederate degenerate to find him sitting in the living room with my mother, silent, with a drink in his hand. I thought maybe he had moved on to the more interesting of the two of us. I was disappointed, but I would have preferred that had I known what was really going on. I said a breezy hello to them and started toward my room. He did not look at me.

He said to my mother, in a voice that filled me with dread, 'I bit into an apple and found a worm in it.'

She waited. I waited too, suspended in that space between fear and hurt, not knowing which one was better. Hurt, I thought. Anticipation is a terrible thing. Then he started talking. About America, about India, about all the things he had encountered during his stay. He hated it all, hated every person he had met during his time here, and hated me most of all, for lying to him about my age, he said, for telling him what I told him that night in his car that had paralysed him for weeks, but his conscience, he said, would not allow him to be silent. After he was done talking relentlessly into the silence and discomfort of that room, he put his glass down and stood up. And then he walked to the door and left. I didn't see him again, not for a long, long time, not for a decade. But he left his words hanging between us, my mother and I, like an opacity that we could neither see nor feel each other through. So now she knew. She knew what I had done, what Varun had done. I waited for her words, but I knew all I would get from her was silence. I was ready for either, I knew what to do with those, they were my friends, her words of hatred, and her silence of negation. But what she said next, was new. I did not expect it.

'Why do you make up such things? Why do you say such things about the one person who has been a father to you? More than your own father, he has loved and supported you. Why would you do this to him? Why do I have to hear these things from everyone?'

I was truly defeated then.

The only person who spoke to me after that day was the baby, the little three-year-old Simi, always delighted to see me, like a little puppy. She would fly into my arms when I came home, 'Ginny! You're home! Play with me, look at my new picture! Read *Babar* to me!' In those days she was my support, my mascot, the thing that kept me sane and alive.

She reminded me that I was loved, I was wanted. She made me want to love someone. I thought of the times when I had hated her, her existence, before I met her in that strange new country, before I had held her squirmy little body, before I had felt the tight grip of her hand around my finger.

Croatians—Dalmatians—were all gorgeous. Yugoslavia, a rush of hormones at thirteen, pouring out of every pore in my mind and body, the beaches, my first bikini, my breasts, small, and though I didn't know or appreciate it then, perfect, Adriatic boys and Adriatic men, a touch, a shade of summer-coloured flush on their bodies, the faces just a blur of young desire in no hurry to be fulfilled. It was a magical place for me. We went to a small island one weekend, Korcula. I was told it was the birthplace of Marco Polo. It was a long boat ride. I could feel salt on my skin. I could feel salt and sea in my hair, curling it impossibly, a mane full of sea creatures. I had not yet learned not to eat things that were slimy, or to dislike the taste of things that were bitter, or resent the texture of things that resisted being chewed. I ate octopus, they were like rubber bands in my mouth, cooked too tough, and went down uncertainly. I had once vowed to try everything, and I did. I ate oysters, fresh from the sea, brought to the table with wedges of lemon and great half loaves of hot bread, every oyster a morsel of ocean, so perfect, sex on a shell. I see it now as awakening, learning, yearning for things that would come later. Then, my sexuality had no gender, no shape or size or smell, nor yet a face, it encompassed everything. It was a feeling that lived in me like a language, a translator of everything I sensed, a filter, sex-coloured glasses. At thirteen, I felt and smelled those colours and textures for what they were. Octopus, oyster, fresh yeasty bread, rough wines we picked up in wicker-encased demijohns from rough villages. But these smells and tastes are familiar now—in bodies, in the smell of someone's breath in the morning, a fusion of spit and my cunt, the taste of a tongue or a foreskin, the feel of a callus made from holding the handlebars of a bicycle for miles and miles, a scalp under my fingertips through thinning hair, no different from a baby's scalp, it is all food, for the senses, for the heart, for the soul.

We went to Trogir, a small town near Split. There was a Turkish sweetshop in the town square, and I bought a square of Turkish delight. It reminded me of a sweet from home, but this one was so hideously sweet that my nipples stood out through the yellow t-shirt I was wearing, surprising me. The street markets of Split: old women, very old women, strawberries big as my fist staining my new white pants, staining my mouth, my lips swelling slightly from the tart acidity, like the strawberries, aching to be eaten. Dubrovnik, rambling roses climbing all the way up the ancient walls, their gaudy scent saturating the air, making me so high I could have fainted from it, any of the young cigani men selling silver in the square could have plucked my rose. And that wild blue Adriatic Sea, it was green pretending to be blue. My sexuality was just that then. It really had no name or number or expectation. I don't know when it all changed. When it became a matter of give and take, of being valued. And I had taken my little sister for granted then, I had been immersed in myself, my mind, my body, the attention of the men around me. Including, but not at all limited to, the father of that lovely baby girl. I didn't want to acknowledge her then, I certainly didn't want to love her. Before that, she was to me the thing that would take my mother from me. I didn't know then, that I would be the one to take her from my mother.

I took a bus downtown. I was of more than half a mind to just not go. But curiosity, as always, got the better of me. I was an hour early for my appointment, so I walked around the shops at Fountain, looking at used and almost antique paperbacks. They were not really shops, just row upon row and stack upon stack of books standing unsteadily on the sidewalk. They were incredibly cheap, but I had very little money, some pocket money, some occasionally stolen bills from my mother's purse. I thought carefully about what I would buy. Some of the vendors were annoyed by my excessive caution, but some were kind. I built a small library from those piles over the years. Westerns, old Nero Wolfe and Modesty Blaise paperbacks, South American writers that I first bought for the luscious covers and then, after I read them, for the luscious words, books on cooking, tattooing, motorcycles, plastic surgery, art, photography, everything under the sun. When the time came for my appointment, I was a few minutes' walk away from the building. I took my time, I hadn't yet made up my mind that I was going to keep the appointment. It was an old building, but lovingly looked after. The banisters were smooth and shiny, and not just from being touched. They were polished, and the old thick walls were painted a sweet yellow, the deep gothic arched windows let in the sunlight, making them glow. It was cheerful in an unassuming way. I walked up three flights of stairs rather than take the cage elevator. The office was off to one side, there were two couches and several dark over-realistic landscapes on the walls. The cheerful yellow ended in this area, the walls here were a pale green and all the furniture was upholstered in hunter green leather. I wasn't sure what to do, there was no receptionist or doorbell. But I was committed now. I sat on the couch and looked at one of the magazines. It was about tattoos. I thought it must have come from the pavement below.

A few minutes later, just as I was settling on what type of tattoo I wanted, the door opened and I saw him for the first time, the person who would guard my sanity for the next several years. He was pale and expressionless, his eyes were like river pebbles set in an elegantly high-cheekboned face. His hair floated in a fine uncertain mist over his head, the light behind him gave him a halo.

'Hi. Virginia?'

'Ginny.'

'Ginny. It's nice to meet you.' He held out a spade of a hand for a handshake.

'You don't know that yet,' I said, putting my hand in his. He covered mine with his other one and said, finally smiling, 'Right now, it's nice to meet you. We'll see if that changes, won't we?'

I followed him into his inner office. There was an ancient desk that took up most of the cosy space, it must have been born there and grown to its present size there, it could not possibly have been brought in fully grown. He went around it and sat with his back to the sunlight that came in through the closed, but uncovered, window.

'No couch?' I asked.

He laughed, a sweet, low growl that was gone before I had had enough of it.

'I like my clients to look at me, and I like to look at them.'

'Clients? Not patients?'

'Clients,' he said, firmly.

I sat for a while without saying anything. He waited, looking at me with his lovely colourless eyes. I gave in first.

'So. What next?'

'It's up to you, Ginny. Is there something you want to talk about?'

'Not really.'

'Hmm. Did you buy that book on the sidewalk?'

'Yes. It's about black and white photography.'

'You do photography?'

'I'd like to. My stepfather gave me an old record player and an even older camera, and all I can afford is black and white film. I'm still learning to use it.'

'That was nice of him,' he said. I knew it was a hook, I knew where this conversation was going, but I went with it. Even though I had decided not to.

'Will you be reporting our conversation to them?'

'Them? I don't know whom you mean, but what we talk about is between you and me, Ginny. I don't take it outside this space, and by this space I mean you and me, not this room.' He seemed to want to say more, but stopped, sensing unerringly my desire to speak. I knew what he was doing every step of the way, and yet I went with it, succumbing to my need to talk to someone who knew nothing about me. And then I remembered that he did know something about me. In fact the things he knew about me were all the things I wanted no one to know about me. The truths he had been told about me were not my truths, they were the truths of the world. They were my mother's truths. She had constructed me the way she wanted me to be seen, and I had not the will to deconstruct and reconstruct myself otherwise. I had no picture of who I wanted to be, of who I wanted to show him. I was suddenly empty and tired, and just sat there, and said no more.

'Ginny,' he said, so softly it felt more like a vibration in my mind than actual words, 'I met your mother last week. She said you needed someone to talk to. That's all I know about you. I like to form my own picture, so I don't know anything about you at all, other than what I see in front of me, and what you will tell me.'

He was reading me like a bad movie. It was unnerving and comforting at the same time. I found myself looking into his unblinking eyes, white as if the white city sky had found its way through his head. He shifted in his chair slightly, and I heard a rustle of wings. I came to a decision. This angel would be mine, and he would see me, as I really was, every last nerve and muscle exposed. He would be the wind that would blow all the leaves and mud off my landscape, he would lay bare the rocks of my being. I smiled.

'Think of something nice?'

'Yes,' I said, and told him what I had been thinking. He laughed again, and I realised I had been waiting for that sound all the time between then and the last time I heard it.

'Me, an angel? Yes, I have an angelic name, but you know, Ginny, Gabriel is not the sort of angel you are looking for!'

'Your name is Gabriel, Dr K?' I asked him, unreasonably delighted by it. 'Why is that? I mean, how did you—I mean . . .' He knew I wasn't going to get that question right, so he answered it.

'My mother is Italian, and my father was a Parsi. I guess my mother prevailed. And they told me that my sister was to be called Carmen, but I was the only child they had, they were both too old for what was considered a polite time to have another child those days. So here I am, the angel Gabriel.'

I talked then. And he listened. I said everything, and nothing at all. I took him into lanes and by-lanes, through every ugly one and every dull one, into every house and store, I showed him the things I had only gazed at and longed for through the plate-glass windows—the headless mannequins, the bras, the boots, I introduced him to everyone that I had ever met that I could remember, every man and dog that I had spoken to, every hour and minute of seventeen years spilled out of me in haphazard sentences between torrents of tears that at first embarrassed me, and then just lubricated my thoughts and words, until I stopped at that closed door of the lie that I would have to live, for as long into the future as I could see from where I stood. And there we both stood, me exhausted and at a blind alley, him at a loss, and, I suppose, out of time. I felt his hand on my head. I did not realise I had put it down.

'Will you come back and see me?'

'Yes,' I said, certain that I would. 'Even if it's just to give you back your handkerchief.'

Bijou was dressed and had eaten breakfast when I got there. A plate with egg smears and bread crusts lay beside him, maybe from the day before, by the look of the bread. I hoped not.

'Let's see them. What do you have?' he said. I smiled. He was never one for good morning or how are you. When I commented one day that a question about my wellbeing would be nice, even polite, he snorted at me. 'If something is wrong you will tell me, and if nothing is wrong, well then, what is there to waste words on?'

I started loading the carousel on the slide projector. I said nothing as I worked, and neither did he. He just watched me. I knew he saw something different from what I saw in the mirror. I saw my face, and hair, and my skin, which looked particularly even that morning, glowing with the slight burn from the week at the beach. He saw movements, muscles and bone. I recognised myself sometimes in his huge canvases, a tiny figure among the crowds of the city, a face among three or four women in a group, once a woman in a mango tree, and then I saw what he saw. I saw the light from his window on the tops of my breasts, the flat luminescence that settled on me like dust through the gulmohar trees outside. The first time he painted me, he didn't tell me. I noticed it one morning, an indistinct figure that may have been a woman or a child, but I knew it was me. I did not like his paintings. They were too blatant, too insistent, too confident, too large for me. They left nothing for me to dream about, no surfaces unsaid. Everything was right there, to be seen, there were no hidden places, no dark spaces, no mystery. The people on some of those vast canvases, I only had to see them once and I knew everything about them that was worth knowing. It sat on their faces. They seemed not to have lives beyond that one moment on that wall. I did not like his work, no, but I also knew he did not make mistakes. For many months I said nothing about that figure. He knew I had noticed, and it became a waiting game between us.

That morning I showed him all my photographs, which were lovely simply because they were ocean and water and sunset, but also the photographs from the morning before. I had gone to buy crabs at the Sassoon Docks. I went there at four in the morning to be there when the fishing boats came in. I often ended up getting this usually expensive item free, if I waited around for the fishermen to throw them overboard from the boat bottoms, caught by mistake in the pomfret and mackerel nets. I had slides of fishermen, of fisherwomen with their sarees worn like pants with a length of the cloth twisted up like a rope and wrenched tight between their legs following their ass cracks. I had big mackerels not quite alive, but not as yet quite dead, twitching in the salt water and slush on the dock, of cats, one-eyed, one-eared, half-tailed and full, scuttling and languid, scrappy and confident, in every colour from white to black. He was thrilled with these. 'I can do a dockyard series,' he said. 'You could wear one of those sarees, I'll paint you.'

'No, thanks,' I said. 'Not my thing.'

He didn't say anything. He had painted me often enough by then, but I had never actually sat for him. One evening, after I had cleaned his brushes and soaked all the rags and wiped his hands clean of the turpentine, and he was particularly mellow after I had made him his second rum and club soda, I had given in and asked about that figure in the painting he had finished months ago.

'That's me in the corner, isn't it?'

He laughed, a small victory.

'Yes. How did you know?'

'The light in that corner has nothing to do with the rest of the painting,' I said.

'Do you like it?'

I was surprised at this question. I answered without thinking of the consequences, honestly, but also because I knew he didn't really care what I thought.

'No. I don't like any of them. I like some colours sometimes, the way they blend ... I like watching you when you are painting. I like how your eyes look. But what you do ... no.'

'Why? Can you articulate a reason? Or is it just your usual impulsive, meaningless likes and dislikes?'

'Impulsive? Well, let me tell you what. I dislike them first, impulsively, and then find the reasons for disliking them. I don't like the finality of your paintings. They look to me like this is it, that nothing happened before or after this moment that you have painted.'

'That is really the stupidest thing I have ever heard. Of course nothing happens before or after the moment in the painting. It's a painting. Come here,' he said suddenly.

I went over to his wheelchair. He pulled me down and kissed me on my mouth.

'You are incredibly stupid, and don't know it yet. And as long as no one else finds out, maybe you will be fine in the world,' he said.

That morning he looked tired, and didn't say much. I knew and he knew that one of those days I would sit for him. But neither of us was ready for it. It had been an odd but impulsive moment, but it had passed, and I perhaps understood him a little better. Perhaps, I thought, I was not the only one who was uncertain here.

He liked the pictures I had brought for him. It was my little gift to him, to bring a little more of the world into his studio than he could easily get to.

'Those are some good images,' he said. 'You seem to have a point of view, they're not just pretty. In fact, many are not. I know a guy who could help you, teach you. Maybe you could work for him, make a better living than what I pay you, and do something that could—you know, end up somewhere for you. I'll call him later, remind me. Now go make me some tea and get me a cigarette. I haven't smoked all morning, and that stupid Raju never showed up today.'

He looked up at me and said, 'I dropped my glasses,' pointing at the floor right beside him. I bent down to pick them up, and he put his hand on the back of my head as I straightened up, and kissed me, looking into my eyes with his dark smudgy ones, smiling a little. Then he released me and said, 'Hmm'.

'How did you bathe and dress today, Bijou?' I asked. If his boy servant had not come that morning, he would have had to do everything for himself, and it was possible, but not easy for him, I thought, for a moment forgetting that I had just been kissed, once again, in a most presumptuous way, perhaps not even noticing it. This man was at least twenty years older than my seventeen years. He had been paralysed in some part of his lower body but not all of it, and though

I was unbearably curious about which parts, I had not found out yet. I did think about it, of course, what, or how sex would be with a paraplegic. Or whatever the right word was for someone in his condition. I'd been kissed anyway. His mouth worked just fine.

The next day he sent Raju over with summons. He lived in the building across from mine, in the same complex, that's how we had met. He needed help with everyday things, and I was always looking for extra income, my downstairs neighbour, the scriptwriter, had put us in touch. I was still asleep when Raju rang the doorbell, which I ignored, he rang it many times, and finally commenced hammering at the door. I got off the mattress on the floor and opened the door to find him standing there. He was probably about thirteen, but to me looked nine. He had terrible teeth, they were rubbed with some black powder—the ashes of something— I'm sure he thought it was good for him, but the abrasions on his enamel must have been pretty deep. He said, 'Bijou wants you to come right now.'

'Have you made some tea?'

'Yes, but you don't have to drink that, I made coffee for you. And I will make you a nice six-egg omelette with green chillies if you come with me right now.'

'You go ahead, I *will* come in a minute.'

He peered around me and looked inside. There wasn't much to see, a record player and a stack of records on the floor in the corner, a stray chair that must have belonged to previous occupants—some lame-duck couple my mother had decided was in dire need of a place to stay because they were doing some world-changing thing that met with her approval—and Roy, asleep on the mattress on the floor, next to his pet plant, which had burst its pot at the roots, and was becoming large enough in height and leaf size to threaten our space. I had dreams of being eaten in my sleep by this plant, but he had had it for years, and wouldn't hear of planting it in the compound.

'Is that your husband?' Raju asked me. 'No,' I said 'he's my friend'.

'A man friend?' he grinned at me.

'Why don't you go, I'll come after I'm dressed.'

'No, I'll wait here. Sahib said I should come back only with you.'

I went to the bathroom and brushed my teeth, peed, and put on a bra, t-shirt, and my jeans that Roy had washed for me. I told him I was across at Bijou's though I was sure he hadn't heard me.

Roy. He was my friend, he was my comfort. He was a gentle soul, straightforward and unpretentious. He didn't want to know too much about me, what I thought or who I was. He liked the simple pleasure of living with me, of being able to tell his friends that that girl on the magazine cover they were all drooling over went to bed with him at night, most nights. We had a pad, which not many people our age did, at a time when I was probably the only woman in that entire city of millions who was quite happy to cohabit without the dread lock of legality. Security, I instinctively knew, was a prison. The warden is as much imprisoned as the prisoner. I didn't keep my eye on Roy, he went to college every day, or most days anyway, I went to whatever job, modelling or assisting a photographer, or as I did that day, to hang out with Bijou, make him tea or order Raju to make it, help mix paint, clean it off his fingers, and cream his hands with some foul-smelling ayurvedic paste that apparently helped with his allergy to turpentine. His hands were always raw and bleeding from the repeated daily assault from chemicals that he could simply not stay away from.

'My curse, just one among many,' he would say. I suggested surgical gloves, and he said 'Condoms during intercourse. Where's the fun in that?'

'Prevention of pregnancy, Bijou, and in your case bleeding fingers,' I said. He didn't smile.

'You are just sharp and no substance. Or, you have not realised your potentiality. If you are not careful, you never will,' he said, not for the first time.

Raju sat on the step outside my flat. He was relieved to see me come out, and we went over to Bijou's. There was someone sitting in the studio with his back to me. Bijou smiled broadly when he saw me.

'I told him not to come back without you. Have you eaten? Is Roy home?'

'Yes, but he's sleeping. We got home late last night, there was a concert at St Anne's school. I took some pictures for you, of stoned kids. They'll be processed tomorrow, but I have no money to pick them up.'

The man sitting in front of him stood up. He was barely my height, and I am not the tallest person in most rooms. He had a comb-over, and his head was greasy. A smell of some oil and soap emanated strongly from him, even over the pervasive smell of turpentine and paint and fresh canvases in the house. He had a nice smile, though, and he held out his hand. 'Kamal Patel,' he said. 'Nice to meet you. Bijoubhai told me all about you.'

I wondered what Bijou had told him about me that could be 'all', but for once, I let it pass without saying anything. I looked over at Bijou, working on a huge cobalt patch that had started in one corner but was beginning to spread over the canvas. It was really a lovely colour, I almost wished he would just cover the whole surface with it. I could spend my life with someone who had eyes that colour. It was liquid, and didn't lose its depth when it dried. Kamal seemed to become uncomfortable with the silence in the room. It wasn't really silent at all, the brush made a sound, the birds on the gulmohar, the autorickshaws outside on the street, Raju making my promised omelette, two dogs in a hostile conversation, all filled the room in a kind of audio image. With the spreading patch of cobalt, it was a moment not to be interfered with. But he spoke into it, unaware of mine, and possibly Bijou's, quietude.

'So . . . what sort of photography do you do?'

I was stuck. What sort? The sort where you point a camera, look through the lens and choose a moment to replay? I didn't think that would be the right answer.

'Just stuff for Bijou. You know, so he can look at stuff. I also take photos of his paintings. He doesn't like what I do, but he doesn't stop me, so . . . that's what I do.'

He seemed to be searching for the next words to fill the perceived silence. He didn't take very long.

'Bijoubhai tells me you have some talent. I am looking for an assistant. Would you be interested?'

I was taken aback. This guy didn't seem the sort to either impress Bijou or—and perhaps I was being uncharitable here and judging his talent by his looks—be a real photographer, one I could learn anything from. I didn't say anything. Bijou put his brush down and began to wipe his hands, wincing slightly.

'Wait, I'll bring you a bowl of water.'

Raju came in with a tray for me, there was a plate with a stack of toasts and a huge omelette, a mug of coffee, and a bottle of ketchup. He smiled sweetly at me, exposing his blackened teeth, and I said 'Thank you, Raju. Please bring Bijou's bowl.'

I put the tray on my lap and began to eat. The food, as always, was delicious. All food to me was always delicious. A cook's dream, that was me. When I was halfway through my first toast, I felt both men looking at me. Bijou had an indulgent smile on his face, and the self-satisfaction of someone who had just earned karma points for feeding a poor starving child, and the other man, I had forgotten his name by then, was looking at me with the curiosity of someone who had seen a poor starving child for the first time. He averted his eyes as soon as I looked at him. 'Would you like some?' I asked him.

Bijou started laughing.

'You may not be able to afford to feed her, Kamal,' he said. 'Besides, she does not take direction well. I mean, she knows what I like and what I need, but,' he said, still smiling as he placed his hands in the bowl of warm water Raju placed in his lap, pausing to say 'Thank you, son, you are a gem when you show up', he looked at me a long moment. 'She may not feel comfortable in your neat and tidy studio.' I was puzzled. He seemed to be dissuading this man from hiring me. Maybe he didn't want me gone morning to evening, which I supposed I would be, if I had a real job. Or maybe he saw my honest dislike of the man.

'Oh, you are funny, Bijoubhai,' Kamal said. 'How can anyone be uncomfortable in a neat and tidy place?'

'Easily.' Bijou said it under his breath.

'Well, maybe she can come to my studio and see how she feels about it. I am going there now, would you like to come with me? It would save you a train trip.'

Before I could answer, Bijou said, 'No, no. She has a lot to do here. Maybe tomorrow would be better, she can go with my driver when he goes to pick up my cheque from the gallery.'

That was that, then.

Kamal stood up to leave. He picked up his camera bag. There was a small sticker on it that said: 'Keep your city clean, eat a pigeon today.'

I laughed. It was unexpected. 'That's funny,' I said.

'Oh yes, I bought this bag from a German photographer from Düsseldorf. The sticker was his. I should take it off, but I am sure it will ruin the leather.'

I didn't say anything. 'I will see you tomorrow then? Bijoubhai's driver knows where my place is. I have a meeting at ten with an agency, so I will be back there at about twelve, or twelve-thirty. You could have lunch with me, and meet the rest of my staff.'

'Okay,' I said, and saw him out the door.

As soon as he was gone I said to Bijou, 'What an asshole!'

Bijou laughed. 'Yes, I suppose he is. I've known him a long time, he is a good person. Did a lot of social work, you know, before he became a photographer. Not your type, I know, bit oily. But he does all right. Does a lot of advertising work, you could learn something.'

'He's creepy, Bijou. "Ruin the leather"? What a schmuck!'

'You are a snob. Can't blame you. Your mother is a snob too. Can't blame you, considering.'

'Considering what?'

'Nothing. You have every reason to be a snob.' He was mocking me, I thought.

'Oh, come on. I'm just saying, the guy seems ... okay, I'll tell you. He really smells awful. And that hair ...'

Bijou ran his hand over his own silver mane.

'And you decide whom you like based on how they smell.'

I thought about it. He was right, I probably did. I remember clearly discussing with myself the way people smelt. Even classifying them by the way they smelled. There was Ami, clean and fresh with a hint of bitterness, just enough to dispel any illusion of sweetness that her pale, fine-boned face might convey. There was Simi, with her cotton clean, kitten milky smell sometimes made interesting by what was bulging in her diaper. There was Roy, an inoffensive boyish smell of the toast and butter he ate endlessly, mixed with some manly aftershave that seemed too manly on him, like a too-large shirt. I wondered what I smelled like. I didn't wear any perfume, or deodorant, but nor did I smoke anything but hashish in those days, and I didn't eat bananas. I asked Bijou. 'If I tell you what you smell like, will you tell me about me?'

'You are extremely odd,' he said, 'but yes, do tell me what I smell like. Turpentine maybe? Rubbing alcohol?'

'No,' I said, closing my eyes and smelling his hair and neck. 'No, that's the top smell, that's not you.' I stopped and took a step back. 'You ate a banana, didn't you?'

'Yes, of course. It helps me shit in the morning, you know, I don't get to walk or jog a lot to move my bowels,' he said dourly.

'Well then, I can't smell you over or under banana. That is the strongest smell there is.'

'Good god. I'll keep my end of the bargain, you can smell me tomorrow before I eat my banana. I ate two, actually. You smell like . . . come here,' he said, pulling me closer, till I was sitting on his lap. He held my face in his hands, looked a minute, and then buried his face in my hair. He stayed that way a long time, breathing gently, saying nothing. Raju came in and collected the tray with my plate. 'Shall I reheat the coffee?' he asked.

'Thanks, yes,' I said, and he left, and still, Bijou sat there with his face in my hair.

'Am I too heavy?' I asked him.

Still he said nothing. I put my arms around him and didn't move. Raju came in and put my hot coffee on the table.

'You smell like earth,' he said finally, 'that has just been rained on. After a long, long dry season. He let go of me, and I stood up. He had tears in his eyes that spilled onto his face. He didn't wipe them, and I didn't say anything about them.

'Let's finish that blue. Just sit there and watch,' he said.

'I could watch all day,' I said.

The studio was in an office building in one of the stand of buildings in Bombay's corporate new south side. There was a small reception area, an even smaller darkroom, and a bathroom. A remarkable-looking young man sat outside in the reception area on a small stool that looked uncomfortable.

He was reading John Hedgecoe's book on photography. I hadn't heard of it or anything, just read the spine. He looked up and nodded and smiled at me. He had Bruce Lee eyes. 'Is Kamal here?' I asked him, in English. He replied in very burred Hindi, I didn't know accented with what. 'No, he's out for a meeting, he said you would come. He will not be back for lunch, he said I should order you food from the canteen. You want to see the menu?'

'No, thank you. Did he say when he would be back?'

'About one o'clock. The studio is locked, but you can wait here. He pointed to one of the clean but old-looking cane chairs. There was a pack of Gold Flake cigarettes and a lighter next to the ashtray on the coffee table.

'Where are you from?' I asked him, just making sure of what I already knew by then.

'Nepal.' He was gorgeous. He wore a dirty white shirt and khaki pants, both were too large for him. But he was very tight-looking. The skin was pulled so taut over his angular cheekbones that it shone.

'Do you work here?'

'I am trying to learn, but he doesn't let me touch the cameras. I just clean, make tea and coffee, and carry the bags. And set up the light stands and backgrounds, things like that. I really want to learn, isn't it? So I can go back home and maybe start a photo studio? People pay a lot of money for pictures, isn't it?'

I didn't know the going rate for family portraits in Kathmandu. But I didn't think it would take much to teach him how to run one of those. I've seen them in the outer suburbs of Bombay, and in small semi-rural towns. They have painted backdrops of scenes from cities, a train, a famous monument, and sometimes there is a plywood cut-out of a scooter or a car. A family would have a photograph of themselves in a car they will never own out on a jaunt in some city they will never go to.

'How long have you worked here?'

'Almost two years, isn't it?' he said.

'What's your name?'

'Veeru,' he said, again flashing that delicious smile.

I fiddled with the cigarettes, and took one out of the pack.

'You smoke?' he asked me.

'No, not really. Sometimes.'

I lit it and inhaled, and then coughed. It was strong. He laughed. Then he looked at his watch. The phone rang, I hadn't noticed it sitting on a table next to him.

'Hello?' he said, and then listened and said 'Yes, sir,' a few times and hung up.

'He says he will be back in thirty minutes and that you should wait.'

Then he reached over and took a cigarette from the pack and was about to put it in his mouth, and I said 'You smoke?' He rewarded me with the smile again, and said, 'Sometimes.'

'Share mine, then,' I told him.

'Don't tell the boss,' he said.

'Absolutely not. I swear.'

And we had a bond then that lasted that whole year. Until, one night, he emptied the studio of all its contents except the cameras and left me a note saying 'Sorry, but I had to go home. I am not a thief, I just needed to go home and live my own life. Your friend, Veeru.'

The boss showed up, not in thirty minutes, but an hour after the phone call. As the first time I had met him at Bijou's, my first sense from him was disapproval. He walked and talked rapidly, his eyes, beady and suspicious at all times, darted about making sure everything was as he had left it. He unlocked the studio door with a key from an enormous bunch. It made me wonder about all the places he locked to keep people out of his things. We walked into a small space—small for a studio that is, surprisingly untidy. He pulled me a chair, and I sat.

'I'll just be a minute,' he said, and ordered Veeru to sweep the floor.

'See, once a day is just not enough. There is a lot of dust, it will affect the transparencies and lenses. You should make sure it is all clean at all times.'

Then he grilled Veeru about all the phone calls he had answered. He seemed annoyed that there were none. 'I called,' he said. 'You should write down every call. Are you sure there were none?'

Then the door swung open and Brianna walked into my life. 'Hi!' she announced loudly and cheerily, dispelling the gloom that was beginning to swamp the room.

'I know, I was supposed to be here at noon, but I only woke up at noon.'

'Woke up at noon? Well, you had an appointment, do you not have an alarm clock?' Kamal asked her, scowling.

I watched her cheer disappearing and said, 'Hey, he only just got here himself, so don't beat yourself up. I've been waiting almost two hours, smoking myself to death!'

His scowl turned on me.

'That's not the point, if you have an appointment you should make sure you will be on time,' he said.

'Yeah, true,' I said, and he seemed to drop the matter for the moment.

'Anyway, let's get down to work. Barina . . .'

'It's Brianna,' she said. 'I told you when we met. Anyway, I really don't like that either. I'm Bree.' She took out a pack of Marlboros from her black patent leather purse and began to peel the cellophane. Kamal kept talking, eyes still darting from her and me to Veeru, interrupting himself to point out a speck of dust that he had missed while sweeping.

'There is a lot of office work, paperwork to be done, filing, billing, filing, challans . . .'

'What?' Brianna and I asked together.

'What what?' he said.

'That word—bills and what?' I said.

'Challans—they're like work orders. You'll learn as you go along. Also, I run a stock picture agency. So you would have to select and show slides to clients, then return them to their place. In fact, all my slides—over ten thousand of them—have to be dealt with, so any spare time would have to be spent doing that—indexing, filing, cleaning.'

Brianna and I looked at each other. She shrugged. She put a cigarette in her mouth and began to root about in that shiny purse for a lighter.

'You can't smoke in here,' he said. I wondered why he hadn't said anything all the time that she was getting around to it, but I let it go. There was no gap to get a word into his steady stream of talk anyway. She put the cigarette carefully back in the pack, saying, 'God, I haven't smoked in an hour—just one in the taxi here!'

He looked at her accusingly and said, 'You took a taxi all the way here?'

She didn't get the question. 'Well, yes, I didn't walk, it's a bit far!'

'I meant, it's cheaper and faster to take the train, isn't it?'

'Yes,' she said, 'I suppose it is, but I didn't feel like going through the hassle'.

He just shook his head, and his disapproval began to settle on us again, like a death shroud.

Veeru finished sweeping. He asked us if we wanted some coffee. I didn't answer, though I was starving hungry, and a cup of coffee would have been welcome. 'Sure, thanks,' Brianna said to him.

'Make sure the cups are washed,' Kamal said to his retreating back. I imagined Veeru sticking out his tongue, or at least grimacing. I had had enough of that high-pitched nag for the rest of my life. I had decided I would say thanks but no thanks to this job. I just wanted to get Brianna's number before I left. She winked at me when Kamal wasn't looking and nodded toward the door, and made a smoking gesture.

'So what's the pay for all this work?' she asked him, 'and do you have work for us both?'

'I would like to do some test shots of you both, to see if I want to offer you a modelling contract first,' he said.

'A what?' I asked.

'A modelling contract. I have an idea that I could use the two of you as house models, so I could give you some fixed amount of money, and whatever you get over and above that you can keep—say fifty per cent?'

She seemed puzzled. I had stopped listening at this point. I was thinking about a way to leave. Roy was surely still asleep, Bijou had probably started painting for the day, I wanted to get back before dinner time, and it was an hour by train.

'You can do test shots, and we will have to talk this over,' Brianna said.

'But you two don't even know each other,' he said, almost angrily.

'We do now,' Brianna said firmly. She stuck out her hand for me to shake. 'Bree. Pleased to meet you.'

'Ginny,' I said. 'Pleased to meet you too.' And we both burst into giggles.

'Ginny? That's short for what?'

'Virginia. My mother is a writer, she's a big fan of Virginia Woolf.'

'Who? Virginia Wolf? She must be a famous writer?' 'Yes,' I said, for once not writing someone off for not knowing Virginia Woolf. Bree could have been a six-toed sloth, I would still have loved her.

'When do you want to do these test shots?' she asked him.

'Now, if you have the time. Because I don't have anything today. The next date I have available is next week. There are several assignments coming up, so today would be best for you too. And when do you fly out again?' he asked her.

'Monday, I have three days in London, so today is fine for me. How about you, Ginny? Do you have to be somewhere?'

I was grateful to her for asking me. 'Today is fine,' I said.

'Well, then, get on with your make-up. I have some clothes that you can wear.'

I had done a few modelling assignments, thanks to Roy's uncle and Bijou's contacts in the advertising world. They always provided make-up people.

'Oh, I'll do your face,' Bree said to me. 'I've just got a whole lot of new Mary Quant stuff from my last trip.'

To him she said, 'First, I have to eat something. So Ginny and I will go eat, and smoke, and then we can do your test shots. Where is a good place to eat?'

'I don't have all day, you know. So you can go to the south Indian place downstairs in the building, but don't be too long.'

She just grinned at him, took my hand and pulled me up. Veeru was surprised to see us leaving. 'We'll be back for the coffee,' I told him. 'Can I get you some food?'

He smiled sweetly at me and shook his head no.

'Ginny, are you ogling that peon boy?' Bree asked me in the elevator, still smiling. 'He's good-looking, but come on, he's a Nep!'

'A Nep?' I asked her. She laughed. 'Nepali, isn't he? Don't be an idiot. Anyway. Tell me about you.'

We came back to the studio an hour later at most, gossiping and giggling like the long-lost sisters we were, full of idlis and nicotine. Kamal looked at his watch but said nothing. Veeru brought in the coffee and received a distinctly unfriendly look from his boss. Bree laid out all her make-up on a table and began to do my face. I watched her face up close to mine, her skin a rich dark café au lait, a few shades darker than mine, her black shiny eyes like beta fighting fish set aslant over the slanted ridges of cheekbones that already had a dusting of shiny powder, perhaps from the night before, her wide mouth with a gentle cleft below a long, not sharp, but finely shaped nose, the nostrils flaring slightly when she smiled as she talked incessantly. I heard about life as an airline hostess, cities I had never been to, the men she had 'balled' in every city, black Arabs, blond Swedes, pink Englishmen, and her boyfriend, a Bombay businessman. I couldn't see myself in the mirror, she had made me sit with my back to it saying, 'You'll see when I finish.' Then she took my hair out of its usual braid and instructed me to bend forward. Then she fluffed it out with her long beautiful fingers, combing the purple nails through it. When she was done, I swung it back and found myself looking in the mirror at a stranger with rainbow eyes and a mane of wild curls.

'What do you think?' she said, unbuttoning my shirt and sticking her hand in my bra to push my breasts up and out. I said nothing. I wasn't sure what to say about her touching me that way, and anyway, I was too stunned by whom I saw in the reflection.

She did her own face then, and announced to Kamal that we were ready.

'Shoot us together!' she said.

He called Veeru in to help with the lights and background. We could see ourselves in the mirror. We coiled together, faces close, we looked into each other's eyes, we looked hard into the camera daring him to take us apart. He didn't try, just shot roll after roll of film, scowling the whole time.

'I need to do some individual shots,' he said. 'I can't show these to clients. You look like lesbians.'

Bree laughed. 'We're done now,' she said. 'Come on, Gin, let's clean up, I'll drop you off.'

We talked and smoked through Bombay commuter traffic, and the hour-long taxi ride was, for me, over too soon.

'Do you want to come up?' I asked her.

'No, I'll pick you up tomorrow, we'll go look at the pictures. Two o'clock. I'll come up then.'

I waved goodbye, and was disappointed. It was the best day I had had in as long as I could remember. Roy wasn't home, and the place was dark. The carpet felt cold and wet when I stepped on it.

Roy. He had left the faucet on. The water had run out in the middle of his shower, and he had neglected to turn it off. Then the city water had come back on, filled the overhead tank, and started flowing through our shower, overflowing out of our bathroom door, soaking the red carpet. It was still running. We had not paid the electricity bill in six months, and it had been turned off. The electricity came in two ways, they called it domestic and power—they forgot to turn off the power. So our fridge worked, but not the house lights. It was the city of Bombay, after all, so it was never dark. But I stood there on the wet carpet listening to the sound of the shower. I wiped my wet face, and I didn't remember when I had begun to cry. And my only thought was, it's a good thing Bree didn't come upstairs with me.

Roy came home soon after I did, and he found me running between the bathroom and the living room carpet with a towel. I laid the towel on the carpet, stepped on it till it had sucked up as much water as it could carry, and then squeezed it out into the bathroom. I had stacked our precious records onto the single chair. They were wet, but would probably survive. I was done crying by the time he came home.

'I met a really cool person and a really creepy person,' I began.

He had his first-year exams coming up, so he declined to help me with the carpet project, but apologised profusely and sincerely for causing the mess. He also promised to try and get some money out of his poor mother, traumatised and angry with her son's uncharacteristic decisiveness in moving in with me, his girlfriend, with no mention or intention of marriage. We agreed that the bills should be paid. We needed light. I left him in the room with the candle and his math, and turned on Bijou's flashlight. I had borrowed it from him a month before and just not returned it because it came in handy when I had to pee in the middle of the night. I didn't care much about the giant roaches that lived with us, but I really didn't want one crawling into my snatch. I wandered around the tiny flat wondering what I could do, I just wasn't ready to sleep. I saw the steel trunk my father had bought me for boarding school in the corner of the tiny bedroom and for some reason, opened it. There was something not right in that trunk. There was an odd smell that wafted out of it as soon as I opened it, but I didn't really pay attention to it at first. I thought it must be the cheap novena candles we bought by the gross outside the Mount Mary church. But I felt an oozy stickiness on my hands when I tried to take out the papers and photographs, and I knew something was wrong. I thought immediately of the acid blood of the *Alien*, and before I knew it, I had let out a howl. Roy came running into the room when he heard me.

'What the hell is it? A rat?'

'No, no, just something in the trunk.'

'What do you mean "something"?' he said, snatching the flashlight from my hand. It went out. He hit it a couple of times, and it glowed back on, a bit reluctantly.

'It's just some contact. Bijou has probably let the batteries sit in there for years and they have probably leaked.'

He shone the light into the trunk. It was odd, what we saw, and we were both puzzled. Everything seemed brownish and gooey. Something brown and slimy dripped from the open lid onto his hand. He calmly put it up to his nose and sniffed.

'Doesn't smell particularly bad,' he said. 'Probably moisture leaked in when it rained, or something. It has been under the window for a while now.'

I thought he might be right. 'Sorry, you go back to your studying, I'll clean up. Or maybe I'll just go to sleep and do it tomorrow.' He nodded, and gave me the flashlight.

'I thought it might be alien blood,' I told him. He smiled. 'Yeah, it looks like alien blood. But it hasn't eaten through everything—the building would have fallen if it was alien blood. Let's move the trunk and see if it has made a hole in the floor.'

'Okay,' I said, and propped the flashlight on the windowsill. There was a moment of silence as I did that, and then we both heard it. There was a crunching chewing sound coming from the trunk. We looked at each other, and the alien blood idea began to take hold in both of us. He put his finger up to his mouth to silence anything I might have said. The crunching was loud and unnerving. I didn't know how we had missed it before. There are rarely moments of silence in that city, there is always the hum of life and buzz of action, no matter what time of day or night. We had missed it before because we had assimilated it into those other sounds that rose up from the streets and filled our two rooms, and in a way, it was one of those sounds. Of rats and small children in garbage, of the rising tide causing the brackish water to rise into the roots of the mangroves beyond our apartment complex, of homeless people snoring on sidewalks, of heroin addicts and flea-infested dogs groaning and scratching their itches in frantic sleep. I clutched his arm. We just stood there for a few moments.

It had been at least a year since I had opened that trunk. Being steel, there was a gap that ran the perimeter of the lid, it was not airtight, and it certainly was not roach-tight. Perhaps, I thought, a small roach had got in and had began to eat my letters to my mother which she had returned to me for safekeeping while they were gone, and my school-leaving certificate, which was impossible to replace, and my composition books, and my photographs of my baby sister that I had kept so carefully under my pillow for those two years in boarding school, and the letters from Akash, who had been so in love with me but then had graduated and left, and I had moved on, but he had kept writing me from his engineering school in the hope that we would meet again and be together, and my mother's letters to me from Split, and Italy and Cologne, and the beaches of Greece, always accompanied by photographs, which this little roach must have eaten too, and he must have fed and fed on the documents and debris and mementos of my life and become fatter and larger and unable to leave the trunk, so full of all its contents was he. This cockroach would have to be my pet now, he was the keeper of my history. I would have to live with him, feed him, work for him, and I would have to love him, or he would slip away through the crack between the door and the floor, taking my past with him.

'Roy,' I said, 'you know that guy who works at the atomic research centre?'

'Yes?'

'Remember what he said about the roaches behind the reactor? Where they couldn't reach?'

'Yes, I know where you are going with this. They are a foot long. You think there is a footlong roach living in this trunk. Do you want to go outside, and I will deal with it, whatever it is? I really don't think it is a footlong roach. Really, Gin. That doesn't happen in the world outside nuclear reactors.'

I was tempted to let him deal with it, but I really wanted to see whatever it was, even if it was a footlong roach. The awful crunching sound continued. I went to a silk factory once, much later, and heard that same sound in the room where they kept the silkworms. That room was filled with that same sound of constant eating, as the worms ate their way through sheaves and heaps of mulberry leaves. It was the idea of worms, or cockroaches, having teeth that caused a reaction on the back of my neck.

'No, I'll stay. Let's do this together.'

'It is alien blood,' he said. 'So come on then, let's move the trunk and see if it has gone through the floor and into Sarin's apartment and into his brain as he slept. Maybe it killed the bastard.'

Sarin was the scriptwriter and theatre actor who lived on the floor below. He had once been a friend of my mother's, he still, to my annoyance, had her books—Shaw's Prefaces,

Graham Greene, Donleavy, books that I would have liked to read but didn't have the gumption to ask him for, even some of her own novels, author's copies that he had borrowed and never returned. I supposed she would get them back when she came back to live there, if she ever did. He was a nasty curmudgeon of a man that we were afraid of, but we had to pass his door to get to our own apartment. Sometimes he would catch us. When we were together it was not so bad. But when he got me alone, he would ask me what I was up to, and he would ask me if 'what's his name, your namby-pamby boyfriend' had finally left. When we first moved in, we actually went to visit him, and tell him we would be living there.

'Oh, your mother lived here, you know. Nothing you do could ever shock me, you know, she did it all already,' he said to us. I didn't quite know what he meant, but it irritated me. Made me feel unimportant. I couldn't put my finger on why, but I am sure that was exactly his intention. He would bang on our door sometimes, when he needed sugar, or wanted one of us to go get him a newspaper, or some food, because his feet were terribly swollen from the gout that plagued him. We got used to the troll under our bridge, we paid the toll sometimes, but never liked him. We hoped that alien blood had dripped down into his apartment and into his bed and killed him painfully and horribly. We hoped to find the hole in our floor under my school trunk. We moved the trunk away from the wall. There was no hole. The terrazzo tiles were, sadly, intact, and quite clean and shiny compared to the rest of the dusty floor. It was not alien blood, then, that was oozing inside the trunk. We stood in the gloom and wondered what to do next. The crunching continued. Roy opened the trunk again and moved the books and papers away to look below. Then he began to throw them all out of the trunk and onto the floor in a small frenzy, stamping on them with his bare feet as he did, shouting, uncharacteristically, 'Bastards, assholes, die!'

I was alarmed. I watched for a couple of seconds and then grabbed his arm, pulling him away from the mess on the floor.

'What the hell is it? Roy, stop!'

He stopped.

'Termites,' he said.

So. That was the end of my memories, at least of the tangible signs of them, of those years spent with my father and his wife, and of the years at boarding school. Photographs, school certificates, letters from lovers and parents, brilliant essays, even a few clothes. They had become termite food. I couldn't sleep there that night, so I went to sleep on the mattress in the living room in the glow of the single candle that Roy studied by for his exams, dreaming of alien blood and, of course, giant termites. When I woke up the next morning Roy was gone, and there was a smell of cockroach spray and little soggy chemical-smelling sculptures stood all over the room. Hopefully, he had killed them all. I was hungry, but all I had in the house was some cold black coffee and very old bread, which tasted almost fresh after I burned it on a pan. I had breakfast, and then cleaned, and threw mounds of tiny termite carcasses into the toilet. When the surface of the water was obscured, I flushed them away. Then I emptied the trunk of all its contents, I looked at each paper and photograph carefully. I wanted to know what I was losing, I wanted to make a mental list of it all. Mary and baby Jesus were unrecognisable on that little card I had had for so many years.

By the time Bree came I had the place looking somewhat normal, and I was actually relieved that it was daylight and she wouldn't notice that we had no electricity. I was beginning to wonder about food. I wanted to go over to Bijou's where Raju would cook me some eggs or give me leftovers from dinner, but didn't want to miss Bree. I heard a car honk insistently. I leaned out of the balcony and waved. She got out and let the taxi go. She stood at my door five minutes later, in what she told me was a catsuit. It was a lime-green pantsuit, and with her large dark glasses and large handbag she looked like a B-movie star. I thought she was gorgeous. She came in and looked around. Then she threw the precious LPs to the ground and sat in the chair. She lit a cigarette and said, 'Whose place is this?'

'Mine,' I said, and explained that my mother had left with her husband and daughter to live in Japan for the next few years. I told her about Roy, my school friend and now boyfriend.

'Where is he?' she asked.

'He went to college, he has exams.'

She was fanning herself with a newspaper. 'Can we turn on the fan, please?'

I was dismayed. And then I simply told her. We couldn't turn on the fan because we had no power because we had not paid the bill because we did not have the money because Roy did not work and neither, really, did I. I didn't cry, though I was close to it, and she didn't say anything for a few moments after I had finished my story. Then she threw the paper on the floor and said, 'Are you hungry?'

I said I was starving. The last time I had eaten was lunch with her the day before, burned bread hadn't done much. She took a large round steel box out of her handbag.

'My mother made roast beef chilli fry this morning, I brought some for us. Do you have some bread?'

I said no. I said I would go get some from Bijou's, and also that I had to check on him. We took the steel box and went over to his house.

Bree was delighted with Bijou, and he with her. We sent Raju to the little corner cigarette kiosk for bread, the bales of fresh rolls that were delivered there by the local bakery every morning. I made a salad while Bree and Bijou got acquainted. I could hear them laughing. I finished slicing onions and cucumbers and tomatoes and garnishing the plate with lime slices and roughly chopped coriander and finely chopped green chillies. I waited in the kitchen for Raju to return with the bread. I heated up the beef, there was a large amount and it looked and smelt like nothing I had seen or tasted, and I popped a piece into my mouth. It was soft, and it was saturated with cloves and pepper. The spices had soaked deep into the meat. I chewed carefully and slowly. I heard Bree laugh again. I didn't want to go back out to the studio. I remembered being in my grandparents' house, in the kitchen with the cook, while they sat at the dining table and spoke in low voices about their daughter, my mother, and her impending divorce. I wouldn't have known what they were saying even if they had spoken audibly, they spoke to each other in German. The language of secrets. Of precision. Of long words. I would find out so much later that it was also the language of passion, of Nietzsche, of love. But I didn't know it just then, I hadn't found my own German then. Then it was the language, for me, of exclusion, and solidarity that

I was not part of, and of plans being made for my life that I had no control over or say in. That day in Bijou's kitchen, I felt that same sense of helpless childhood as adult voices drifted in to me, rising and murmuring, laughter and secrets that I was not part of, and could never be.

We ate the meal together, laughing and talking like old friends though we were new ones. I looked at Bijou's dark face as he spoke to Bree, I watched him run his dark long fingers through his steel hair. He looked like a defeated god, asexual, physically powerless, yet one of the strongest people I would ever meet, though perhaps I didn't really see it that way then.

When we went back to Kamal's studio there were people inside. Veeru sat us down in the foyer and went inside to inform his boss that we were there. He came out with a stack of contact prints in colour and black and white for us to look at, and made us coffee. We pored over the photos together. I did not really recognise myself. I looked old, or older than my eighteen years, and there was something else there that I couldn't put my finger on. I had been photographed before, of course. By smalltime photographers, not the real ones. I had never liked the way I looked in pictures, and on film even less. I didn't usually get to see the results until my face appeared in some corner of some magazine in a half-page ad for some tea or biscuit. These had a different quality. And there was the undeniable dynamic of Bree and me together—

we looked like young goddesses, like we could take on everyone together. With bad intent. It was no wonder that I had the feeling the photographer was afraid of us. He had every reason to be. Bree was thrilled with the images too, judging from her squeals as she pointed out the best and the very best ones to me.

'Oh, my god,' she said, 'we are so fucking beautiful!'

I wouldn't have put it quite that way, but I saw her point. We were not bad individually, but together we were undeniably stunning. I wondered what use these images would be to anyone.

Veeru stood around with us looking at the pictures, taking them from me as I finished with each sheet, and he looked again and again from the pictures to the two of us. Bree was always well put together—it was probably her stewardess training. She wore high heels, she had lipstick on her mouth, she had fine soft hair always tied back from her face emphasising that long neck. She wore a huge gold Nefertiti head on a short gold chain, she knew it was a representation of her. And me, in my jeans and faded checked madras shirts that Roy and I shared, so they were large and hung unflatteringly on me, my hair uncombed and beginning to mat and dread. Neither of us looked like we did in those photographs.

The door opened and the boss walked out and three people followed him out. He made assurances to them about deliveries, and then they left.

'So, do you like your pictures?' he asked, smiling at us, but not before sending a warning scowl Veeru's way that all of us saw and none of us understood the reason for. We were not smoking, we were not being too loud, but he must have found some reason.

'The pictures are fabulous,' Bree said. 'With the two of us together, you couldn't go wrong! Maybe we should take these to ad agencies—or even other photographers . . .'

'No, you can't,' he said quickly. 'These are mine, I have copyright.'

We were both surprised at this reaction. 'Well, you could give us a few prints, can't you?' Bree asked, undaunted by his authoritative refusal.

'I don't have to, I did these for myself.'

'Well, then, you can't use them without our written permission either, can you?' she said, smiling sweetly at him. I was impressed with her unwillingness to back down. My instinct at that point was to find an excuse to leave and never come back.

'What about the job?' he said, opening the door to the studio just as Bree took her cigarettes out of her purse. She didn't move, she took two out of the pack and lit them, handing me one. He scowled some more, shut the door again, hard.

'We haven't thought about the job yet. I have a job already, I am out on flights about once a week, and mostly to Jeddah, so I can't promise how many days I can work. What about you, Gin? Have you spoken to Bijou yet?'

'No, I haven't had a chance to. But I don't think I can work here either. It's too far, I'd have to commute by train every day. I'm not sure I want to get into that mess.'

His scowl deepened. 'I thought you were interested in learning photography, that's what Bijou said.'

'I am.'

Bree looked at me. 'Really?' she said, 'you should have told me! I know all the big photographers in the city! I can take you to meet—oh, eight or nine of them, and you can choose whom you want to learn from!'

'No one wants assistants right now,' he said, obviously not liking this line of conversation at all. 'And none of them would pay you to learn.'

'And you will?' Bree asked, a little sarcastically, but I detected some interest too.

'I would, yes. I would pay you for the work you do on my stock picture agency, and I would also give you modelling jobs. Obviously, if you were here, you would get jobs that come my way, if, of course, the client approves either of you.'

Bree said nothing for a moment, taking quick puffs from her cigarette. The ash grew and fell to the floor.

'Look, don't let the ash fall everywhere. It gets on shoes and gets into the studio and then it could affect my lenses and transparencies.'

Veeru came in with a dustpan and swept it up, keeping his eyes on the ground.

'We'll think about it,' Bree said, getting up to go.

'Oh, don't you want to see the transparencies? I had Veeru set up the projector for me to see them, so you can, if you want.'

I looked at Bree. She shrugged. 'Should we?'

I nodded. We went into the studio and sat in the chairs. Veeru turned off the lights and started the projector. We looked at ourselves in colour and larger, much larger than life, and we were both again stunned into silence. The photographs were not great. The lighting and composition, even to my amateur eye, were ordinary, in bad taste, like posters and calendars from the Marathi and south Indian language magazines that couldn't afford anything but bad stock photography. It was all flat, standard. And he had no eye for what should not be in a frame. It wasn't bad, but there was just nothing to it. What worked was the something between the two people in the photographs, the series. It was hard to pin down the relationship. The two women could have been sisters, or friends, or lovers. 'Goddesses' best described us in those pictures. No one seeing those images would have believed that the two people in those intimate, utterly sexual yet utterly innocent pictures had met less than an hour before they were taken. Looking back now, I wonder whether it was the friendship or the pictures that came first, whether we tried to live up to those first images of two goddesses, those moments that were not really real, that were caught by some voyeur, a photographer who just happened to be there when some instant but fleeting magic happened.

Bree and I left after looking at the slides. We were both aware that we had seen something that meant something. I think we knew that there was a future for us together, but neither of us knew what it was, what shape it would take, what shape we wanted it to take. We took a taxi to the train station. 'There won't be any crowds in the ladies' compartment,' she said. She was right. We sat below the ubiquitous Pearl Centre posters. I told her of my experience. She didn't say much, just nodded, like she knew exactly what I had been through.

'I'm Syrian Christian,' she told me. I didn't know what that
meant, other than that she could not have abortions. She said
she had two brothers and two sisters, and she was exactly
between her siblings. 'My mother may have been better off if
she had gone to Pearl Centre a few times,' she said. And
then, after a pause she said, laughing, 'Who knows, maybe
she did!'

'Her cooking is fantastic,' I said, it was all I could think of.
I told her I had a baby sister and a dead brother and another
whole family somewhere in the frozen north of Canada. Her
stop was after mine, but she got out with me, we had
decided to go talk to Bijou about this job offer.

We took an autorickshaw home instead of walking the
distance, the sky was white hot and there was steam rising
off the ground, and neither of us felt up to it.

Bijou was almost done with the canvas he had been working
on for months. But it had looked done to me months ago.
Blue had spread all over.

'How do you know when to stop?' I had asked him, not
once, many times. He had never answered the question. I
thought he was either thinking about it or did not know the
answer. Or maybe it was different for each painting. 'My
wife asked me that question all the time,' he had told me.
'She always wanted to know if I was done. Always. Every
morning, she would wake up, early enough, but still long
after me, and ask me if I had finished.'

His wife had left him for reasons unknown to him. She did
not have a lover, she had not, to his knowledge, been
unhappy, she had never said anything negative about him in

stories and interviews that inevitably followed the breakup of a famous couple—in this case a very successful painter and a heavenly nymph of a dancer—that gave any clue to why she had left him. It was not the paralysis, he had been that way five years before she left. He simply did not know. He didn't think it had anything to do with him, or their relationship. He thought, like a painting that was finished when it was finished, their relationship was finished. There had been nothing more left to do, or say, that would or could, add to it. He had been on a gallery tour in Europe; when he came back, she had left. She called him, and they spoke once after she left. But that was all. Niharika, once one part of a beautiful couple, was no longer any part of Bijou's life, and other than casual references to her that any person talking about Bharat Natyam would make, she might never have been. Bree asked me about them, if I knew anything. I really did not. I told her she could ask Bijou herself, hoping that she would. But she said, 'Why would I talk to him about something that must have been so painful to him? I wouldn't want to bring it up even if I knew him well enough, which I don't.'

It puzzled me. Why would it be a painful part of his life? I thought. He didn't show any pain, he didn't talk about it, but neither did he avoid it. To me, the more I thought about it, the more it seemed like a finished canvas in his life. Why would that make him sad? I was convinced that it did not.

Bijou began to laugh when we told him about Kamal.

'It doesn't seem as if you two like him very much,' he said, still laughing.

'That's an understatement Bijou. Even his photography is awful.'

'How do you mean?' he said, suddenly serious.

'It's just bad,' I said.

'No, explain,' he said, and waited.

'Well, he seems to have no intention,' I said, trying to put into words what was a feeling somewhere between contempt and frustration. I knew what I felt, but as always had a hard time conveying it to another person. I found it easier to just say something was the best, or in this case, the worst thing in the universe, and leave it there, and hope that I was understood. Usually I was. But Bijou would never take superlatives as explanation for anything. He would make me articulate exactly what I felt, or thought, and would not let me get away with 'You know . . .' So I tried. And both he and Bree looked at me intently as I struggled with real words. I felt cornered, but also liked that he wanted to know what I thought.

'What do you mean by intention?' Bijou asked me, to perhaps make it easier for me.

'I mean there seems to be no purpose, no point of view to his photography. It seems to be nothing more than recording — no, it is not recording either, because even that is a legitimate intention. I mean, he has no purpose. Other than perhaps to have something he can sell to someone.'

'That is exactly what he does. He is not an artist, or even a photographer. He is a businessman, and he uses photography as a means to make money. I am glad, actually, that you get that, because then you won't expect to learn anything from him. Just learn how to use the things he has, the tools. How to switch things on and off, how to process film, how to use a light meter perhaps.'

'Wait. What makes you think I plan to go work with him? I couldn't bear to be in the same room with him for more than ten minutes, and if it wasn't for Bree, not even that long!'

'Ginny,' he said, kindly, and there was something in his voice that made us both be quiet and listen, 'you never know what can come from what. This may be an opportunity.'

And then he smiled and said, 'Hey, if you really hate him that much, forget it. You can always work here for no money, get nowhere, and watch me paint. Would you like that?'

'Yes I would, thank you Bijou,' I said.

I took the contact print sheet out of my bag that I had taken from the studio to show him. Bree was shocked and delighted.

'You stole it! Clever girl!' she squealed. I like being called a clever girl. My mother did that sometimes, and when it was not said sarcastically, it made me swell.

'I didn't steal it, I just took it. You know he would have refused to lend it to us even to show Bijou.'

Bijou looked over the pictures.

'These are truly terrible,' he declared. 'But you two look beautiful together, like Lakshmi and Saraswati.' That's what I had thought. We were goddesses. More like twin Kalis than Lakshmi or Saraswati. But I felt no power alone. And Bree, in my eyes, could have been any goddess she chose to be.

The day went by in a hurry as it always did when things were sweet. Raju cooked rice and rajma, and chopped cucumbers and onions to make a raita. Bijou played the smelling game with me, and I knew he did it to show off my olfactory skills to Bree.

'What's for lunch?' he asked me, and then to Bree, 'watch this'.

I got into it. 'Rice, and it is not basmati, it's Ambemohar.'

'What?' she asked me, smiling.

'Ambemohar. It's a kind of rice that grows on the coast of Maharashtra. It grows among or near the mango trees, and smells of mango blossoms.'

'Really? I never knew that!'

'You would have to be from Maharashtra to know that,' Bijou informed her.

'What?' she asked.

'You'd have to be from that part of the world. Never mind, Bree, you wouldn't know. You're from Kerala?'

'Well, my mother's Goan and my father is a Syrian Christian from Kerala, yes. But I really grew up near the docks here in Bombay. Born and brought up here.'

'On the wrong side of the tracks,' Bijou said. Bree said nothing, but took no offence.

'What else is for lunch?' he asked me again.

'Rajma. Lots of cumin. Maybe too much. And garlic, but no ginger. And Raju is right now taking the skin off the onions, and has stopped to scratch his arse.'

They burst out laughing. 'You are so funny,' Bree said.

'Yes, she is, aren't you Ginny?'

I was surprised at that. I had never thought of myself as funny. In fact I thought I was pretty serious and often even melancholy. But they had been laughing all evening, mostly at things I said. The doorbell rang, and I went to open the door, since Raju was busy. It was Roy. He smiled broadly and said, 'I'm just in time for dinner, right? I can smell the rajma-chawal all the way down the street. I was hoping it was coming from here and not that horrid Sarin's house!'

We all laughed now.

Life with Bree. We did modelling jobs together, thanks to her contacts with the real photographers in the city. We got calendar and poster jobs, and I had a little money. Not enough to be flush, but enough to eat better. Enough to have some small treats sometimes, a meal in a restaurant, a new pair of shoes. I ran through it pretty quickly though, there were two of us, and Roy's parents were not giving him very much beyond college fees. We had to buy his train pass, some textbooks for the new year, lab fees, a pair of jeans. Bree was on Europe flights for a few weeks. I missed her. One Friday, Roy and I walked down to the corner where Pedder Road met Carmichael Road. There was a house on that corner, overgrown garden, weedy, densely wooded, and a low cement wall surrounded it. Baloo usually hung around there, smoking his beedis and waiting for late-evening takers. Like us. It was Friday night, we had a hundred rupees between us. That should have got us a good chunk of reasonably good hashish at the lumber market, Victoria Terminus, and a thousand other dark and not so dark corners of the city, but we didn't have the time to go looking. Unfortunately for us, this was the most snotty part of town. Everything was expensive here, including the drugs. We just hoped Baloo would give us something smokable, and not Bombay Black. Bombay Black is poor-quality hashish that has been cut with anything off the bottoms of the dealer's shoes, which in Bombay was dog shit and tar if we were lucky, or some poor quality opium if we were not. Not much effect other than a plugged digestive system from the opium. Inconvenient, but nothing drastic. And there was usually at least enough hash in it to get us happy.

Baloo was there all right, and showed us some mouldy-looking, musty-smelling stuff that had barely any of the precious aroma of hash. He of course claimed it was Afghani, and tried very hard to get all the money we had out of us.

'Baloo,' I said to him, 'you stupid sister-fucker, do you think I have never seen Afghani? Do you think you can pick up the turd you produce every morning, cut it up, and sell it to me to smoke? I am sure it will have a degree of charas in it, but really, it's never going to be Afghani, unless you are Afghani, which I know you are not.'

Roy was a bit alarmed. 'Babe, you better stop hassling him.'

'Roy, you stupid ass,' I said, looking up at his face—he was six feet tall, at least—'do you think this piece of shit is going to be able to do anything to us? Let's just take all his dope and leave!'

Roy's suspicions were confirmed, I was up to no good. I had had enough of this little gnome, he had sold us so much bad stuff, we had paid him so much money for so little product, we had nine bad and one good from every ten deals this guy had pushed on us, and I somehow lost my temper that day. We had so little money, that might have been part of it.

'Please Gin, I'll take you to Chor Bazaar.'

'Roy, would you look at the size of this guy and stop wimping out! I'm going to put this shit in my pocket and walk away. I will come back on Monday and pay him if it turns out to be worth paying for.' I turned to Baloo and looked down at him. 'Right?'

'Didi, please, I have to pay my boss.'

'That's your problem,' I told him, and then I walked away, Roy trailed behind, he didn't dare give Baloo the money, even though he had it in his wallet. Baloo followed us for a bit, and then gave up and went back to his spot. He knew he hadn't lost that much, and he knew we would surely be back.

'Babe, you're going to get in trouble one of these days.'

'And, my darling, you're going to get me out of it. You're a big guy. He knows it, even if you don't!'

Roy didn't say much about the whole exchange. We went to meet some friends of his from college. They were already smoking when we got there. It smelt like something very good, and it was. It was mellow and green and very clean, nothing in it at all that shouldn't be in it. Pure charas. Most of them were crowding in a narrow part of the balcony, admiring and exclaiming over the size of a dog that was hanging around in the maidan across the street.

'My god, have you ever seen anything that big?'

'It must be a brown Rottweiler!'

'Rottweilers don't come in brown, don't be an ass.'

'It must be a pi-dog, he's just grown huge.'

'Maybe he belongs to a restaurant or something.'

'He's really huge.'

I was curious. I pushed through them to look at this beast of a dog.

'It's a small brown cow, you guys,' I told them. They were silent.

I went over to the guy in the corner of the balcony who was doing all the rolling. He seemed lost and lonely, I thought I could maybe score a bit from him. He had the most amazing smile on him. It came on slow and lit up his funny little face. 'Want some?' he said, and pulled out a lump from his pocket the size of a cricket ball.

'How much?' I asked, thinking I probably, surely, couldn't afford it.

'I have a gin calendar over my bed . . .' he said, and put his hand on my thigh.

That would be the one with photographs by one of Bombay's best-known glamour photographers, a friend of a friend of Bree. Where I wore nothing but black gauze and gothic makeup. It was one of my first big jobs. His hand wasn't just lying on my thigh, he was beginning to squeeze pretty hard.

'How much do you want for all of it?' I asked him, without flinching. I thought, Roy, and also Bree, would be delighted with a stash that size and that good, we could make it last us a month.

'Just a kiss,' he said.

I took the ball from his hand. I kissed him like I meant it, holding the ball hard in my hand. He had my head in a grip like he was going to break my neck.

'What the fuck, man!' I heard Roy right behind me. He let go.

I held up my hand to ward Roy off. 'It's okay, babe, really.'

'How's it okay?' Of course, nothing was going to happen in a hurry, everyone had been smoking for hours, we were all pretty mellow. Slow. Slug-like. We may have run for a piece of cake, but I doubt it. Someone kissing your girlfriend wasn't going to cause any major uproar.

'Where is this stuff from?' I asked him.

'Manali. I was there on a family holiday. It costs 300 bucks a tola,' he said.

The next morning, Saturday, we woke up very late, but very clear. No opiate hangover. I had had an idea. We made some coffee, and I talked to Roy about it. To my delight, Bree came over toward late afternoon with her mother's divine roast beef chilly fry. We talked some more. We went downtown to find Baloo. He came whining up to us for his money. Roy spoke to him. He showed him a very small chunk from the cricket ball. After one look and one sniff, Baloo offered us 300 rupees for it. Roy grinned at me and put the chunk back in his pocket.

'It's fucking Afghani, Baloo,' he said, 'I'll give it to you for five hundred.'

Baloo took a wad of notes from his pocket, counted out five c-notes, handed them over to Roy. Then he said, 'If you can get me half—or one kilo of this, I can pay you in advance.'

Roy, Bree and I bought tickets to Delhi. We would take a bus up to Manali from there. We left three days later, on a slow train north. It took all day and overnight, through the central bandit plains, through Rajasthan. The food was dirty and very tasty, the tea was less spicy and sweeter as we crossed state lines, the night was dark and starry and we sat on at the door smoking the wonderful stuff I had bought with a kiss, and finally we went back to our bunks to sleep a deep, cool sleep that ended when the train stopped at New Delhi station, cold and polluted from smoke of a thousand wood fires. We were starving. We walked through the station toward the bus depot. There were enough French, German, and Russian travellers at the booths buying tickets north that we were sure we had made the right choice.

On the bus I had some trouble sitting with Roy and Bree and listening to their endless talk about trips they had had before, that stoners' competition of who was stupidest or foolhardiest on some occasion when stoned immaculate, and how they were here to relate that hairy tale. They never seemed to tire of it. They all do it, get stoned, talk about other times they had been stoned, how stoned, who said what and how lucky they had been to be alive, to have all their limbs or their penises or their freedom and on and on. I walked to the front of the bus and sat down next to a very dirty white girl. She was gorgeous, with huge boobs. I love breasts. I'm glad I have my own, but I'm delighted with all the boobs in the world. This girl also had pale pinkish hair matted with dirt. She smiled at me, and started talking to me in very disjointed words, with gestures and a lot of touching, and then she gave up and took out a second pair of headphones which she stuck into her walkman and put in my ears. The sounds of The Wall filled my head, and I started dozing. When I woke up I had my head comfortably on the girl's chest, she and I were asleep all over each other. I was okay with it, she was very soft and welcoming. I loved her for that moment, mouth open, arms around me, I went back to sleep. What must have been hours later, the bus driver's yelling jolted us all out of our cocoons. The windows were all fogged, the whole busload of passengers was standing up and exiting the bus. My pillow girl and I disentangled from each other. We were halfway up to the Kulu valley where we were headed. This was a bathroom stop, and a rare one. He was a callous fellow, the driver, and we had to pee and stretch our legs when he let us. The bathrooms were horrific. Bree and I went in together, holding our shirts over our faces. The cold kept some of the smells down, but we literally could not find a single stall that was even remotely clean enough to squat down and take a piss in.

'Outside!' I said, choking on the fumes. We ran outside and found my Scandinavian girl squatting down in some bushes, quite content. I sat down next to her and peed, the release was intense. And Bree beside me, the three of us watched the pee run down the slight slope and intermingle. We had a moment of hysteria, the girl shared her toilet paper with us, and we went back to the bus, feeling lighter and ready for the next four-hour stretch. There were many joints already rolled and lit up in the bus, and no one paid any attention to the driver's objections. He slammed the bus up that little hill without any regard to mortality. The foothills of the Himalayas did not impress him at all, neither did the dark descending around our windows like a flag over a coffin. He just kept going relentlessly. I wondered for a second whether he would drive over some Himalayan edge and kill us all, but the thought did not concern me much, it came and was gone with the next exhalation of the best ganja I had had in my life. I was back in my seat with Roy, he was very sweet and protective, keeping his arm between my head and the hard edges of the bus windows. I took advantage and slept some more. I could see Bree in the seat behind us, she had the whole seat to herself, and had stretched out and passed out, probably hallucinating and unafraid of any dire fate that was likely to befall us at any moment. Like the bus plunging down and waking up one of the sleepy ravines. We travelled through the night, when I woke it was because the bus wasn't moving any more. The first thing I saw was a very white face, blond hair, blue eyes, and gems of every colour encrusted on his ears. He wore a bright yellow jumpsuit, and was stretching his long limbs. Roy came up behind him with a cup of tea in each hand.

'Only an hour to go to Kulu, babe, you want some?'

'Why have we stopped?' Bree asked from behind me.

'Some trouble. With the—I don't know. Something,' Roy told her, vague as usual.

The people around us, Germans, my zaftig princess, some Italians, and a whole lot of locals who must have boarded the bus while we were sleeping, all began to gather up their stuff. They were going to start walking, everyone said Kulu was a few hours' walk, and we were sure to get picked up by army vehicles on the way. Everyone but Bree thought this was a good idea, a good way to see the area, and, since it was six in the morning, it would only get warmer.

The walk was beautiful, pine trees, cows, camaraderie, lovely morning joints, we walked, a lot of languages were spoken, we talked a lot, even Bree was glad we didn't stay behind. A small tea shop supplied us with breakfast—sugar cookies and very milky tea, and a sign proclaimed it the highest tea shop in the world. We may have been the highest people in the world too. As we finished our tea and got up to go, an army truck came rumbling up and we all piled in the back. That was a nice ride up to Kulu, about an hour, but because we were all crammed together, we didn't feel the bumps and lack of suspension. Plus, we were stoned.

As we approached Kulu, we could see the smoke rising from the ground all around the valley town, as though the hills ringing it were on fire, or had been. They were smouldering. I asked the poor jawan who had been thrown in the back with us. He said the army burned the ganja that grew on the hills every six months. To prevent people from smoking it and rubbing the charas out of it and selling it. And to prevent the cows from grazing on it because the army bought its milk supply from these people, and they all had to drink this cannabis-laced milk. I was open-mouthed from these gems of information. He was right, of course, now I think about it, everything comes through in breast milk, whether in women or cows. I translated as best I could for my fellow passengers, who were as delighted with the stories as I was. We were all in paroxysms at the picture of the Indian army staggering about, stoned from ganja-milk. And, the entire population of Kulu valley got pretty high from the smoke that settled in it like down pillows, because of the cold air. When we got into Kulu, we learned the awful truth. The next day was when the great Kulu fair started. There was no hotel room to be had for money, of which we had very little, and no one loved me enough to offer us a bed, even among our little band of hippies, breaking up fast now, as they all found their way to their previously booked hotel rooms.

We soon realised that we had a bit of a journey up to Manali. Kulu valley was not really where we were headed. We said goodbye to our remaining fellow travellers and found a bus to take us up to Manali. On this bus I sat next to Richard from Los Angeles, who told us we'd be better off going up to a village even further north of Manali called Vashisht, where a local villager would rent us his barn, or some such, for very little, and there were hot sulphur springs up there, and the hashish was cheaper and better. Bree and Roy were beginning to show signs of impatience with me, Bree accused me of being ever ready to break away from them and take up with whatever 'moth-eaten, flea-bitten' guy or girl came along. They were right, of course, I was, but I just thought this was part of the whole experience. We weren't there just to buy hashish, surely.

Richard was right, there was a local who came up to us in the Vashisht market where the bus let us off, and offered us a room. It was a small room with two wooden khaats—wood frames with hemp woven crisscross on it to form a sleeping surface. There was hay all over the floor. There was no bathroom anywhere in the whole village. I was okay with it, I was quite willing to squat by the swiftly flowing Beas river that this village was built around. I was sure we would find a bit of privacy if we went upriver a bit, into the mountains behind the house. Roy and Bree were both fed up with me and were openly hostile. They had begun to talk about me and my ridiculous schemes. I realised they were just tired and irritable and I thought some food and a big fat smoke would definitely settle the atmosphere, so I took out my cigarettes and sat down on the hillside outside our room to empty out one. I was amazed when the tobacco from the cigarette poured out into my hand as soon as I upturned it. The humidity of Bombay would have held the strands inside and they would have fought being pulled out to the last one. Roy laughed at my joy at such a simple thing and started burning a bit of the remaining kiss-chunk.

We smoked, and the atmosphere improved dramatically. Then we walked down to the springs. For five rupees we got to go inside and sit in the hot water, it smelled like hell was supposed to. There were warning signs telling us we could only be in for forty minutes or we would feel 'undesirable side-effects'. My curiosity got the better of me. Side-effects are always interesting, and are not always undesirable after all. Bree and I were in the women's section, there was no one there but us, we were naked and sulphurised, and we stayed an hour. Nothing happened to either of us, but we did get clean and warm and all my silver turned gunmetal blue. And there was a row of clean toilet stalls. And outside in the shadow of the Himalayas there was a waiter called Narpat with an embroidered Kulu cap who brought us hot tea and home fries sprinkled with salt and cayenne, and life had never looked so wonderful. And then Richard came striding up the hill, with another man. And I nearly wet my pants when he introduced us. Jamaal. He could have knocked me over with a nod of his head. I was in love. No, really in love. Kashmiri, with sapphire eyes and pale edible skin and dark eyelashes and a mouth to die for and long elegant fingers and that ropy leanness that comes from years of walking up and down mountains, and then he opened his beautiful mouth and spoke, and I clutched at Bree's hand. She told me later, sarcastically, that there were flecks of drool on my mouth. His voice, his out-of-place, unexpected English accent made me think I would lay down my life for just a look from him. Richard said that Jamaal would help us with as much hashish as we wanted. He had some tea with us, made a date to meet us the next day a mile up the hill at a Tibetan restaurant.

That night was too long and too cold, Roy was not nearly warm enough, but we woke up surprisingly refreshed in the morning and went down to the river to brush our teeth. The owner of our barn had provided us with hot tea, Bree and I drank it as we watched Roy freeze his gums from rinsing with the melted Himalayan snow that was the Beas river. He howled and complained, but what really got him upset was the guy I pointed out to him, a little upriver from us, who was washing his ass in the river after having taken a dump. Bree and I decided to brush our teeth later, when we went down to the springs before our date with Jamaal.

The Tibetan place was just that—a restaurant run by Tibetans. It smelled really good, but there was no space for us, so we had to wait outside in the cold. I tried to get Roy to talk to the man at the register, to see if he would let us wait inside, or if he would give us tea. Roy was stoned, and that made him even more reluctant to do anything than he normally was. I went inside myself and complained about the weather. The man offered me tea with yak milk butter in it. And then told me to go and sit in the room next door to the restaurant. We opened the door and went in. There were two cots inside, one with a thin man lying down on it. We sat down on the other one. Soon enough the man awoke and sat up. He was very thin, sepulchrally gaunt, and did not pay us any attention, nor did he make eye contact. He opened a small drawer on the bedside table and took out stuff that I have seen many times since, but that was the first time. He cooked his stuff, whatever it was, in a small steel bowl. He filled a syringe with the stuff. It had an alarmingly large bore needle. He wrapped a piece of black rubber—like a huge rubber band—around his arm. I was fascinated by what he was doing, but his face drew my eyes. He was in there, in that needle, that arm, that vein, nothing else existed. I looked out at the Himalayas, blood-rimmed by the setting light, the vein in that arm that seemed to run over them. Roy and Bree were stuck on that arm, watching the fluid go in, watching the in-out-in-out as he sucked the blood into the glass and sent it back in his arm three-four times before pulling out the syringe and wiping it on his pants. He put everything back in the drawer and shut it, and then suddenly made eye contact with me and grinned from ear to ear; his eyes were clear grey and shining, and he said something to me. I recognised it as German, but didn't get it. And before we could start talking, Jamaal came in and I forgot the man and everything else.

We ate momos and drank more tea. Bree had kept me from sitting next to Jamaal by slipping in next to me quickly and pushing me against the wall, but he was in front of me, and I could feel his knees against mine. I don't think I could have stood up.

She said later, 'He must be some two-bit dealer, to be dealing with us!'

I reminded her that the only reason he had stayed talking to us was because I had his knees between mine. When he heard how little money we had, he had started to get up, only my obviously sexual interest in him had kept him at our table long enough to negotiate enough of a sale to make our trip worthwhile.

I thought my story with Jamaal was over. But he showed up months later in Bombay. My brain dropped between my legs on sight of him as it had done the first time I saw him, and stayed there until—well, until I came to my senses.

Roy and Bree and I bought what was for us a huge amount of hashish from him on that trip. About six- seven kilos each. We wrapped it carefully and stuffed it in our backpacks, and walked down to Kulu, where we had to stay overnight in a small hotel because the bus that would take us to Delhi left too early in the morning to make that walk. It would have been too dark, too cold, and we would probably have got lost. The next morning, one of us, and I really don't remember which of us, but I could probably take credit for this idea without much guilt, decided to skip out without paying the hotel bill. The room, we convinced ourselves, was not worth paying for. There were no sheets on the old thin mattress, and the pillows were like mouldy toasts, the bathrooms were hell on earth, there was no hot water, the owner had been rude to us when we checked in, he knew there were hardly any rooms available so he had quoted a ridiculous rate, and we felt quite justified in sneaking out without parting with what little cash we had left. In fact we knew we were doing the right thing. The only way to the bus station was, unfortunately, right past the front of the hotel. We made it past, and were high from our little achievement, when we heard a man yelling behind us. We stopped. We confronted him. We paid our bill.

The bus left Kulu right on time. We were tired from the long walk down the mountain the evening before, the misadventure with the hotelier, and the resulting feeling of failure. All three of us fell into a deep sleep, though I tried to stay awake to see the magnificent Himalayan vistas, and also, I wanted to be awake for my demise, in case it occurred, which was a distinct possibility the way this driver, like his brother on the way up, threw the bus down that snaking road.

We made it alive to New Delhi station and to our train to Bombay with our precious cargo. We settled into our train compartment with a renewed feeling of accomplishment. Some hours later, the train stopped. We could see nothing but empty tracks. An hour went by, nothing happened. We all knew that these things happened on trains sometimes. Something was wrong, it would be eventually be put right, the train would move on. We had no connections to make, at worst we would get home later than we had anticipated. But soon, there was an announcement. There had been a massive derailment of a goods train on the tracks ahead, there had been several deaths, our train would not be moving forward. All passengers were to exit the train and walk to the nearest town. It was a big town, we would probably find transport to Bombay from there. We shrugged, like everyone else, jumped down from the train onto the tracks, and began to walk with all the other passengers, men, women, children, talking and sharing food and water. As we neared the front of the train we could see the carnage on the tracks. The oncoming train had gone off the tracks on a slight curve, gouging the ground as it overturned, the round tanks lay scattered everywhere, some leaking black oil into the ground. And there were some remains of people. They were covered in white sheets, and I wondered where the white sheets came from. In highway accidents, even miles and miles from civilisation, the bodies of the dead were covered in white sheets.

At the town bus station we were told that there were absolutely no buses available, the accident had severed all train traffic from the north to the south of India. Every train going through had been divested of its passengers and they

were all here looking for a way south. I had the bright idea
that we should give up on the buses and hitchhike. There
didn't seem to be another way. Roy was not happy with this
idea at all. We stood by the side of the highway and held out
our thumbs every time a car approached, but they all passed
by, possibly without knowing what it was we were doing
standing by the roadside with our thumbs held out. We
began to feel like morons. I saw a truck-stop a little way
down across the road. We were hungry and thirsty, so we
walked there and sat at one of the tables. There were truckers
at every table, and there was a loud discussion about the
tremendous shortage of diesel, and which nearest station it
was available at. I had another bright idea. I told Roy to ask
the truckers if anyone was going to Bombay, and if they
could give us a ride. He thought it was a terrible idea. But
Bree agreed with me.

'But what if they rob us and kill us and rape you and Bree
before they rob us and kill us?'

'Oh, if they are going to rape us, they will rape you too,
darling. But the option is,' I told him cheerfully, 'we could
stay here for the rest of our lives. So we could risk the
possibility of rape, I mean, be optimistic, they may not kill
us, and get home in the back of a truck.'

'What if they rob us?'

'Roy,' Bree told him, 'they don't know what we have, and
they won't know if you don't act so squirrelly.'

We bullied him into talking to the drivers sitting around.
One of them said there was a truck leaving for Bombay soon,
the driver was asleep but would soon be there. He pointed
to behind the kitchen area where there were rows of cots
under the trees. Men, and some young boys, were sleeping
off their long drives. We ate some of the delicious curry of

indeterminate flesh with daal and fresh hot tandoori rotis, and waited. A huge man with long hair and a waist-long beard came up to us and asked us if we were the ones wanting a ride to Bombay.

'Let's go then,' he said. He looked sleepy. A small, wiry, teenager lurked behind him.

'Now?' Roy said.

'Now,' he said firmly, 'if we want to get there in twenty-four hours, we have to leave now. Not much diesel available.'

We stood up and followed him to his truck. It was a lovely parrot green, and was laden with something we couldn't see, it was covered with tarpaulin and tied down. So we would not be riding in the back. He opened the passenger-side door and hurried us in. The cab was surprisingly large, there were two rows of seats—sort of, the one seat in the back was just big enough for one small person, and the sulky youth became even sulkier when his boss signalled him to get in it. Somehow, Bree ended up next to the driver, with the gear shift between her legs. The driver said nothing more, just got in and took off. We talked to him, but after getting no reply, gave up and talked amongst ourselves, and eventually fell asleep. It was dark and rainy when I was awoken by Bree urgently shaking me and saying, 'He grabbed my tit! Wake up, we have to change places. Roy! Get up, fool!' He woke up, and rubbed his eyes. 'He grabbed my tit!' she said again. 'Move over and sit next to him!'

'But what if he grabs my tit?' Roy said sleepily. We didn't move, it was impossible to do so, but we all stayed awake after that, and the sun rose, and there was no more grabbing of tit or anything else. Then Roy said to me urgently, 'Tell him to stop, I have to take a crap. Now.'

'You tell him,' I said, beginning to laugh.

'Please, tell him, I really have to take a crap.' He sounded like he really did. I said nothing, and neither did Bree, but we were beginning to giggle. Roy kept at it, whining and getting more and more desperate, and Bree and I got more and more hysterical with every passing kilometre.

'Look, there's a good place to stop, there are some bushes, you guys,'

And again in a few seconds, 'Please, you guys, I have got to unload, it hurts.'

The driver suddenly turned to Roy and said, 'You have to shit?'

'Oh yes, I do, I do have to shit.'

Our driver pulled over to the side of the road. We got out and Roy shot off into the scrub that delicately lined the road and squatted behind the largest one. Not two minutes later, he came running back.

We got in and started off again. A few minutes later, he said, 'I didn't finish. And my asshole hurts, I wiped it with some dry leaves. I think they might have been poisonous.'

'For fuck's sake, Roy, why didn't you finish?' I asked him.

'I thought he might run away with you guys, so I just—I came back.'

It was sweet of him, but I was exasperated. 'Roy,' I said, 'if he wanted to do anything to us, you couldn't stop him. He'd kill you and throw you in the bushes. Or just throw you in the bushes.'

Roy glanced miserably at the driver. Then he said to him, 'I have to shit again. And I need water to wash my ass.'

'Sure,' the driver said. 'I was going to give you some, but you just ran off.'

He stopped the truck and growled at the youth, who got out an empty paint can, filled it with water from a large jerry can, and handed it to Roy. He came back from the bushes smiling this time. At 4 am the next day, after numerous stops at gas stations to fill whatever diesel was available, without running out even once, we were dropped off at the side of the road, on the outskirts of Bombay, safe, fed, having paid for the long ride with nothing but a tit-grab. Our driver, when we offered him whatever little money we had left, refused to take any. And we had our stash of fine hashish that would see us through six months of bills and food. Mission accomplished.

It wasn't until the next day that we found out. We were all asleep in the apartment though it was well past noon. The doorbell rang several times, and then stopped when none of us bothered to open the door. Then there was a banging on the door that would not stop. Bree was the one who finally got up and opened the door. Raju stood there.

'He is very sick, he is in the hospital. He is asking for you, you must come now,' he said, and began to weep.

The funeral was a series of speeches by people who had not seen him in years, I thought. Roy and Bree sat on either side of me and held one hand each. Bree squeezed hard, Roy held gently. I had never been in a crematorium before, and nor had I seen a person I knew that well, someone I had touched and who had touched me in so many ways, dead. His wife was there, a few rows in front of me. She wore a black silk saree and a blouse that plunged low and deep, and her saree hung low, casually, seemingly unintentionally exposing the tops of her breasts. I thought about Bijou's head on those breasts, his silver hair brushing the unseen nipples, his large peeling hands on the exaggerated double-bass curve of her waist. The thought that he would never have another orgasm left me breathless with fear and sorrow, and I began to sob, finally. I put my head on Bree's fine dark breasts, and sobbed. I could feel her large nipple on my cheek. I couldn't stop crying.

'Let's go outside, baby,' she said. It was better in the sunshine. We sat and smoked a cigarette, the three of us, and looked at the white sky. Raju came out to tell us that the cremation would take place soon, if we wanted to go back in. I declined. I was happy to remember my friend the way I had last seen him, painting perfect blue.

We did nothing much the next few days. Some men came to the apartment to deliver my inheritance. Bijou had left me thirty or so unsold paintings, and also almost thirty that were in a friend's warehouse that I would have to collect. *Blue* was among them. I realised that he would have to have made a will at some point, and that he must have known he was going to die.

I had no job, and no long-term way to make a living, three kilos of the finest hashish money could buy, almost sixty works by one of the premier painters in the country, and a termite-infested apartment to put them in. I looked at my two friends. One was drinking coffee and reading a newspaper he had stolen from the troll's doorstep, the other was rolling a joint. It was eight in the morning on a Sunday in June in Bombay. The monsoon was in the air. Life was uncertain, but we didn't see it that way.

I didn't know the paths I could have taken. I didn't see choices. Sometimes, in life, later, much later, and earlier than then, I have had some image of myself, of who I would be, or at least wanted to be. This was not one of those times. I have no memory of a thought in that time, of a girl in a green bathing suit, of a gesture, of a look I could flaunt. I had no self-image to build on, to turn toward. I had no destination I wanted to get to. It was a moment of blankness. I was a page to be used for someone's absent doodles as they spoke on the phone. I was a shirt to be worn between the game and the shower. I was a storage box for unwanted mementos, that you didn't really want but couldn't really throw away.

The year after Bijou died became what I think of as the year of Jamaal. It ended with riots that rocked my usually lazy city and my intellectually lazy life. I took it for granted, life, until then. I lived from one day to the next, with no thought for the next week, let alone a future. Perhaps I clung hard to the present because the future was so precarious, so unformed, so uncharted. If a day passed with at least one meal, if we sold enough of our dwindling supply of hashish to make enough for a week's worth of lazing about, if Bree or I did a modelling job once in a while, life was fine. I got to know some of the photographers, some of them got to know me. We had a working phone finally, because we had enough money to pay the past bills and bribe the technician, so it was reconnected. We had our power turned on, so that there was light, and there was music. I even cooked meals in the once dusty and abandoned kitchen, and made coffee every morning, or noon, whenever we woke up. Roy began to drift away, he didn't come home every night anymore, he stayed at his parents' home more and more. I was sad, but not so much that I made any real fuss about it. We didn't sleep together much, and were never much more than very good friends anyhow.

I could have done better with the modelling had I not answered the phone one October morning and heard a voice that wired a thrill down my belly and between my legs once more. Jamaal. I never found out how he got my number, but I did find out that it wasn't too hard for someone like him.

'Ginny. Good morning, this is Jamaal.'

I was silent so long that he said again, 'Hello?'

'Yes, it's me. Are you in town?' I asked stupidly. I ran through that whole first conversation in my head many times, and changed it to incorporate all the pretty things I could have said. But in reality, I was stunned into stupidity by the sound of his voice. Bree was asleep, I spoke quietly so that she would not hear me, I hoped the sound of the ringing had not woken her, I don't know why. Roy was there that day, but he was not one to be awoken by a mere ringing phone. I set up a time to meet Jamaal at the Irani place for lunch the next day. I was comfortable there, I thought somehow that would make me feel better about meeting him. I was nervous all the rest of the day. I spent a long time trying to figure out a way to get rid of Bree and Roy, or make up some story that would give me the next day without them, but could not think of anything. Roy was easy, he would go off to college some time after he woke up. I could wake him early. But Bree and I were too tied together for me to do anything without her knowing. I was almost resigned to telling her when she woke up and came into the kitchen.

'The van will be here at five tomorrow morning, I have a flight to Jeddah. Damn. Do you want to come with me to the parlour? I need to wax. And my hair is so fucked. Shall I make an appointment?'

I was thrilled. She would not only not be there the next day, but I could get my hair washed and blow-dried so it wouldn't frizz around my head, I could get my legs and anything else I wanted waxed, I would look, hopefully, better than I had when Jamaal had last seen me in the mountains all cold and bundled up in Roy's huge sweater.

'Yes, call. I'll do everything you're doing. I have enough money for once, to do everything at the same time,' I said to Bree. And she made me feel really bad about not telling her Jamaal had called by saying, 'I'll treat you, it's covered, and I never use the whole allowance.' I didn't feel bad enough to tell her though.

We got to our appointment at Shakira's after a quick lunch of samosas and salty lassi at a small shop outside the beauty parlour. The parlour was run by a gaggle of happy women.

Shakira, the owner, was a small sylph of a woman with huge green eyes and the straightest hair I had ever seen. I told her I wanted my hair to be that straight. 'We'll do it,' she said, touching my hair. 'It's very wild. I like it, but it's not in these days, you know. But you should not straighten it too often, you'll ruin it. Shall we henna it? You'll get nice red highlights, the brownish dry ends will look better. And let's trim all these splits off too. You really should come in more often. And why are you growing these eyebrows?' She was clearly appalled and personally offended by my eyebrows, which met heavily in the middle of my face. 'You look like a ram,' she said. 'Let's thread those off. You go do your waxing with Bree, and then come to me after your hair has been washed.' I did not want my eyebrows forced into the unnatural arch every person in the parlour, employees and clients, sported. I hoped she would forget. I told Bree in the waxing room, as we lay side by side and got our fur yanked off by an expert and extremely pregnant waxer.

'I'll tell her not to,' Bree said. 'I like your eyebrows.'

I looked at the pregnant girl as she held my skin taut and applied the very warm wax to the bushes in my armpits. As she stroked the piece of cloth in preparation for ripping it off, I said to Bree, 'I need to have an IUD put in.'

Bree didn't hear me over Abba. 'What?' she asked, and I told her again.

'Why? What have you been doing all this time?'

'Nothing,' I said, hoping she would let it pass.

'Nothing? What do you mean, you're not fucking him, or you are not using any birth control? Ginny, please say it's the first.'

I said nothing.

'Oh Jesus, you guys take the cake. And the baker and the bakery too. I'll take you to my gyny when I get back.'

She said no more about it, and somehow the conversation turned to intestinal parasites. The pregnant girl's other child had worms, she discussed and complained about it in great detail, and Bree, of course, had a remedy. I already knew more about intestinal worms than I wanted to.

Once a year, my mother would give me a spoonful of some vile syrup, oversweetened to hide the awful bitterness. One year, at the age of five, I asked her what it was. My mother's policy was to answer all questions honestly and straightforwardly, and she did it this time too, same as always. 'It's for worms,' she said.

I wondered for a moment what she meant. Then, since she was still there washing out the spoon and corking the dark brown apothecary bottle, I asked her 'What worms?'

'Oh, you play in the dirt and eat things, and sometimes things get under your fingernails, like worm eggs. You could have worms in your stomach, they'll all come out with that medicine.'

I swallowed and digested this information as she went about her business, still standing there in the middle of the kitchen. I looked out of the kitchen door and saw the black cat, Fitzie, lying in the dirt and licking herself clean, imagining the worm eggs entering her pink mouth and hatching in her stomach. She blinked her green eyes at me and went to sleep.

I stopped going to the bathroom that day. I had visions of worms crawling out of my ass, I tried to imagine what sort of worms these might be, and came up with earthworms. It was the monsoon season, and we had a special kind of earthworms that crawled out of the wet ooze at that time of year to further fuel my imagination. They were a rich dark red, they lived in mounds, writhing and slipping on each other, hundreds of them in a single heap, a single being all knotted and tangled together so you couldn't tell where each one began and ended. Three days of holding it in, and I realised I would have to stop eating too. I began to avoid mealtimes, or eat a few bites and hide the uneaten food, or slide it back in the pot, or wait till everyone had left the table to wash their hands and then sneak it into the garbage. My grandmother was the first to notice that something was not quite right with me.

'Does your stomach hurt?' she asked me one day. I heard her later, in consultation with my mother. I didn't quite understand, but there was talk of soap. Then they both called me into the kitchen and took out a cobalt blue bottle. A large spoonful of what looked like thick milk was poured out into a giant serving spoon.

'Open your mouth,' my grandmother said. She was not a soft-hearted woman, at least not to me.

'No,' I said.

'Child, you have to have this. It's for your stomach.'

'My stomach is fine,' I said.

'You haven't been to the bathroom in four days. It's not fine. This will make you go.'

'No,' I said, and burst into tears.

'Child, what is it?' my grandmother said, looking at my mother, who stood beside her shaking her head, impatient. 'Is this for some other worms?' I asked, through my tears.

'Worms?' my grandmother was puzzled.
'Will they bite me when they come out?'

Bree and I walked out of the parlour looking sufficiently like models that people turned when we passed. My hair was a glossy red, and fell straight down in a single sheaf. It swung when I moved. My arms, legs, every part of me was smooth and free of stubble. We had been in the parlour almost six hours, and it was close to dinner time. Bree asked if I wanted to go with her to her parents' house, she needed to pick up her airline uniform. I was hesitant. But in all the time I had known her, she had never invited me home, and I was curious enough to not say no.

'Come, you can meet my brothers and sisters, it will be fun.'

We took the train to the docks. I had never been in that part of the city.

The train ride was thirty minutes. We were in the ladies' second class, and had not a moment to talk to each other. Little boys swarmed around us with goodies to sell. One had purses and handbags and wallets of some material he insisted was real leather, but it didn't resemble the hide of any animal that I had ever seen. Bree shooed him away when he correctly read my interest in a particularly vile pink patent leather purse with a shiny golden chain handle. Another had condoms, they were re-packaged in glossy magazine covers, six to a pack, and I couldn't figure out at first what he was

selling. His little face was full of lechery that hinted at things
he couldn't possibly know at his age, but he managed with
various suggestions and gestures to convey penetration. We
finally understood when he said, 'Raincoat!' and pointed at
his crotch. I bought a pack out of curiosity. There were
plastic combs and hair accessories. I bought a set of bobby
pins decorated with peaches, bananas and mangoes. I was
fulfilling childhood yearnings— these had been popular when
I was ten years old, after the release of *Bobby*, a film in which
the heroine wore them in rows on both sides of her head. I
had never been able to afford them, and my hair was always
too short anyway, but I had wished for and wanted those
rows of fruit-infested bobby pins. I had wanted them so
much that I had actually asked my mother for some. She had
said, 'Don't be silly.' They were ridiculous looking, and I
would never wear them today, but now I owned them, and
I could try them on. And of course the train boys sold food.
Minuscule plastic bags with more cayenne than peanuts in
them. Cookies in packaging that imitated famous brands, but
were obviously low-quality rip-offs. Sliced guavas with salt
and cumin, only the white ones were for sale, but on display
were ripe pink ones that lay open on green leaves like
disembodied cunts. Deep purple figs nested in deep purple
leaves, imperfect and slightly bruised, bursting at their seams,
oozing the barest trickle of juice. I was hungry.

'Don't even think of buying any of this stuff, it will poison
you for sure,' Bree warned me, only half joking. I couldn't
resist. I stopped the guava boy as he sauntered by for the
tenth time, leering at me with his child mouth.

'Ginny, stop it,' she said, clearly annoyed. 'This is all
unwashed fruit fertilised by shit—they are grown in places
that are used as toilets. There is probably something in it that

will make you shit yourself blind, if not dead,' she said, and quite firmly told the boy to vanish, threatening him with a slap if he didn't. I hoped she wasn't serious, but the boy thought she was, and left with his poisonous fruit, spewing bilious words at us both. I thought of a poem I had read which had fascinated and consumed me as a pre-adolescent. It was about two sisters, Lizzie and Laura. I had found it in an issue of *Playboy* magazine I had come across in the house on the beach. I sneaked it into my school bag while my mother and the owner of the house and the magazine were otherwise occupied, so I could look at it later. It was the woman on the cover that had drawn me at first, of course, her wide mouth and upturned nose, her large very white teeth, her freckle-dusted white breasts and huge rosy nipples that I would never have, the many shades of orange in her straight shiny hair—but after examining her assets in the centrefold, it was the poem that I returned to most often. It was explicitly illustrated, the hideous goblins tempting the sisters with fruit, not just any fruit, but 'plump unpecked cherries' and 'bloom-down-cheeked peaches'. The fruits in the pictures were hybrids of peaches and breasts, pomegranates and pears were barely disguised clitorises, grapes and nipples and bananas and penises merged into a Bosco-esque garden of unholy delights. Like Bree, Lizzie warned her sister against the goblins' fruit—

'No,' said Lizzie, 'No, no, no;

Their offers should not charm us,

Their evil gifts would harm us'

but Laura succumbed to their sensuous lures, and sickened and faded in her terrible longing and yearning for another taste. I thought of my own lust for ripe peaches and strawberries bursting with seeds and juices, and the slow release of my own juices over the years that I had read the poem and looked at those detailed drawings of skilled goblins ravishing poor Laura. But I ended up identifying with her and wishing for a goblin market that I would be lured into. I decided eventually that the yearning and longing I would be left with was probably worth the pleasures of a taste of that forbidden fruit. That magazine was now termite shit, along with everything else I had treasured that once lived safely in my steel trunk.

Bree's home was in a congested alley a few minutes' walk from the railway station. We stopped at one of a row of open doors. A faded, but once brightly printed frayed cotton curtain was flung over the door. I could see a hugely fat woman sitting on a sofa with a dog and a child on either side of her. There was a blue TV glow in the room, and they wore the vacant faces of TV-watchers. I followed Bree up the six steps, stepping carefully to avoid the pots full of flowers and herbs that lined both sides of the stoop three deep, and the woman caught sight of us and jumped up and screamed. Her face spilt into a toothful smile.

'I knew you would come home today, I told everyone. See?' she said to the dog and others in the room I couldn't see yet. 'I even told Laz to go out and buy some Limca for you!'

She enveloped Bree in a hug that hid her from my sight for a moment. Bree's mother. She noticed me. 'Ginny? You are Ginny.' She smiled all over her pretty face, a plump, but not much older version of Bree's. I could see where Bree got her eyes and mouth.

'Oh, how rude of me, making you stand on the step like that, come, come and sit, I'll get dinner ready,' she said, and let go of Bree. They both went through another printed cotton curtain into the next room. The dog, a small and handsome brown mutt, jumped on me as soon as I sat down on the sofa. The child, a sweet-faced little girl, in fact a little-girl version of Bree, moved closer to me.

'Hi, Ginny,' she said. I was at a loss, so I said 'Hi.'

'My name is Pearl. I'm in kindergarten. My dog's name is Tiger. Bree is my favourite aunty. Granny made bombil curry. And ladyfingers. And bangra fry. I love bangra fry. My mummy takes out all the bones for me. My daddy works in the mutton shop.' I was quite amazed by her. I didn't ever speak to anyone, let alone a stranger I had not even been introduced to, at least not when I was Pearl's age. I let her prattle on and nodded occasionally. Bree came out and admonished her for chewing my ear off.

'It's fine,' I said, and Pearl looked adoringly at me and moved even closer to me. She put her hand on mine and fiddled with my bangles. She kept on talking. About her dolls, her uncle Laz, her other uncle Michael, her precious Bree, all the things that Bree had brought for her when she went away on her trips. I listened absently. Bree came out and informed me that dinner would be ready in a minute. I could smell it, and I was hungry, my tongue was ready for it. I could not only smell but hear the sizzling fish as it was dropped into boiling oil. Bree came out again and opened a small cupboard next to the TV. She took out two white plates from a stack of what was obviously the good china, and went back in, giving Pearl a little pat on the head on her way. Pearl kept on chattering.

'Why is your hair so straight? It's so pretty, like the Barbie

Aunty Bree brought for me. I can comb her hair, she has a set of combs, and brushes, and hair curlers. Do you have hair curlers? I want to curl my dolly's hair, but the curlers don't work. Can you make your hair curly?'

I tried to think of a time I had talked that much at one time to any one person. I couldn't think of one. I talked to the baby sometimes, and she talked to me. I wondered how she was, if she missed me or even remembered me. Of course she did, it had been barely a year since they had gone away. I wondered if my mother talked about me, if she reminded Simi about me, kept her memory of me alive, or if she let it die a little every day, so that when I saw her next she wouldn't even know me.

'Do you go on planes too, like Aunty Bree? Do you go to the parlour to paint your nails? Aunty Bree took me to the parlour last week and Aunty Shakira painted my nails. See?' Pearl showed me a set of small hands with chipping pink nail polish.

And then finally Bree called out to us, 'Come inside, you two, let's eat.'

Pearl held my hand tightly in hers. I stepped through the curtain into an unexpectedly large kitchen. There was a dining table large enough to seat twenty people, and as we stepped into the room, two young men appeared through the back door on the opposite side of the room.

'Hi Sissy, hi Mom, hi Pearly,' I saw the family resemblance. These would be Michael and Lazarus, Bree's younger brothers.

'Say hi to Ginny,' Bree said.

Laz, the taller and older of the two said, 'Hi Ginny.' Michael just smiled. He, of all the people in the room, looked most like Bree. There was something soft and gentle about him, the way he moved, the way he put his arm around his mother before he helped her with the massive pots of food. Bree's two sisters joined us before we had even sat down at the table, one from the front door and one from the back. They both took after their mother in girth, Bree was the only svelte sister. But all of them, all five siblings, were undeniably beautiful. Laz had a piece of fish almost into his open mouth when his mother slapped it out of his hand. 'Say grace,' she said, and they all did. I sat and watched the suddenly still faces, eyes all shut. All but Pearl's, who grinned at me. The food was some of the best I had ever eaten, and the conversation never stopped. They all teased each other with the familiarity of people who had known each other's weaknesses all their lives.

'How many brothers and sisters do you have?' Pearl asked, as soon as the prayer was done.

'Just one sister, she's a baby. Well, not a baby any more, she is four.'

'Why didn't you bring her?'

'She lives in Japan.'

There was a sudden lull in the conversation at the table, and everyone was looking at me, waiting for an explanation. I explained.

'They live in Japan. My mother teaches English at the university. Her husband works in a bank.'

I was done explaining, they waited for more. I had nothing to say, and Bree sensed my discomfort.

'We are thinking about taking on that job I told you about, Ma, with that photographer.'

'Oh, the creepy guy? Why? What's wrong with your job?'

'Ma, I told you, I'm tired of flying. This won't pay as much, but I will see you more often.'

'Brianna, that is no reason. You think about this carefully

before you do anything drastic. Maybe you should get Laz to meet this photographer. Make sure he is, you know, not a bad person.'

'Ma! I'm old enough not to have to take my brother to check people out.'

Laz and the other two sisters, whose names I found out were Maria and Josie, got into a tangled argument about some incident in their childhood that involved bullying, the details of which they could not agree on. There was tremendous shouting and eating and slapping of backs, and mostly laughter that filled the room. Pearl sat with her hands clapped dramatically over her ears, and said to me, 'Always, every night, they all shout like this. It's because Grandpa is not here.'

'They don't shout when Grandpa is here?' I asked her, wondering where Grandpa was, I had not noticed his absence until then.

'No, when he is here it is even louder,' she told me.

I sat there quietly, eating huge amounts of rice and bombil curry, the fish cooked to perfect sliminess in a curry as bright orange in taste as it was in colour. The fried mackerel was, as Pearl promised, full of long springy bones that slid out of the dense salty flesh. The fish had an old-sock taste brightened by the lashings of lime from the mound in the middle of the table and was perfect against my teeth. I watched this family, which had spent so many years with each other, knowing and loving and hating and baiting each other, and it struck me that I had had nothing like it. They were fat and thin and poor of course, Bree's generation was obviously the one that supported them all, if not Bree by herself. They were devoutly Catholic, Bree's mother had admonished each one for not going to church enough, for not helping some neighbour with preparations for some saint's feast, for not wearing a crucifix one day, and there seemed to be some underlying tension about the boyfriend of one of the sisters being a Hindu-boy. But they just looked so simply happy.

After dinner Bree was in a hurry to leave, and Pearl began to cry. I rummaged in my bag and took out the bobby pins. She looked at me with such devotion that I was embarrassed and somewhat alarmed.

'Will you come back soon?' she asked.

Bree hugged her and her mother, and we left. As we walked down the lane toward the main street that led to the railway station, I felt someone next to me. It was Michael.

'Ma sent a box of food for you,' he said, a bit out of breath. I realised it was the first time I had heard him speak. He had an oddly flat tone to his voice, but he didn't say any more, he turned and started back before I could even say thanks.

'He's deaf, you know,' Bree said. 'He learned to speak before he went deaf, but he can't hear a thing. And he learned to lipread, so he can understand you fine as long as he is looking right at you. Actually, I think he can understand more than most people who can hear. I think he can read people's minds.'

'I like your family,' I said to her, 'thanks for taking me.'

'You really don't have any family at all, so I thought you may as well meet mine. Now you have one, they will look after you. If you ever have any trouble with anyone, call Laz. I'll give you the home number. I am very serious, Ginny, don't laugh. I am not surely sure what my big brother does for a living, but I suspect it's not very—you know, legal. Anyway, he's good at solving problems.'

I was not entirely comfortable with calling Laz with my problems. I couldn't imagine what problems I might have, and I said as much.

'What if, for example, a cop catches you for selling stuff to someone? I'm just saying, what if?'

'What can Laz do then?'

'He'll call someone. Or pay someone. And make the trouble go away.'

'Oh,' was all I could come up with. And then I remembered my date with Jamaal.

The riots started in our neighbourhood and spread through the city. Someone had left a dead pig outside the mosque during the night. Hundreds were killed and hundreds more terrorised and traumatised before it was found out that the pig had met its death by a car speeding in the early hours of that Friday the week before, and not at the hands of an intrepid and malevolent Hindu. It was not an act of incitement but of fate. The pig had been just one of thousands of the dark, rank, hairy boarlike creatures that we took for granted, along with brown dogs, multi-coloured cats, bandicoots, cows—I had even seen a small black bear once, probably escaped from its owner. There were no forests near the city that he could go live in, and even if there were, he would not survive there after his life in captivity. I experienced a silly moment of joy, nevertheless. Another moment of clinging to the present in the face of an obviously nasty future. The riots happened, and there was no turning back the death or damage. I doubt that anyone learned any lessons from the incident. It was the brutal release of bad energy from a seemingly endless reservoir of hatred and resentment that was ignored because it was just too much trouble to do anything about. We all forgot it existed, or accepted it as part of the landscape. The carcasses of burned buses and cars became playgrounds, installations on the streets for street children. The hatred, the destruction, blended into life. No one asked why the riots always started in the poorest neighbourhoods, why the sunrise apartments on the south side or the walled complexes on the seaface didn't erupt.

I was lying face down on the platform of Bandra station, feeling the police running over me. My fingers were mashed. They took months to heal. I wasn't hit by stray bullets. I did know what that sound was I was hearing, pops and thuds of gunfire, utterly familiar and yet somehow a sound I rejected completely, a sound I had heard in the movies. I stayed down there, the smell of piss and paan spit and sweat, my own, soaked into my head. I couldn't believe I was going to be injured (I never thought I was going to die) in someone else's battles.

I think, even before that, though I was not aware that any question was forming in my mind, I must have wondered about Jamaal, small-time drug and arms dealer, love of my life for a few moments of it, heartless sapphire eyes. I ignored the questions, but some part of me wondered what he was in it for. He did talk a lot of Islam and jihad, but I could see that he just liked the money and the power. I was unable to get used to the fear. His commands, his sex, however narco-exotic because of that crisp English accent, were still harsh. I recognised, at least in the time that I spent with him, that he would let me die if he needed to. Some questions arose and were answered by that backroom of my mind in those moments, lying on a filthy railway platform while people tried to kill each other, not afraid of what might happen then, but relieved that I knew what to do next. For once, I knew.

I went to the station on time for our train to New Delhi, and stood waiting in the shadows until it ground out of Victoria Terminus. Jamaal. I saw him glance around the platform once as he lit his Marlboro, standing at the door, his always white kurta catching the wind, his eyes, maybe he saw me, maybe not, but it was the last time I saw him. I cried, from loss and relief and the knowledge that I had somehow saved my own life.

It had been so easy to get him out of my life, or for me to get out of his, that I was puzzled. I had tried so hard, I had enlisted the help of others that I would never dream of going to for anything at all, I had agonised, lied, done things that I would look back on and not believe were me. And in the end, all it took was not getting on that train. Since that second time we met, the day after I waxed and primped myself for this lover, until the moment that the train was out of sight, I had been in a haze of existence. Nothing had seemed real, nothing had any form or solidness. That first meeting we had lunch together, I hardly remember where we were or what we ate, I was so enthralled by the feeling of sinking into something I had no control over. It was a kind of freedom. The freedom from self-awareness, from self-interest, from intelligence. We went to an apartment then, miles above the city, with plate-glass windows and abstract paintings and black leather and steel and glass so '70s chic, I didn't notice the edges of decay, fraying carpets and peeling paint and a dripping faucet in the black marble bathroom that I went into to wash off the remains of some passionless conquest. There was no holding, no touching, no lying in the sheets in the fading orange sunlight, just the sex, like a period at the end of a sentence that was precisely spelt and grammatically correct. And knowing all of this, having been there for all of this, I still turned to pulp every time I heard his voice on the phone calling me to meet him there, in that apartment. The reality of how it was never impinged upon my images of how it was going to be, and that kept me going back again and again for more. And then one day he asked me if I would go with him to Colombo. He said he had some business there. I had a passport, he would buy my ticket, I had no reason to say no and every reason to go. I dreamed of walking on the beach with him, of waking up after a night of gazing into his dark-rimmed gemstone eyes and making his coffee, of things that had never happened and I knew never would. But it was the dreams that had held me to him for the short time we had together, and I went.

It was a stunning country. Jamaal left me alone in our hotel room most of the time, and of the week that we were there, he was gone altogether for two days. He left me a car and driver, and a large sum of spending money, and told me to go and check out the duty-free shops in the city. I did, and I bought two Dior swimsuits for myself, a Halston dress for Bree, and a Geoffrey Beene cologne for him, Grey Flannel.

He laughed when I gave it to him. 'You don't like the way I smell?'

We were out at a restaurant for dinner one night, gorging on a shrimp curry that was searing my palate. The food in Sri Lanka was incredibly spicy. It scorched the skin off the roof of my mouth in the first bite, and then a kind of numbness took over, and then a slow persistent burn reached all the way to my ears, eyes and throat. I had never had anything like it.

'This is where the best spices come from,' Jamaal told me.

He had smoked a lot of the mild island ganja, he seemed more approachable than usual. He actually asked questions about me. I mistook this mood for openness, and asked him why he was in Sri Lanka, and where he had been the two days he had been gone. He looked at me strangely, and still, I thought he was going to tell me, and then tell me about himself.

'Don't ask me things you don't need to,' he said, and that was the end of my visions of being his confidante. I was nothing more than what I was, he had been clear about it. There was no relationship, there was some talk, some sex, he thought I was happy to be there, and mostly, and out of curiosity, I was. I wondered what Bijou might have said to all this. Or my mother. I did not have to wonder what Bree thought of Jamaal, or of what she called my 'behaviour', she took every opportunity to tell me what she thought.

'You should stop seeing him, you should not even take his calls,' she told me when I was showering before running off to meet him one time. When I told her I was going on a trip with him she was really angry, more than I had ever seen her.

'This is really stupid. We bought hash from this guy. What

the hell do you think he does for a living? What if something happens and you are there with him?'

'What do you mean "something happens"? Bree, do you think we're in a movie, or what? Nothing is going to happen. I haven't seen any drugs around him at all in all this time.'

'What if he is into something worse?'

It was the '80s, terrorists were not foremost on our minds then. The only one I knew by name was Imad Mugniyeh, the Osama of our time. There was no Internet to inform and fuel our fears, and I couldn't imagine what Jamaal might be up to that might be a danger to me.

Eventually, I caught on. He either began to trust me more, or care less about my safety, I like to think it was the former, but knew it was the latter. I wasn't always the only one at the apartment anymore, there were sometimes men there whom he would send away if I arrived while they were there. Then he stopped doing that too, and would continue his conversations with them in my presence. He spoke French very well, I discovered this when a tall angular-faced man came to see him one night at the apartment. I was in the bedroom, and could hear them talking. When I went out to get a glass of water, just to see who the faceless voice was, I saw him, and heard them, speaking to each other in rapid French. Jamaal spoke it normally, as he did English or Hindi. I couldn't tell if he was fluent, but it seemed normal to him. There was a handgun on the coffee table.

One of those hazy, lazy days, I was home when the phone rang. It was Roy. I had almost lost touch with him, he came and went at different times, if I was home at all I would not wake up until noon, Bree and I took to sleeping in the bedroom because he had to be at college early, he came home less and less and stayed at his parents' house more and more.

'Hey you,' he said, half surprised that I had actually answered the phone. 'Are you home? I'd like us to meet sometime, you know, I'd like to talk to you, all I've heard the last few months is a growl in the morning.'

'I'm home,' I said, 'and will be all day, and tomorrow too.'

'Is Bree around?'

'No, she went on a flight.'

'Good. I'll come over in twenty minutes.'

Roy and I, both thinking the other would expect it, kissed each other in a friendly but desultory way and then, when we both knew it was going nowhere, gave that up in favour of talking. It was as awkward as the touching, at first, but then our old friendship settled into the cracks of the discomfort. We talked for a long time, we went over old times, in school, when we had met at the railway station waiting for a train to boarding school, about our life there in that little apartment for the time we had lived in it, the trips we took in that room and out of it, the friends who had crashed there, literally and psychologically, we took that last trip back through all those memories, comparing notes, laughing, being amazed that we remembered the same times so differently.

'Remember Farouq?' he asked me.

'Who?'

'That guy, who was too stoned to walk and then drank someone's rum, and then was afraid to go home?'

I remembered. It was after a rock concert in the St Anne school grounds, and we had been elected to take care of him because we had our own place, and we could get him back in shape before an adult sighting. Roy and I had somehow dragged him up the three flights of stairs, past the troll's house. The troll had grunted at us from the inside of his apartment to keep it down, but luckily for us, his feet must have hurt too much for him to come and open the door. Roy had wanted to lay Farouq down in his wet clothes—it had been raining at the concert—but I was afraid he would get pneumonia, so I had undressed him down to his skin, towelled him dry, and zipped him up in a sleeping bag.

'You know,' Roy said, 'he woke up the next morning, and you were in the kitchen making coffee for us, and he looked down at himself and said, "Thanks for taking off my wet clothes, man," and I said to him, "You can thank Ginny for that," and he was just mortified, and said, "She saw me naked?" and I nodded, and he said, "No one has seen me naked since I was six years old." And he didn't thank you for that, did he?'

I laughed. I had forgotten the whole story.

'I have to move back to my parents', I won't come home that much anymore,' he said. I knew that he meant that he would not come home anymore at all. We had no ill will toward each other, we had never made that kind of commitment. We lived together because we were friends, now it was better for him to move back home.

'Has Bree moved in?' he asked me, out of curiosity more than anything else.

'Not really, but she does live here a lot. She still has her paying guest place, and she goes home often, but I've been to her parents' place, there's not much space there for her. Or for anyone. There are eight or nine people in two rooms. I guess they are used to it, that's where she grew up. But yes, she does live here quite often.'

I helped him pack up his few things. There was a backpack, and two boxes. He looked at the stack of LPs on the chair and said, 'You keep those. I don't have a player anyway.'

'You can take them when you have one,' I told him, and we were done.

A car honked insistently, and before I could express my irritation, he said, 'That's my friend, he said he would drive me back, I thought this would be too much stuff to lug in the train.' It was, the crowds were crushing at that time.

'Call me if you see alien blood anywhere, babe,' he said, and we hugged, and he left. And that was that.

I wonder sometimes, when I think of someone from my past that I am no longer in touch with, when the last time was that I saw them. Some partings are like that one I had with Roy, it was clear and it was a definite goodbye. I did see him occasionally after that time, but I remember that parting. Or Jamaal, I saw him one last time as he left on a northbound train. It was not a goodbye, but I remember it. Some people, you suddenly remember them—a girl I went to school with, whom I walked to the bus with every day, a two-mile walk, even though we took different buses. We were not friends, we were co-walkers in one of the walks of life that seem at the time like you will do them forever. I don't know the last time that I saw her. I don't even remember her name. But there are people who really meant something, who changed my life, in good or bad ways, who helped me get where I am today. And they are gone, and I don't know where they are, or how to find them, and I cannot remember the last time I saw them, and there was no goodbye, no decisive parting, just a wearing away, just one day after the next came and went without seeing them, and then they were no longer part of my life.

Like Bree. I cannot remember ever saying goodbye to her, or deciding we had to go our separate ways, nor did she marry, or move away, nor did anything happen that would mean us not being part of each others' lives anymore. But I cannot remember the last time I saw Bree. We did spend some five years with each other, through good jobs and bad, through one very bad job, through her boyfriends, through her almost marriage, through the loss of Lazarus. I had my second and better childhood with Bree. She treated me sometimes as her sister, sometimes her daughter, but most often she was my friend, and one time she was my lover. But she went away eventually, in a slow and imperceptible way, until one day, we were living lives that did not include each other.

Bree didn't live with me, but sometimes, a few times a month, she stayed over. The airport was close, so it was usually on days when she had a flight the next day, or on Fridays, when she would come back late at night, almost early morning, and then we would spend the weekend looking at the shopping she had done, for her, and also for me. She always brought back things for me. Girlie things. Make-up kits, bikinis, bras, shiny shirts of fabrics close to plastic that I had never worn next to my skin before. She made me try on one of her bras before she left once, because she had gone out shopping with a colleague and wished she had known my size. Then the next trip she came back with a dozen for me. She didn't bring white and pink lacy ones for me like the ones she wore. I got black ones with a fine mesh that showed the skin through. A red one with matching panties that had gold thread woven into it which was itchy, but had the nasty look that she claimed was me. There were turquoise and camouflage-patterned ones, oranges and yellows, and my favourite was a white one with circular stitching on it like an old-style bra, there was something raunchy about it. The label said 'Gaultier'. I didn't know Gaultier back then, but I could have sold it for a bit of money had I kept it for a few years. It was not much good as a bra, it gave me weirdly pointed breasts when I wore it under clothing. I enjoyed just wearing it with nothing else and walking around the house. It made me feel like Wonder Woman. Except, I always thought, being an Amazon, I would have only one breast—I had read somewhere that Amazon women burned off one breast because it got in the way of shooting arrows. I ignored that bit of the story when I pretended to be Wonder Woman in my Gaultier bra. I liked the symmetry of having both breasts even, though they are asymmetrically sized. The right one has always been a whole cup size bigger than the left. Maybe that was where the Amazon legend came from. The asymmetry was emphasised as they grew older, because of their archery, or spear-throwing. In any case, I was an Amazon warrior with both breasts.

One evening, we were trying on coloured mascaras and an eyelash curler Bree had bought on her trip, when the phone rang. She answered it. I listened absently as I ate my cup of instant noodles, and got the impression that she was not entirely happy to be talking to whoever was on the other side. I gathered as the conversation went on that it was Kamal, and he was calling to give us a modelling job together. She was silent most of the time, he obviously wouldn't let her get a word in edgewise. I was glad it was she who had answered the phone.

'I couldn't forget, you have told me everything twelve times already,' she said loudly and suddenly, it sounded as if she was cutting him off, 'I will talk to her and let you know, maybe tomorrow.' Then she listened some more, and said, 'Okay, in a couple of hours. We will call you after dinner.'

'What the hell was that?' I asked her.

'That stupid guy. He has a calendar job for the two of us, some client liked the photos he did of us together. What is strange is, he instructed me again and again, that if any other photographer or agency or anyone calls and offers us this job we should say no. The only thing is . . .' she paused and looked at me, and said, 'it's twelve pages, it will take a week at the beach to shoot it, and we have to go with him to Goa and it will be all paid for.'

'There is a catch? What only thing?'

'The only thing is, these will be topless photos.'

We just sat there for a while and said nothing.

'Is it a lot of money?' I asked her.

'He didn't say, he said he would tell us if we were interested in the job.'

'But we might be interested if it is a lot of money, wouldn't we?'

'Yes, I think so. I don't know. My parents would probably not like it. Laz would really be mad. But hey, he might never see it. And you know, we don't really look like us in photos, with all that make-up, and if we did our hair a bit differently, maybe no one would ever know. I should call him back and tell him we would be interested if there's enough money. Right?'

'Let's make him wait,' I said, 'and maybe the money will increase?'

We shrugged and went back to our new make-up and cold noodles, talking about the job occasionally. The idea of going on a week's holiday to Goa was appealing. I didn't much care about being naked on a calendar, I had no aspirations that would be thwarted if the entire city saw me naked. I didn't want to be a film star in the movie industry, nor did I want to be married. Not to a man who would mind public nakedness anyway. Not that I thought about marriage or this prospective objector at that time. But if I had, it would not have been a consideration.

The phone rang again an hour later. I let Bree answer it again. We both thought it was Kamal, but it was not.

'No, this is Brianna, the other girl in the photos. Virginia is here . . .' and she stuck out her tongue at me and mouthed 'Virginia' at me as she listened to the woman at the other end. I could hear it was a woman. Bree gestured to me for something to write with. I gave her an old bus ticket and a pen, and she said to the woman, 'Hold on a minute, let me get a piece of paper and write all this down so I get it right.'

I gave her a paper bag, it was bigger than the bus ticket. Then she began to write things on it. First, dates. Then some stuff about binding contracts and liquor companies. And finally, she wrote down some numbers. I took one look and thought there was something wrong. If that was money, it was more money than I had ever had in my entire life. It must be for the two of us, I thought. I lost track of what Bree was saying, and finally she said 'Goodbye' and 'Thank you very much', and hung up. Then she screamed and hugged me. I waited. She picked up the paper bag and explained to me that we would do the calendar for this company, we would make that amount of money, yes, not together, but each of us would get that much, and we would be going, not to Goa, but to Sri Lanka, not for one week but for two, because this other photographer, whose manager had just called us, had not one, but two projects, and the second project would be paid for separately, and did not involve any nakedness.

And then we just sat there and stared at each other because we did not know what else to do.

When the phone rang again, we ignored it. Bree picked up her handbag, threw my half-eaten noodles in the trash, and said, 'Let's go out and party.' The phone stopped ringing but started up again as we stepped out of the door. Poor Kamal, I thought. And that may well have been the one and only time I ever felt sorry for him.

It had been too long, I thought, that morning as we packed for our trip to Sri Lanka, since I had seen Gabriel. I remembered our last meeting clearly, it had been the day what family I had left me. I was heartbroken. I had to say goodbye to the one person in the world who had loved me unconditionally. She had clung to me and cried and howled. I had carried her the whole time we stood in the check-in line, and then, because we were early for their flight, we sat in the coffee shop. Varun had a scotch and soda, my mother drank a Coke, Simi just sat there miserably on my lap with her head in my neck. I was hoping she would fall asleep, that way I could just hand her to my mother and be gone. Roy was with us too, he had offered to drive to the airport and then deliver the car to the man who had bought it. Apart from a French couple who looked relieved to be leaving, probably, I imagined, after a physically and spiritually brutal Indian sojourn, we were the only people in the coffee shop. There were crowds milling about outside, but the café was obscenely expensive, presumably that was the reason not many people came in. I could see people through the plate glass walls. There were crying children, distraught mothers, nervous older people seeing their children off to foreign lands, or themselves travelling to places they didn't really want to go, but had to, to visit those children they had sent off. There was a stifling anxiety that drenched us all in a cold unhappy sweat.

Our time there, as time does, came to an end, and we got up and trudged to the security line. There was not much to be said. It had all been said in the weeks before. Varun had been transferred to the Tokyo branch of the bank, and they would be going. I would not be going. I had the apartment to live in, they had made sure the couple living in it would be gone a week before I had to move in. I had no choice in the matter, my mother had made it clear that if I was not going to college, she had no further responsibility for me or my life, and no reason to discuss it any further with me.

'I will pay for college, if you choose to go back and complete your education,' she said to me in the course of the talk she had with me. They would be leaving to go away to Japan for two, maybe three, maybe even five years.

'I do not think it is a good idea for you to come with us. There will be nothing for you to do there, and I think it will be good for us to have this time apart.' They had worked it all out, the two of them, and there was nothing for me to say.

'What about Simi?' I asked, stupidly, because there was no answer to that question. What about my baby sister? She would go away with them, and I would not see her again for a long, long time. I recognised that at four, even a year is long enough to forget your whole little life before that. And it began to sink into me that she would grow up, she would forget me, she would probably not know who I was the next time we met. There was so much anger in that room that day, that my mother did not even answer my question.

'I will pay for you to see Dr K,' she said. 'It would be a good thing if you keep seeing him at least once a week, he might help you resolve whatever you have lurking in that heart of yours. It would help you to understand that you need not take revenge on me for things that you imagine I have done to you. Perhaps you will stop being a liar. I doubt it, Virginia, because once you begin to lie, once it becomes easy, it is hard to learn that you do not have to. I don't know where your . . .' and she paused for a long time, so long that I thought she would not complete that sentence. But she did.

'Morality. I do not know where you learned it from. Perhaps it is genetic, and you got it from your father. But you are amoral. You are a liar.' I went through so many answers to her words, but said nothing. She went on.

'I hope all that will change. Or maybe he will teach you to alter your behaviour, in spite of whatever is in your heart. So that you could have a decent life.'

At the airport, before she pried Simi's tiny hands apart from where they were tightly clasped around my neck, she gave me a long hug. Varun did too, and then he shook Roy's hand and thanked him for driving and looking after the logistics with the car. And then he quickly walked toward the gate without turning back, saying to my mother, 'Come on, we had better go now.'

'Take care of yourself,' she said, and then strode into the security gates. I could hear Simi screaming a long time after I had lost sight of them. I turned and hid my face in Roy's body, and he put his arms awkwardly but firmly around me and held on until I had stopped shaking. We stopped for coffee on the way back from the airport, it was morning, the streets were empty, and the sun was beginning to rise. Bombay looked beautiful to me. I had intended to drink just a cup of coffee, but when Roy ordered breakfast for himself, I knew I was hungry, and ate a plateful of idlis too. And then, when we were at what was to be our apartment for the first time, we lay on the single mattress on the floor, and he accepted my urgent sex that he must have known came from anger and betrayal and misery and abandonment. And then we slept through the morning, until it was time for me to leave for my appointment with my angel Gabriel that evening.

I was always his last client, and that day was no different. It was different, though, that I walked into his office and sat down, and before he could say anything, I put my head in my hands and cried. It was fifteen minutes before I was able to stop. All I could think of, every time I stopped, was Simi's breath on my face when she kissed me, her hands in my hair, pulling it when she thought she was brushing it, her tiny voice squealing when she saw me after even an hour's absence. It wasn't just that I missed her so much, in such a physical way, but that I knew how she missed me, how she would miss me with her whole body, and I knew how that hurt, that terrible pain that made you want to wring your hands and pull your hair and bite the insides of your wrists or mouth. till you could taste the blood. I also knew how the only way to stop the pain was to cover it up, to crush it under the weight of normalcy, of lunch, homework, dreamless sleep. And then I thought of how she would forget me, day by day, as children do, in the way I had forgotten so many people, and that made me cry even more. Gabriel just waited patiently. I had no feeling that he would prefer me to stop. I was not embarrassed, and I cried more sitting on that green upholstered chair than I have ever cried in anyone's presence.

We talked, of course. But what I remember most about that day was that he came around to my side of the desk and stood in front of me, and I put my arms around him and he patted and stroked my head. I could tell from vibrations from his stomach that he was saying something to me, but I could not make out the words. When I let him go, there was an embarrassing patch of snot and tears on his pants, and I apologised, and he said, 'It's fine, Ginny, it's fine.' He gave me his handkerchief.

I talked about the time before Simi, when my mother and I had moved in with the man who would be Simi's father, but then he was still my father. Varun lived on the south side of the city, the posh side. It was the opposite end of the city from where we had lived, and the opposite end of the city from my school. I told Gabriel about the monsoon. 'It hit Bombay every year on the eighth of June,' I started, and Gabriel laughed out loud. It was not the eighth of June absolutely, but it seemed to me it always came on the first day of the new school year. I had new notebooks and textbooks. I didn't have too many other new things. Most of my clothes were bought for reasons to do with dire need, and were not usually my choice, and the cheapest money could buy. Books, however, were books. Parents found the money to buy the books the school told them to buy, whatever the cost. Parents, even my mother, bought them. They were brand new textbooks, history and geography, full of maps and photographs of the places in the world I would never see. Some I didn't want to, I was content to see them in those books. I never even imagined myself in those places, the ones with naked natives on tiny islands claustrophobic in a huge open sea.

The monsoon was a living breathing crying thing that laid its accumulated sorrows upon us every year. We ignored it every year, we got involved in the practicalities of living with the lachrymose beast, sometimes just dripping and sometimes ranting. In the face of so much wind and water, there was no time for why. I took it personally, its thoughts and feelings, its Niobe-esque misery. But it was only a wind, soggy and heavy with what it stole from the Arabian Sea.

My school principal heard from somewhere, it could not have been over the phone—phones lines were the first to go and the last to come back—that the city was flooding. The combination of a high tide and this endlessly weeping monsoon meant that the water had nowhere to recede to. It rained, the tide pushed seawater up the sea walls and up the drains, and they met in the coastal streets. School was closed for the day. I walked to the bus stop, waited, didn't get on the first or the second, they were too full. I took the third, and settled myself in that coveted front seat on the upper deck of the double-decker bus. The ride on normal weather days was about an hour. That day the bus lumbered through the flooded city slowly and carefully, picking up people, dropping them off, everything had the feeling of moving through sorrow. The bus stopped where the water was too deep for it to go through. It had a low-slung carriage, it would have stalled had the driver attempted it. So he stopped where all the other southbound buses had given up, and we all got out. They assured us there would be buses on the other side of the water, and our tickets would be honoured. I was small, but not light enough to float, and I could not imagine swimming in that brew of filth, of backed-up sewers and dead cats. Besides, I could not swim. The water began to lap against my underwear. I held my school bag over my head. I had just that weekend covered each notebook with brown paper and each textbook with old wrapping paper and magazine pages. They were new, and I did not want them wet. My bag was a canvas backpack, it would soak up the water if I let it even skim the surface. A raft of large brown hard-shelled cockroaches floated by me. I saw when it got closer that it was a plank of wood to which they all clung, but it was hardly visible, so thickly did they cover it. The water was getting deeper, and I tried to walk closer to another person, but people were walking fast, and seemed not to be as afraid as I was. I waded through the water placing one foot carefully in front of the other. I could fall into an open manhole and never be heard of again, or at least until the monsoon was over and the waters receded. This is something that happened regularly—and I mean at least once every year—so any amount of caution and paranoia was not unwarranted.

Gabriel stopped me with a question. 'Where was your mother?'

'I didn't know, and I didn't think she would come for me. And I knew she would not worry until an hour after I was supposed to be home.'

I walked on through the water, and saw a brown dog swimming toward me. He was not worried, just going to where he needed to go. If he couldn't walk, why then, he swam. I said, 'Hey, can you swim next to me?'

He just looked at me and kept on swimming. I wished he were going my way, I would have walked with him. But he had some purpose on the other side.

And then, all of a sudden, I heard my mother's voice.

'What are you doing?' she said, before my relief overwhelmed me. She snatched my bag from me and took my wrist in a firm grip.

'They closed the school, so I had to leave.'

'Goddamned bastards,' was all she said, and marched us both home.

'She must have been really worried about you,' Gabriel said.

'Worried? She was probably mad as hell to have me home early.'

'I doubt it,' he said.

It was time for me to go back to him and tell him about my life. About where it was going and where it wasn't. I decided I would go right after Bree and I got back from our trip. In fact I was so determined that I picked up the phone and called him there and then. I did not expect him to answer, it was late, and the usual method was to leave a message and then he would call back.

'Dr K,' he said.

'Gabriel, it's Ginny. I want to come see you.'

'Ginny. It's been a while. Are you well? Is it an emergency?'

'Emergency? No!' I said, thinking of the sorts of emergencies he might have to deal with. I was embarrassed. I wasn't suicidal, or manic depressive, or even sad. I just missed talking to him.

'I just miss you,' I said. 'I'm going on a two-week trip to Sri Lanka. Can I come after I get back?'

'Sri Lanka, how nice. What for?' he asked.

'A photo shoot. I'm going to be naked on the beach, it's for a calendar. I'm going to make a ton of money too.'

He laughed. 'Call me when you get back then. And bring me back some *watalluppam*.'

'Some what?' I asked.

'It's a Sri Lankan dessert. Just eat some for me. I used to go there as a child. Have you been before?' he said.

'No.' I hadn't told him about Jamaal. I had a lot to tell him. It had been over a year since our last meeting.

'You will love it, it's a beautiful place. It will fill your heart.' I was quiet, this was not like him at all. I knew how beautiful it was, but I had only really seen the inside of my hotel room, the view from our window, which was no doubt spectacular, and the inside of the building that housed the duty-free shops.

'Call me when you get back, Ginny, and have a wonderful time.'

'Thanks, Dr K, I'll see you soon,' I said, and hung up as Bree came in with her toothbrush.

'Who were you talking to?'

'A guy.'

'Yes, what guy? Are you hiding something?'

'No. Yes.'

'One Jamaal not enough for you? Are you stupid? I think you are,' she said, shoving our bras and panties into a pillowcase.

'He's not really a guy like that.'

'Tell me,' she said, and I did.

'A psychiatrist? Really? Did you try to kill yourself or something?'

I laughed. But that was how it was. You didn't get taken to a psychiatrist unless you tried to kill either yourself or someone else. Or at least ran naked in the street. I told her that my parents thought I needed someone to talk to.

'They probably didn't want to deal with it, and they have the money to pay for expensive doctors. My mother sent us to the priest. I suppose it is the same thing. And confession. That's the same thing too, isn't it?'

'Yes.'

It was the very early '80s. Sri Lanka was beginning to open up to products. Cosmetic companies and foreign investors began to trickle in, a lot of Japanese building machinery companies came in as construction began to boom. Products meant advertising agencies. Indian agencies opened branches in Colombo, or did business with them from Bombay. But they had no local models there then, it was still a very conservative society. Indian models were being recruited for ad campaigns. You needed a passport to go over, so some

were automatically weeded out. Most, because their parents
would simply not let them go 'abroad' with ad agency execs.
That meant Bree and I, ever ready to whip out passport and
whip off bra after the initial hesitation, began to get a lot of
work. I became a travel addict, I would go anywhere for just
the expenses, if it was new and exciting. Bree wasn't always
with me, but she sometimes, in the beginning, would negotiate
my fees anyway, when she found I would agree to any paltry
amount. After our first modelling trip to Colombo, I let it be
known that I would go there anytime for ticket and hotel
only, I did not need any modelling fee. Sri Lanka was what
I had been looking for all my life. I always felt, when I went
to Goa, or Manali, that these places were great, but not 'the
place'. Sri Lanka was 'the place'. Great untouched beaches,
plenty of cheap, clean, mellow weed, European travellers,
wonderful food, Gabriel was right, I was truly in heaven,
and, I was an angel.

On that trip, my second and Bree's first, we stayed at the
Lanka Oberoi. Bree, faster than me, immediately shacked up
with the French photographer, and I had our room mostly to
myself. The hotel was new, all marble and chrome. Forty-
foot-long locally made batik hung in the lobby, the staff was,
like every Sri Lankan I have ever met, lovely. Everything, to
me, was just perfect. One night, having a late drink at the bar
with the agency folk, we were introduced to a whole bunch
of college students one of the girls knew. I didn't register any
of the faces but one. His name was Ellie. He probably had a
long, tongue-numbing Tamil name, but I never found out
what it was. He was very tall, for a Sri Lankan, dark enough

to cause total eclipse when he came into a room, he seemed to draw in light, he had that matte blackness like coal, a soft, velvet black. And his eyes, they were the shiniest deepest black I had ever seen. He and I were on each other like (no, not flies on shit) two young people who had found each other. Smelled each other. He was about twenty, he had just finished his Bachelor's degree in some kind of chemistry. From that first night in my room, the only time we were apart was when I had to do my shots. Even to turn my face to get made up was hard, we had to stop kissing. I was offered another small job when Bree and I finished with the calendar job, and she had to go on a flight. She still had her airline job, her mother had convinced her not to give it up. I stayed another week, made a little more money, and enjoyed a few more daylight and night time hours with tall, dark and handsome Ellie.

I went back to Colombo almost three months later, to do a film for a famous brand of face cream. It was called a 're-entry' film, because the brand was going back to that market after many years. I thought of it as the Ellie re-entry film. But that was not to be. I called Ellie, he did come and see me. But he had a girlfriend. I wasn't too hurt or upset, he was too gorgeous to wait about for someone whom he may never see again. But it was disappointing to be there for two weeks and not have him. The next day, though, Ellie came to see me on the set of the film, which was not really a set, but the home of the president of some bank. It was a colonial masterpiece of a house, all dark wood and whitewashed walls, palms and bananas and birds of paradise, brass everywhere, bearers in starch-white sarongs and brass-buttoned jackets waiting on us, fifteen of India's most beautiful and succulent fruits, pale, tan, dark-eyed and light, tall, short, small breasts, large, and me, in between. Ellie brought with him a gift for me, a sort of apology present. His name was Damir. He was as different from Ellie as anyone could possibly be. He was cream and had faded khaki eyes, and smelt so European, so clean and vanilla compared to Ellie's spicy muskiness. I thought of him as pudding, after a curry main course. Lots of vanilla pudding. I had as much enthusiasm for him that visit as I had had for Ellie the time before. The director of this film, a woman who had been quite snappy with me until Ellie and Damir showed up, was suddenly extra nice to me. Best of all, she made my stay by moving the girl who was sharing my room out, so I had it to myself. After the film was done, I stayed on in Colombo another two weeks. Ellie took me to his place, a large guest house. His mother ran it after his father's premature death, and Damir rented one of the rooms there for the summer.

After the first couple of days of being inside Damir's room and coming out to the common dining room only for Ellie's mother's searing curries with rice noodles, we got over ourselves a little, and began to hang out with Ellie and his friends. Damir talked about his home, Yugoslavia, then still a whole country. He was at first disbelieving, and then thrilled that I had been there. When he found I had actually been to his home town, Split, he got all excited and hugged and kissed me. Ellie and his friends, about five other boys and three girls, talked a lot about Jaffna, and the north.

About Tamil liberation. About attacking the government, about having their own state. I didn't pay too much attention to all this, I was happier smoking grass, having Damir wrapped around me, sitting there in the semi-dark late hours of night into the early hours of day, talking endlessly. It started getting more and more specific, they spoke of people they knew in the north, they spoke of times, places, attacks on police stations, colleges, the Ceylon broadcasting station, a library in Jaffna. I was, by the end of the week, beginning to get uneasy. Damir laughed at me, he said we were foreign, we didn't count. The agency knew I was still in Colombo, they called me to check if I would do another film there for a toothpaste. They said they could pay me three hundred dollars because there were no travel expenses. I had to stay another two weeks, while they got it all together. I was delighted, and Damir and I went down the coast to Hikkaduwa with the advance money they gave me. We stayed a week, and came back to Ellie's late on a Friday evening. I remember it was a Friday because Sri Lanka closes on Fridays, it's their Sabbath, sort of. There were two new people at the guest house. Damir's room had been given to one of the men, and we had to stay in a smaller room that faced the back. It was actually a prettier view, there was a small slab jutting out from the back door, with a wooden swing in a small garden. We put our stuff away and took a shower. I remember Damir was sunburnt, I put face cream on him (I had a lot of jars), he was not in pain, but quite uncomfortable. He couldn't put a shirt on. We went to dinner like that, everyone laughed at him. Ellie sat with us, I noticed he did not introduce us to the new people. They sat by themselves in a corner of the dining room, not at the main central table. At night, when we went to Ellie's part of the house to smoke and talk and eat dessert—as Gabriel had promised, I encountered watalluppam, it was a custard made from coconut milk and jaggery—the two men were there, again apart from everyone else, in chairs at the far end of the verandah where we sat. We stayed a long time, and this time just talked of nothing and everything, laughed and had a really sweet time. I remember it as a very special evening and night and early morning, it must have been 2 am before Damir and I went to bed. He lay on his stomach with his burning back, and we were both a little sad that night. It seemed to be ending, our time together. I had to report to work in the next few days. Though I would see him every day, it didn't feel like it would be the same.

After the toothpaste commercial was done, I booked my return a few days later, so I would have a little more time with Damir. He said he would be going back to Yugoslavia soon, the summer was coming to an end, he had to go and do his compulsory military service. We spent those days very carefully, very gently, holding them to us like they were precious, and they were. We were not in love, but we were lovers, we were friends, we had been, in heart and spirit and body for however short a time, together. And we were sad. We both knew we would never be that way again, even if we ever saw each other again, which was unlikely.

That night, fast asleep after good food, vanilla ice cream (Damir loved his ice cream), making love long and sweet and very quiet, we woke up to violence. There was thumping and shouting, I could hear people running down the passage outside our room. Damir was wide awake and off the bed before I could get my thoughts together. He pulled me to my feet, wrapped the sheet around me, and pushed me out of the back door. We jumped off the cement slab that was the patio thing, and were going to run when lights went on in the rooms on both sides of us. He shoved me to the ground and whispered to me to go under the slab. I was terrified. Of snakes and scorpions. He pushed me, rolled me, and then rolled under with me. We went right to the back, till we hit the wall of the building. I could feel cobwebs, thick, that had never been disturbed. We crawled still back, into a section that had a tamarind tree in front of it on the outside. He lay by me, put his arms around me, and held me hard and close, like we were one. Nothing happened for the longest time, all we heard was each other's heartbeats, and breathing, his slow and steady, mine all jagged. It wasn't that long before our door was kicked or somehow forced open, footsteps came out on top of us. Lights came on. We could see shadows and lights and hear people, men, talking aloud, neither of us understood Sinhalese. They shouted, presumably calling someone. Then we heard someone shout from the other side of our room, and the men ran off. Damir and I lay there, we lay a long time, breathing, touching, eventually finding each other in the dirt there, comfort, relief, goodbye, all of it coming together in the sweetest saddest time we had ever had.

When we got out of there in the early morning light, we went back to our room, showered, him in pain from the scrapes on his poor back, then we dressed and went to eat breakfast. Ellie was there, smoking, shaken, obviously he had been awake all night. The police had been there, they had taken away the two men. When I asked who they were, he said they were from the north, you know. I didn't, not really.

I didn't meet Ellie again, though I went back to Sri Lanka many times after that. I found his guest house, when I went there to find him, partly burned down, and abandoned, they said he and his mother had sold the land and moved to Jaffna. The neighbour I asked said, '*Kotiya*?' and made a gesture of dismissal. Damir went back to Yugoslavia. I thought about him when the images of war and the NATO bombings filled the papers and the news. I think of him sometimes when I eat vanilla ice cream. I hope he still eats it, and I hope he remembers me when he does, or when he feeds it to his children.

Sri Lanka was not done with me. Thanks to the troubles there, the work eventually dried up, and we were not willing to risk our lives to go there to do what little came our way. The last time I was there was in the summer of 1983. The country, and the city of Colombo, was in hell, and I was too.

Bree and I did some work with Kamal on and off. He didn't get the high-end glamour jobs, but he did have a steady stream of work that gave us a steady stream of income when there was nothing else to be had. He had his low-end clients, people who did their calendars every year with him, or greeting cards, companies that made metal boxes and playing cards that went to him for images. He was unbearable to be around, he was always officious and picky about everything. He treated the help and the staff with contempt and impatience, he yelled at everyone all the time, it was no fun being at his studio. But we went anyway. I managed to avoid going there without Bree, but we both knew the time would come. It came when I was low on funds, and couldn't afford to say no to the job. On top of his normal crabbiness, he had never forgiven us for doing that first calendar job with the French photographer in spite of his repeated pleas to us not to. We didn't refer to it after the first time we met, but it was there.

'It was unprofessional of you to do it when I had called you first,' he had said.

'It was unprofessional of you to attempt to keep more than half the modelling fees,' Bree had said.

'But if word spreads that you two don't keep your word, you won't get any more work,' he had said.

At which point I lost my temper and said, 'Oh, give it a break. We have done lots and lots of work, everyone knows us together and individually, and your threats sound just stupid.'

He was almost shocked that I had been the one to speak, and he stared at me and said nothing more. He did yell at poor Veeru about a speck of dust on the cup of coffee he had just been handed.

158 / Urmilla Deshpande

That morning I was late for the job. The trains were crowded, and I let two go without fighting through the throngs. By the time I got there I was thirty-four minutes late. I was ready for a lecture on the virtues of punctuality. To my surprise, he said nothing about it. In fact he asked me what I had eaten for breakfast and if I wanted some coffee. Then he sent Veeru to order me a plate of idlis and make me a cup of coffee.

'Where's everyone?' I asked. There were no make-up and hair people, no agency reps, no client there. I wondered if I had the time wrong.

'Actually, the shoot isn't until noon,' he said. 'I wanted to talk to you alone.'

I was angry, but more surprised. 'You could have told me, I would have taken a less crowded train,' I said. He ignored that.

'I wanted to talk about this job I have.'

'I'm not interested in that job,' I said, before he could get into it. His usual scowl deepened, still, he held his temper in check.

'I thought you wanted to learn photography, at least that's what Bijou told me.'

I sighed. Bijou had not crossed my mind in weeks, if not months. I felt a little sad at the thought. His paintings still sat in a huge stack against the bedroom wall, taking up most of the small space. I was afraid the termites would get to them, and I checked occasionally, but there was no sign of them. Roy had killed them all. And the friend who had the rest of my inheritance sent me an official-looking letter with a list of my paintings, name, size, medium, date, all detailed on it. He also told me to put that letter in a bank vault, in case something happened to him and I needed proof that those paintings did indeed belong to me. Kamal had been talking incessantly all the time I was thinking about Bijou. I heard him finally, when he said, quite loudly, 'So? What do you have to say?'

'About what?'

'Have you not been listening to me?'

Suddenly, he sighed. He put his hand on mine and started over. 'Look, Ginny, you really need help, don't you? You must have been heartbroken when he died, he was like a father to you, wasn't he?'

I did not show my amusement, but I wanted to laugh out loud. I guess Bijou was like a father to me, he would have jumped in bed with me if he could have jumped at all. I didn't laugh, but I watched Kamal's face uncomfortably close to mine, full of uncharacteristic concern.

'Are your parents here?'

I had to think about that question carefully. I could lie, and say no. Or I could tell the truth, that my father, and his wife, did in fact live in the city. I chose the second.

'My father lives here,' I said. He drew back his hand from my arm in a hurry.

'Really? Why don't you live with him then?' he asked, embarrassed and covering up by reaching for his coffee.

'They were divorced. I grew up with my mother. I don't get along with his wife. Many reasons.'

He said nothing for a while. Then, 'Well, let's talk about this job. I know you said you are not interested. But let me talk to you about it, maybe I can get you to change your mind.'

He talked about the kinds of jobs he got, the kind of things I would learn. He did a lot of industrial work, he said, which meant there was a lot of the technical part of photography and lighting that I would learn.

'I don't do a lot of glamour work, I do more food, and factories. I do a lot of hotels and interiors. It would mean hard work, carrying bags, doing complicated lighting set-ups, in hard conditions sometimes. I should probably hire a man to do it, but I thought I owed it to Bijou to ask you first.'

I was intrigued, and slightly tempted. I imagined myself with cameras slung around my neck, dressed in khakis with many pockets, Dennis Hopper in *Apocalypse Now*, taking photos in the midst of death and burning. And then he said something that, now I look back on it, must have convinced me.

'I should tell you upfront, there will be a lot of travel. This may be hard on your other career, but you should look at it as an investment. You would learn a skill, and you would make a lot of contacts.'

Contacts. I didn't have any. I learned later that this man had no friends at all, only contacts. That everything he did, he did with some calculation in his mind that ended up, even if mistakenly, being advantageous to him. I didn't know that about him then. I didn't know he instinctively, almost, moved through the world working everything in a way that diminished those around him and so built him up. I saw it, in small ways, in the way he dealt with Veeru, or the thin hardworking boy who brought the coffee and food from the building canteen. He was always smiling, that little boy, until he encountered Kamal's distaste. I didn't understand then, that Kamal would not survive without crushing everyone around him. I didn't understand that he had so little self-worth that all he could do was be bigger than everyone around him to be any size at all. I just thought of him as a pompous ass. I was wrong. Pompous asses are easy to deal with. I didn't know my own deficiencies, and I didn't know that they fell squarely in opposition to his. I was the perfect muse, the perfect take-down for his build-up.

I agreed to think about the job. I agreed to come in a few days a week and see how it felt. There would be travel, I thought, and that sucked me in. In a few months, I was on my way to being a film processor, a carrier of bags, a setter-up of lights, a librarian for boxes and boxes of slides, a make-up artist. What I was not, was on my way to being a photographer. But I was hooked. I had a place I went to every day, I had a routine, I was needed, and I was determined to make myself indispensable.

The year and a half of being free and open to my own life, to my own growth, was over. Before I knew it, I was one tenth of a couple. It was Kamal and Ginny now, I was no longer just Ginny, who had her own pad, her own life, her own career, who was at the fringe of the counterculture. I was uncomfortable, in some parts of my mind, but those parts grew number and number in the comfort this adult gave me. I looked for those parts of myself sometimes, when Bree and I met, which was not often, when she offered me a cigarette and I looked nervously around to see if he was there, and wondered why and who I was afraid of. She saw it too, and tried to point it out to me. I listened, at first, when she said, 'You never did what anyone told you. It's one of the things that infuriated me about you. But it was the thing I loved most about you. What's going on?'

'It's good for me to not smoke, he's right about that.'

'I'm not talking about smoking, Ginny. I'm talking about you. I'm talking about him telling you what's good or bad for you.'

'I don't know what you mean, Bree. He doesn't tell me what's good or bad for me.'

But Bree didn't crash with me so much anymore, she kept away from jobs with me. Maybe there were not that many, but I didn't see her as much as I used to.

It was easy, in some ways, with Kamal. I didn't have to think about where my next meal was coming from, I didn't have to think where my next job was coming from. He said he calculated an amount for me, a salary, and that he deducted my expenses from it. I didn't realise that this meant I had no money saved because I ate lunch every day, I didn't ask, I just trusted him. I didn't realise that he paid me nothing for all the modelling jobs he brought in, because he figured he would give me twenty per cent, which covered my expenses. I didn't realise that he didn't pay me for all the work I did for him as an assistant because he was teaching me photography, and I was an apprentice, and apprentices don't get paid. I think I should have been paid for sleeping with him then, surely, the few miserable times that I did. I didn't think anymore that that was supposed to be a joyous thing—he blamed me for his premature ejaculations, he blamed me for being too passive, or too hasty, or not enthusiastic enough. I was grateful that this did not happen too often. He had beady suspicious little eyes, and smelled of something I could not recognise. His was going bald in a bad way too. I never thought baldness was ugly, it never put me off, if it was a normal accepted condition. But his was greasy, an uneasy baldness that no one acknowledged, because he did not. It hung like a fart in the room that everyone knew came from him, because it surrounded him, because everyone knew it wasn't them.

We had fun together too, not everything was dreary. We went to places I might never have gone to, we saw things I might never have seen. I even fell in love one wintry smog-filled Bombay day. Kamal had moved in to my place by then, he had abandoned his pregnant wife and small boy in a flat in a distant suburb on the north side. I had met her just once, when he had invited Bree and me to go to his home after a photo shoot in the vicinity. She was a small, sharp, attractive woman with kohl-lined eyes and long beautiful oiled hair, dressed in a flowered cotton sari. She was polite and friendly and served us tea and snacks. I was uncomfortable around her, I felt, as I always did, over-dressed and over-made-up. I wondered why Bree never felt that way, in spite of being twice as dressed and made-up as I was. She was more grown up, I always thought, than I could ever be. Comfortable in her skin, so much so that I was comfortable in her skin too. I remember thinking that day that I hoped she would always be with me.

We woke up very early to pick up the processed film from a lab halfway between home and his studio. I waited in the taxi when he went in to pick it up. He came out with another man. I didn't catch his name, I didn't hear anything that was said after I laid eyes on him. He had long eyes framed by dark lacy eyelashes, and his expression was an arrogant sneer, but that may have been because he spoke out of the side of his mouth that did not have his cigarette. He threw it out of the window and took a pack of Marlboros out of his many-pocketed khaki jacket and offered me one. I took one. Kamal shot me a poisonous look, I ignored it. I leaned toward the front seat for it to be lit, and looked deeper into those eyes. After that the two men ignored me and talked about the price of lenses and the trouble with film, and I was free to examine his silky dark hair and listen, without understanding a word, to his silky dark voice. I had to see him again.

And then one morning, after I had given up hope of it, and hadn't figured out a way to get information about him out of Kamal without bringing his ever present suspicions to a boil, he walked in the door of the studio. I was alone. My pulse hit some high and erratic rhythm, and I was reduced to talking in monosyllables, and he formed an impression of me then that has persisted over decades: that I was a silly child.

'Where's your creepy boyfriend?' were his opening words. I wanted to say, 'He's creepy, but he's not my boyfriend, I don't know or care where he is, and by the way, can we go find an island together?', but I said, under my breath because I did not trust my voice, 'He's out, he'll be back in an hour, would you like some coffee?'

He lit a cigarette, and I did not dare tell him he couldn't

smoke there. 'I'll have coffee,' he said, and began to go through the boxes of slides that sat beside me. I did not tell him he should not.

'What's your name?' he asked me, but I did not get the impression that he would care if I didn't tell him, or remember if I did.

'Ginny,' I said anyway.

He didn't say anything more. I went outside to ask Veeru to make a coffee. I left the door open and hoped that the smoke inside the studio would dissipate before Kamal returned. And then I sat and worked on the slides, stamping every single one with a copyright stamp, and glancing at the man I knew I loved. He looked up suddenly and caught me. He took a piece of paper from the desk and wrote on it, and said, handing it to me, 'Call me.'

The paper had his number and name on it. Avi Suarez. So. I knew that name, of course. Anyone who had any interest in photography did. I put it in the pocket of my jeans.

Kamal walked in and slammed the door shut. He threw his bag on the floor and said to me, in a controlled temper, 'Why is there smoke all over the place?'

And then, 'Avi. What do you want? Put that cigarette out. Please.'

Avi laughed and kept smoking.

'I need to borrow some lights and an assistant, if you have one.'

'Borrow? I can rent you my lights if you want. And no, I don't have an assistant to spare.'

'I'm not paying you rent, man,' Avi laughed again. It

looked as if he was going to win this battle. He did. Immediately.

'When do you need the equipment?'

'Tomorrow morning, I need it delivered at the Oberoi, I'm doing their interiors.'

'Really? Why can't you pay rent for it then? You're surely not working for free, are you?'

'Oh come on, Kamal, you fucking businessman, I'll buy you a drink, how's that?'

Kamal just glowered at him.

'What about an assistant?' Avi asked. I gasped internally. He was completely shameless, and obviously knew he was going to get everything he wanted.

'The boy making the coffee—you can have him, if you want. He's a Nepali boy.'

Avi said nothing for a moment, and for some reason I didn't know then, Kamal said, 'Oh, I'm so sorry, I didn't mean . . .' Avi cut him off. 'It's fine. Give me the boy and Ginny here, can she do lights?'

'I'm his assistant, of course I can do lights,' I said, and received another toxic look from Kamal.

'You have to finish filing all these slides, you can't go running around with him.'

'You mean I have nothing to learn from the great Avi Suarez?' I asked, not believing my own audacity.

Avi laughed again, infuriating Kamal. He made a list and gave it to Kamal. 'Here's what I'll need, and send them around 10 am, we don't start till after lunch, so I'll set up and feed them, and have them back to you by midnight. I'll need them for three days.'

He got up to leave when Veeru came in with his coffee. He sat back down, much to Kamal's further annoyance. I hadn't expected him to. I kept doing what I was doing, but my hands were shaky. I felt a sense of irritation, as if I wanted to be somewhere else, doing something else. I felt trapped in the moment, and all I could do was fantasise. His voice soothed me, and smoothed my edgy thoughts, and brought me back into the room a few times. But I kept going back to them. I am aware of reality, but I have and take and give myself the liberty to violate that reality at least within my own head. I imagined being single again, having my place be mine again, messy and termite-infested, with months of unpaid bills and roaches crunching on the kitchen counter at night, Bree or Roy or both asleep on the floor, Bijou waiting for me to come and show him slides of faces in markets. I felt a sting of tears. I didn't think either of the men in the room noticed or cared.

Avi said, 'So will you come to the hotel in the morning?' but there was something else I thought I heard in his voice, a promise, an acknowledgement.

'Yes, I'll be there,' I said, and smiled, and my tears went back into the ducts from whence they had threatened.

After he left, Kamal complained bitterly about his bullying.

'He has really survived because of all that the photography community has done to help him, you know. He has no idea, and acts as if the world owes him.'

'Why do you fall for it then?'

'Because I have a conscience. I do the right thing.'

'The right thing? It's your stuff, you could say no.' I

couldn't stop. 'Maybe you just want to be able to tell people that you helped him, because he is someone. He is undeniably one of the greats, and not just here, but in the world. Maybe you just like that.'

Kamal was angry now. I had hit a raw nerve, or perhaps come so close to the truth that it actually made him uncomfortable.

'You don't know anything about it. Just make sure you get every piece of equipment back.'

'And what do you mean by that?' I asked, sensing a past.

'He's not very good at returning stuff. He has, in days gone by, actually borrowed things and not only not returned them, but sold them.'

'Yours?'

'No, but I've heard. From reliable sources.'

'Right,' I said, and didn't bother to hide my sarcasm.

'Look. I don't care what you believe, just make sure every light and wire and every last thing is accounted for. It's your responsibility.'

'Why don't I just give him the whole lot and then run away with him?' I asked.

'And why would he want to run away with someone who can't even support herself? What would you do without me?' he asked, and turned back to Avi's list, dismissing me.

The question rang in my head. I got up to go outside.

'Where are you going? You need to finish this.' I ignored him and left the studio. Veeru stood up hastily, thinking it was Kamal, and smiled when he saw me.

'Shall I make a coffee for you?' he asked, nearly breaking my dam of held-in tears. I shook my head, no.

'A cigarette?' I asked, and he took one from a pack from his pocket, and lit it for me.

We stood in silence for awhile, and then he went off into the darkroom to avoid being yelled at by his boss. I thought about that question Kamal had asked me: 'Where would you be without me?'

I was twenty years old. I had been living with, working with, dissolving myself in the needs and wants and demands of this man more than twice my age, for almost three years. It had happened slowly, almost unbeknownst to me, somehow. Days filled with hard labour and protests and resentment led me to where I was. I fantasised more and more about where I would be, and none of those fantasies had any chance of becoming real if I continued on the trajectory I was on, and certainly not if the man I spent my days with had any say in the matter. Where *would* I be without him? I would be in my little apartment, with Bree, perhaps, or Roy, or Avi, or that other man I knew was out there. I smoked my cigarette and ignored Kamal's voice calling me. We had things we owned together. A car I could not drive, equipment, antique silver. Memories. But those were mine as much as they were his, and I could take them with me. I would rather have left it all behind, especially the memories, but I was stuck with those. It had been a practical existence with him, there was no emotional connection I felt other than what he had somehow unintentionally, I'm sure, pointed out to me—the fear of being without him. I thought about where I would go, what I would do if I could do exactly as I pleased at that moment. And I thought of Simi. I thought of my mother. I decided I would talk to him about that, about a ticket to Japan. I thought I would be a traveller again, be alone in the world, on the lookout for other lonely travellers in need of a temporary companion, a meal with a friend, a night of comfort. There was someone out there for me, who would know me as I would know him, as soon as our eyes met. It was an unspoken, almost unacknowledged thought, and wish, but it was always there. I did understand that this invention of Him and Me had no place in reality, in the world, in his life, whoever he was, or mine. It only lived in thoughts and dreams, in odd little fragmentary images, a tall shiny man with navy blue eyes. My fiction. I found it almost heroic to allow his existence even in these forms, regardless of the consequences to my real self, or even my life, and those of others I inhabited as a person outside that invention— Kamal, Veeru, Bree, the make-up people and photographers and light-boys and models that I met each day. Sometimes they were the fiction, and the contents of my head were my reality. I felt alone again, suddenly, and it struck me then— I had no family, and for the first time in a long time, I had no friends. Just contacts.

Narita airport was dark and empty. Mine was the first flight to land there in the early morning. My heart was pounding and my mouth was dry with fear and apprehension that threatened to overwhelm me. Would she recognise me? I clutched the polar bear I had bought for her at Hong Kong airport at the World Wildlife Fund store. He was big and white and had blue translucent eyes with big black pupils. I had loved him the moment I saw him, with his shiny silver-tipped hair and his sad, away-from-home face, and I knew she would too. But as I approached the exit, I wasn't so sure.

It wasn't the polar bear, it was me I wasn't so sure about. The fear of not being recognised was thrilling somehow. It was familiar, and somewhat comforting even.

It had been a battle with Kamal to be there at all. There had been days and nights of bitter quarrels, about money, mostly. He had made me put all my modelling money into a joint account that allowed him equal access to the funds. He had kept records of everything, and they all showed I had no money. I couldn't understand where it had gone, and said so repeatedly.

'How do you think the bills get paid?' he said. 'You just come and find the light comes on when you flick the switch. How do you think that happens? How do you think the car has petrol in it? How do you think Veeru gets paid? Or the canteen bill for when you order your lunch every day?'

I asked him about the many calendar photos he had sold of me. 'I pay for the film, and the processing. And I have invested in all the equipment, you know how expensive that is. Who do you think pays for that? You?'

I was stuck. I thought he would look after my interests. I had trusted him. I was close to tears, one day, after arguing and screaming, when I began to laugh. I would call Laz, I thought, and make this man go away. Or I could find Jamaal again, maybe he would help me. And when I could find no solution even in my imagination, I got a call for a job. It was an ad film for an aftershave, and the money would be enough for me to buy my ticket, and have enough left over to spend, too. I didn't tell Kamal about it. I negotiated with the director, who made no secret of his utter contempt for

Kamal and distaste for our relationship even in Kamal's presence, that he pay me cash. He was fine with it as long as I signed a model release form and a receipt. He was even more eager to help me when I told him what I was going to do with the money.

'You should have nothing to do with that asshole,' he said, as he always did. 'Come work in my company. I know you'll learn fast. You can direct, or assist the cameramen. I'll fix you up, just get away from him. You're worth more than that.' I was grateful for his words. Nobody, certainly not my mother—who, to be fair, didn't know the details of it—not even Bree said it so bluntly. And much to Kamal's anger, I had my ticket. It was a bonus that I looked really good in the film, and it was shown everywhere and helped get more work lined up for me for when I returned, and that infuriated him even more. I was done with him. I was empowered, at least momentarily, and I took urgent advantage of my power for fear it would fade.

I told him, 'I want you to get your things out of my place before I return. Leave the key with Mr Sarin downstairs.'

He was beside himself, first with rage and then, and this surprised me, tears.

'I love you, Ginny, how will I manage without you?' he said, and I looked at him in utter disbelief and walked out. I moved in with Bree for a few days. I thought I was done with Kamal, and that episode of stupidity in my life. I believed he would be gone, when I returned. I was wrong.

Simi let go of our mother's hand and ran to me as soon as she saw me. I dropped the polar bear to the ground and grabbed her, and she was so much heavier than when I had last held her. She buried her face in my hair and said not a word. And then my mother was there, and hugging me. The three of us stood there, and for those moments, we were just a crowd of family. There were no memories, no words, and I thought, we could begin again. I could be inside that circle again. And then I remembered the last time we had been at an airport together, when Simi had cried because she was going away from me, and my mother was dry-eyed and relieved that I would be away from her. But there was a time before that, when my mother had clung to me and cried so much that I thought she would break, and I hadn't understood why, she was going to see me in a month, she said. But it had not been a month, it had been two years before I saw her again.

Those years, living with a father I had never known, though he was really my father, a sister I had never met, though she was really my sister, and a stepmother from the bowels of hell, was another, different journey. My mother must have known I was not going back to her in a month, or she would not have come apart as she had done. But that was another journey, and it was behind me that day. That day, at an airport in Japan, everything was behind me. Betrayal, loneliness, fear, being high, being low, it was all gone. Because there was Simi, again in my arms, my mother wrapped around us both, and I wished that moment never would end.

They lived on a hill just past the cemetery for foreigners. My mother laughed as she pointed it out to me through the huge windows of the bus that brought us into Kobe.

'That's where they will put me if I die here,' she said.

The walk from the bus depot was long, and we dragged my suitcase through the streets like a dog on a leash, taking turns because it was unwieldy. Simi got tired as we walked, and I picked her up and carried her piggyback.

'Oh, put her down, she can walk,' my mother said. I didn't.

The feelings of warmth and relief which I had thought were mutual dissipated perceptibly as we made our way through smaller and narrower lanes. Ami pointed things out to us in her usual way—Chiba dogs with curly tails, noodle stalls, never-seen-before vegetables and foods, a man selling hats, a drunk lying under a bench near a bus stop. People didn't look at us as we passed them in their little shops and vegetable stalls, nor did other walkers, mostly women, with small children tied to their backs and fronts. I soon became aware that no one made eye contact. We were an odd group, and spoke loudly, but my mother explained that since we were *gaijin*, we were allowed any odd behaviour, in fact it was expected of us. But I began to feel invisible, as if we could see them, but they could not see us. Over the month I was in that country, the feeling only grew.

We got to the top of the hill finally, and to a small house with a tiled roof. She opened the door and walked in ahead of me, and then held the door open as I carried Simi through. This was by far the smallest house I had ever been in. It was neat and sparsely furnished, and the floor was covered with tatami. My mother told me to take the bag upstairs, to the bedroom at the back that I would share with Simi. It was tiny, and there was a single tiny bed in it. But there was a huge french window, and the hill rose steeply outside, covered in tangled bushes and vines, almost tropical in its green muscular energy. Simi stood behind me, rubbing her eyes.

'Do you want to take a nap?' I asked her.

'Will you take a nap with me?' she asked me. I wasn't sure what to do. I was hungry. Then we heard Ami calling to us, and without saying anything, we went downstairs again. She was in the kitchen.

'Do you want a drink?' she said, and I saw she had a big chunky glass half full of amber. She took out a club soda from the fridge, poured it in, and took a long gulp, downing half the glass. Then she poured the rest of the soda into it and sat down.

'I'll have some water. And I'm a bit hungry.'

'Oh, dinner will be ready in ten minutes. I made moussaka, and a feta salad, and potatoes, and your father will be home soon. Can you wait that long, or do you want some cookies?'

I said I would wait. And then we talked of what we would do the next few days, and where we would go, and all the temples and shops we would visit, and the trails in the mountains we would hike. I told her about Bijou, about Roy, Bree, Kamal, even Jamaal. The letters we wrote each other were few and far between, maybe I had written two, and she had written me four or five at most. She listened to me with an air of impatience. She drank her drink, and refilled it when it was gone. Simi sat in the living room and watched Japanese cartoons.

'Have you been seeing Dr K at all?' was her only question.

'Yes, I have seen him a few times.'

'Why only a few? You should see him at least once a week,' she said. I said nothing, I didn't even sigh. 'Ami, my father is moving to Canada,' I said to her.

'Canada? Why?'

'He applied for immigration. He got it. So they are all moving at the end of the year. I don't know much about it, he called me just last week. I didn't go see him, I was busy with all this visa and ticket stuff.'

She considered a moment, and then said, 'Stupid man. I suppose he will do better there, they won't notice what kind of person he is. He'll fit right in.'

I thought she would ask about her other daughter. But she didn't right then. I showed her and Simi some magazines with my picture on the cover. Simi was so excited.

'Can I put these in my room? Please?'

'Of course,' I said. She had looked different to me when I saw her at the airport, more angular, her hair was short, like mine had been at her age. She looked like a little boy, as I had. I had dressed her in sweet flowery dresses and silly bows when we were together. There was nothing frilly or silly on her anymore. She wore little jeans and a white t-shirt. Even her shoes were white, no-nonsense trainers. I noticed a small bangle on one wrist. She took the magazines from me and ran up to her room.

'Are you learning any photography? Or are you going to just model until you can't anymore?'

'I'm learning, but not much. Lighting, meters, that sort of thing. It will be a while before I can do commercial work.'

'Soma called me a month ago,' she said. I waited. Soma had been her friend for a very long time. I had not been in touch with her after they had left, I found her dry and depressing, she always found the misery in any situation, no matter how happy.

'She told me a few things about this Kamal of yours. He's living in the flat with you?'

'Yes,' I said.

'He's married, and has children?'

'Yes,' I said again. I felt again at the edge of that vortex of uncertainty and fear. But, I thought, she couldn't threaten me with silence anymore. I was an adult. She would have to talk to me. But I also knew that she didn't have to. She could stop, and be silent, if not in words then in her thoughts, she would block me out of her thoughts and feelings, if she had not done that already, a long time ago.

'How old is this man?' she asked me suddenly, almost angrily. I was relieved to hear her voice again, but also her anger. It said to me that she was still there, aware, and cared where I was in my life, and with whom.

'He's old,' I said, beginning to smile, and somehow warm to the conversation that would happen between us, because I was ready to tell her what an awful man he was, how he was losing his hair in the worst way, how he smelled like a barber shop by the railway station that we sometimes went to, with his hair oil and vegetable soap, how he had no sense of what was pretty and what was just not acceptable, how he had suspicious eyes and how he made sure somehow, in a logical, accountable, legal way, that I had no money at all, how badly he treated everyone around him, as if stepping on us all made him taller than his puny self. She waited. I had said nothing, but I was going to say all of it. And make her laugh like she used to when we went on walks by the beach and I pointed out people and made rude comments about one and all, and she would say, 'Oh, that's just terrible, you're a bad girl,' but laugh anyway. And sometimes she would laugh loudly, when I compared a man to a breed of dog, as I often did, and say, 'You are such a clever girl!'

'He's an old pug, but he doesn't know it. He thinks he's a watchdog,' I began, and looked for a sign of a smile, but there was none on her face.

'Ami, he's old enough to be my father,' I said, and this time I knew it was the wrong thing before I had finished my sentence. She didn't look at me when she took another sip of her unending drink. I saw her jaw clench, but before she could say anything, the front door opened, and I heard his voice from the foyer. Varun.

'Hello! Anyone home? Where are you girls?' And we got up and went out, and I collided with Simi who had come running down the stairs. I picked her up and stood there while he kissed my mother.

'Hi, how was the trip?' he asked me, and then, to my mother, 'Oh, you've had your drink already? Well, I'll get one and join you in a few minutes.'

Dinner was delicious, the ground lamb and aubergine complementing each other perfectly, the cinnamon joining them in a wonderful trio. The salad was rich with olives and great chunks of feta. Simi refused to eat any of it. Her plate lay in front of her, and she sat in front of it, not making a move to put a bite in her mouth.

'You will get that for breakfast tomorrow, and lunch, and dinner too, if you don't eat it,' my mother said.

'I'll feed her,' I said. 'Is there any ketchup in the kitchen?'

'Ketchup? You're going to put ketchup on the food? She should learn to eat different things. The shitty child just eats hamburgers, and nothing else. I am really sick and tired of her.'

'Oh, she'll like it with ketchup, I'm sure, she loves her ketchup, don't you, Simsy-mimsy?'

Simi giggled and said she would try it. I poured a big puddle of ketchup in her plate and began to feed her, soaking each bite. Then, when she was eating without looking, I gave her a bite now and again without any ketchup. She didn't notice and kept on eating. My mother noticed though, and said, 'See? Didn't I tell you? It's not the food. The goddamned child only fusses so she can get back at me.'

Varun, who had been forcibly cheerful all through dinner, got up to refill his glass. He had not made eye contact with me in all the time we had been in the same room.

'Get me another drink too, please,' she said to him.

The days in Japan went by in a flurry of exactly beautiful temples, ethereal castles, gardens continuously tended to maintain their perfect form and balance—I saw a gardener pick up a leaf as soon as it floated down, almost before it touched the spirals of sand below—and we got to all these places on high-tech fast trains that made me feel I was in a science fiction movie, or another planet altogether. Everyone we met or spoke to was unfailingly polite, and yet so distant as to seem rude. The year was fading, we went to see the fall colours up in Nara. I had never seen fall before. The maple forests seemed to be on fire. The year wasn't fading here, it was going out in a blaze of glory. There were biscuit-vending machines to feed the hordes of deer that infested the area. They were aggressive and almost ugly, domesticated in that way, unafraid and hanging around like cows. They reminded me of the monkeys in the hills in Lonavala where my mother had taken me along once to an office picnic. I had never had good luck with semi-wild creatures. I reminded her of it. I had been eating a banana, which I rarely did after I was master of my own diet, and a large brown male rhesus monkey with an evil grin came right up to me and snatched it from me. I was quite angry, if he had asked for it, I would have given it to him, and would have even been grateful to him because I didn't have to eat it. She remembered it vaguely.

'It wasn't right out of your hand, it was from the picnic table next to you. You are exaggerating as usual.'

Simi loved the story, and believed it. On the train home she said, 'Tell me again about the thief monkey!' and I did, and in this iteration he was larger and meaner, and he slapped me on the side of my head as he ran off with my banana. Simi giggled, and my mother looked at me, smiling, but shaking her head.

'Ginny, you lie very well,' she said. 'You always could. You're a born liar.'

This was the first of many times to come over the years, when Simi and I would be carted off to see sights or experience the world in ways that our mother thought would expand our minds. We saw Shinto shrines in Kyoto, a white floating castle in Himeji, the imperial gardens of Tokyo. Still to come were the orange trees in Seville, the great mosque of Cordoba, some now forgotten temple in Ulsan, the race course in Hong Kong's inaccurately named, at least for me, Happy Valley. There were good times, of course, and I am grateful that I saw some of those places. But though I remember some of them, mostly what I have memories of is an abiding fear that I would be lost, left behind, that my Simi would be kidnapped by a Chinese, Japanese, Korean, Croatian stranger. We would get lost in parts of towns that no tourist would ever see. She would not ask for directions, our mother, even when she knew perfectly well that we were lost. Even when she knew that the largest shrine in Japan was not anywhere close to the street we were on, with stalls on both sides selling huge plastic buckets, huge tools, materials related to some specific industry that we could not identify. Or that time we walked through some part of Bombay that I have never in all my years there been able to find again, where there was a man making a stew that had lizards in it, and people had lined up to eat it, in spite of the stomach-turning smell. We had left home to do nothing more mundane than see a movie, but she had decided to take a short cut. We would trail uncertainly behind her, propelled by little hope and a lot of fear that we would never leave there, whatever bizarre spot there happened to be. At a railway station somewhere outside Tokyo she boarded the train without waiting for us, and before Simi and I made it, the doors closed, the train pulled out, and we were left there in a panic. I assured Simi that we would be fine, and she of course, believed me. We took the next train that came in, I figured it was as good as any other, I couldn't read Kanji anyway, and we found our mother at the next stop, not particularly gleeful at having managed to lose both her remaining daughters, but not very anxious either. When I began to express my indignation she said, 'Well, you're here, aren't you?' She had a point. She always did.

Then there was the farm that she bought a few years later. The farm, in the drought-plagued midlands of Maharashtra, was far away from any town, and her land was in fact separated from the access road by a small lake. The only way to get to the house was either to swim across, which my mother could do easily, but there were not too many of the rest of us who could, or stand on the shore and hope that she would row across in her little wooden boat and get us. We would need her to want us there for this to happen, which wasn't always the case.

My mother lived on that farm for a few years, on and off. She went there on the days of the week that she wasn't teaching at the university, she spent her weekends there, and sometimes longer periods of time, when she was writing a novel, or just getting away from people, from us, her husband, her children, her friends. We would visit her occasionally. She would call me, and persuade me to go spend some time with her. Bombay was not so distant in terms of miles, but it did take most of a day started very early to get there by dinnertime. She would tell me how pretty it was, how it had rained for a week and the lake was full, there were birds visiting, black-necked storks and grey herons, it was cool and pleasant. I would forget my last visit, and the one before that, or in fact every visit there that had been a disaster for one reason or another, when either I had had to leave or lose my sanity forever, or she had made it clear that I was no longer welcome. She would somehow make me think of long walks and hours spent rowing on the lake, games of Trivial Pursuit and scrabble and canasta, of meals of fresh vegetables from the backyard, of moonlit nights on the wraparound porch smoking menthol cigarettes and drinking, she her rum, and I a weak whiskey sour, mostly lemon juice and water with a few drops of whiskey so I could call it by its fancy name.

One morning, one of the many boys who worked on the farm came running up the path to the house, shouting for her. He told her he had seen a pink bird, maybe even two, on the way to work that morning, in the upper lake. Simi was about eleven years old by then, and home from school for the summer. She and I wished his words back in his mouth as soon as he said them. This lake was no more than five miles as the crow flies from the house. We looked at each other with a shared premonition of things to come. My mother declared that they had to be flamingos, those pink birds. And we knew a trip to the lake was in the works of my mother's mind. I knew we had not the choice to say no. The next morning, we left before breakfast. Simi said she was hungry, but our mother shushed her and said we would either find something in the village, or then we'd be back by lunchtime anyway. She ate a few glucose biscuits hastily. We walked the five miles to the lake, and found there was no water in it, it was just a bog. Simi and I exchanged another of the millions of meaningful looks we used to communicate in her presence, and I shook my head. Not imperceptibly—quite vigorously, in fact, our mother had her back to us, and was telling us she could clearly see the birds, and that we should step into the bog, and start walking toward them. She then stepped into the bog and began to sink. We did not follow her. Every squelching step she took, the already distant two birds—and there were two birds—squawked loudly at her and retreated.

Thankfully for us, later than we would have liked, she did give up and squelched her way back to us. We were relieved that there was some chance we would be heading home now. As soon as she turned around, from the height of the hill, standing there on the dam, she spied the red roof of her house among the sparse trees, the only slightly green area in the whole valley, that she herself had planted and tended.

She pointed, 'Look, we can see the house—it's straight ahead. If we cut through the fields, we'll be home in fifteen minutes.'

She started down the hill, and we followed. As always, she strode off into the middle distance, and I found myself in that familiar role again, one that I had played all over the world with these same two people—my mother in front trying to lose us both, and Simi, lagging far behind, dragging her feet, hoping our mother really would lose us. I tried to keep track of the guide in front of me and the child behind me. It was easier here than it had been in Japan, or China, where the streets were full of people careless of my dilemma. Four hours later, the mud from the bog had dried and caked and fallen off my mother's pants in tempting looking chocolate wafers. We were hungry and thirsty and tired, the sun was making us drier and hotter, and there was no sign of our house. There was no way to know where we were, the dam was the highest point, it was all downhill from there.

My mother stopped in front of a large acacia tree. 'Climb up on that,' she said to me matter-of-factly, 'and see how far we are from the house. It looks tall enough.'

I looked at the tree. Every branch had two-inch long thorns thickly spread on the bark. My options were to climb the tree or to tell my mother I would not. The second did not occur to me then. I climbed. I got scratched, and in a couple of places, impaled. I got up into the lower branches, and that was enough to see the red roof of the house, not too far, directly in front of us. I yelled unnecessarily and cheerfully to Simi and her, 'I can see it, it's right ahead!'

She took off with her long insistent strides, she was out of sight by the time I extricated myself from the thorns and got down off the tree, leaving us behind to figure out our way home. The boy who had told us of the flamingos was startled to see us appear from the blond grass behind the house.

'Where did you come from?' he said. 'From seeing pink birds,' I told him. He sensed, but didn't comprehend, my sarcasm, annoyance, tiredness. We got home, and found our mother sitting at the kitchen table with three inches of rum in a crystal glass. I put some kindling into the water heater and sat down heavily at the table. I must have been particularly tired, I just sat there examining the holes in my wrist and palms, one of the thorns had pierced the webbing between my thumb and forefinger. It hurt.

'It's only acacia, you'll be fine,' she said.

'I'm sure I will be, but right now, it really hurts,' I said, with some heat.

She swallowed the rest of her rum and looked right at me,

and said, 'I don't know why I bother to do all this for you ungrateful bastards.'

The Japanese sojourn ended too soon. Before I knew it, I was at another airport with a weeping Simi in my arms, assuring her that I wouldn't be gone too long, that I would see her soon, that she would be fine, that I would write to her every week. She seemed sad but not devastated when I finally put her down and walked away. It was I who was devastated. It was not Simi that I felt so wrenched about leaving, though I did miss her already as I walked away. It was my mother. Every parting took us further and further away from each other. She didn't cry when she said goodbye to me as she had done when she sent me away to live with my father. But now she didn't even seem sad. She just gave me a quick, cursory hug that seemed disinterested more than anything. I had thought that the time together, after Varun left for a trip to Tokyo to his head office, would be like old times, when she and I had first moved to Bombay, only better because we had Simi now. But it was not. I had found myself always between her and Simi. It wasn't about where we went and what we saw. It was about the food Simi would not eat, the homework she would not do, the speed she would not walk at, the books she would not read. And it was about my mother wanting to get home and have her drink in peace.

'It's the one thing I look forward to,' she said. 'I cook, I clean, I wash her clothes, I take her to school, and all she can do is find the worst possible things to say to me. I am really at my wits' end.'

We were sitting in the living room a few days before I was to leave. She had had many drinks, I had lost count. She refilled her glass with club soda, and then poured the rum, or whiskey, into that, so I didn't really know how many drinks it added up to. All I knew was, it made her at first open and talkative, and then, as the evening wore into night, she became maudlin, and then angry, and I had learned in my first week there to go to bed before the onset of that acrid anger.

'I am tired, Ginny.' I was startled by her use of my name. 'This year has been hard on me. You see how Simi talks to me, when she does. I don't know why she hates me so much, really.'

'Ami, she's only a baby. She's not even six years old. She doesn't really hate you, you know, she's probably confused about where she is, and maybe she feels awkward in school, you know, all those little girls are so different from her, with their long hair and bangs and non-existent noses.' I thought there was a moment there that she was going to listen to what I had to say, all because she called me Ginny.

'Don't be silly. That's just psychobabble. She knows they are Japanese and she is not. No, she has just taken against me. And now you are taking against me too. You think just because she is a child she doesn't know what's what. She knows how exactly to hurt me. You've been here, you have seen it. She calls me fat, and old. That's not something a person who does not understand would say. But why should you take my side? You never have, after all.' To my horror, she began to weep silently. I summoned up all my courage and did what all instinct told me not to. I went and sat next to her and put my arm around her. She put her head on my shoulder for a moment, and then stood up and went to the kitchen to add to her dwindling glass. I sat there without moving, wondering what to do next. I would leave soon, go back to my life, whatever that would be. I knew why Simi was so angry with her mother. She had taken her away from the one person she had loved and trusted implicitly. Me. I knew that her anger would only get larger, stronger, blinder as Simi grew older. I knew she would turn some of it on me, though that was unreasonable, for abandoning her to this hated life. She didn't know that I had no choice.

Ami came out of the kitchen and put her glass, still empty, down hard on the table, and said, as if she had made some sort of decision, 'I think you should know this before you go. Your father told me not to tell you until—well, until later. But I think you should know. We are sending Simi to boarding school. He says that if we continue like this, we will end up hating each other.'

Before I could say anything, I heard something, or maybe just felt her presence behind me. Simi was standing at the bottom of the stairs holding the white polar bear Nanuk to her chest, looking at me over his head. I got up and took the two strides to her and put my arms around her and her bear.

The three of us stood there for a long time, and this time our mother did not come. She was back in the kitchen. I could hear the sound of the ice tray being banged against the sink to loosen the cubes for another drink.

'I have always been an inconvenience,' I told Gabriel. I had to see him after the visit. He was happy to see me, as always. It made me wonder if he was that way with all his patients.

'Why?' he asked, in his characteristic way.

'They all seemed to want to lose me, forget me.'

'They all?'

'All my parents.'

He waited this time, saying nothing. I knew I didn't have to say anything, but I did.

'My mother was always late to pick me up from school,' I said. It wasn't exactly fair to put it that way. She got off work at five, like everyone else in the world, and the commute to my school was an hour. She took the train from the Victoria Terminus, and then a bus to my school. She was there at the dot of six every single day, unless it was a particularly soggy day in the monsoon. I sat there under the same tree every single day, where I could see everyone coming into the school. I didn't take my eyes off the road until I saw her. I cried every single day, from the moment school let out, at four, until I saw her. Then I would wipe my eyes one last time and stand up, pick up my bag, and walk toward her. The teachers gave up trying to tell me that she would be there. They knew I would cry anyway.

'Why do you think you cried?' Gabriel asked me.

I didn't answer him though I knew the answer, because it embarrassed me, even years later.

'What did you think?' he asked again. This time I knew I had to answer. He knew what it was, too, that made me cry every single day. I looked into his pale angelic eyes.

'I knew that one day she wouldn't come. Every day I thought, "This is the day she won't come." I knew she didn't want me.'

I remembered the feeling so clearly, I closed my eyes and was back under that tree. Other girls sat around and read books, or talked with each other. There was a teacher who had an evening sewing class for the girls. Those girls were never leaving that place, it was an orphanage. They were the ones whose mothers or fathers had not returned for them. I almost wished some days that she would not come, then this terrible waiting would be over. Like Virginia Woolf, I was so afraid of death that I wanted to kill myself to get away from the daily, insistent fear.

'Ginny. You are old enough to know now that she was having a hard time. She was working a job, and bringing up a child alone in a time when most women stayed home, and hardly any woman was divorced.' He said it firmly, but he reached across and held my hand when he did.

'I know that, Gabriel, I just didn't know it then.'

'Yes. You were a child. That child is still with you, but you are not that child anymore.'

I told him about my trip. I told him everything in detail. At the end of our time that day he said, 'Do you think the drinking is a problem?'

I hadn't thought about it that way. I had thought of it as unpleasantness for me, and for Simi, that she became so unbearable when she had passed the three- or four-drink mark.

'Sister Joan told me to go upstairs and put away Nanuk so we could go to the dining hall for lunch.' Simi wasn't crying, she didn't even look particularly disturbed. But there was a detachment to her that made me hold back the desire to hold her close. We sat in a restaurant close to the convent, the first time I had seen her after she had been sent away to the Catholic boarding school. She looked different. Confident, quiet, taller of course, but mostly she looked centred.

'When I came back down, they were gone. I didn't know what to think, and I would have liked to cry, and yell, but there was something about Sister Joan that didn't allow it. I just stood there staring at the road that led away from the school. The car that brought us there was gone.'

I didn't know what to say to her. I wondered if our mother had cried all the way back, or if she had looked out of the window, at the red sky of sunset, always red in that part of the world because it was so dry and dusty. I wondered if she had seen the single heron against the burning sky, if it had brought to her the same bitterness, loneliness, mortality that it brought to me. I had asked her once, if white herons at sunset made her feel sad. She had just smiled at me. I wondered if she had remembered another elective separation from another daughter.

That separation had always puzzled me. When she married Varun, and they had to go away for his job, I was still an androgynous child. I was her child, I had not known, or in any case did not remember any other parent. She had told me that I was going to be with my father for a month, so that he could spend some time with me before I left the country with her. She said he had demanded his time with me, and the courts did not give her the choice to say no, that I had to go. She said the four weeks would be over soon, and we would be together again, and we would go on an adventure after that, to a new country, a new life. But in the taxi to the airport she was strangely silent, and held my hand, and clenched her jaw the whole way. I did not have any idea still, of what was to happen. I hugged her, uncertain, but not afraid, I knew, I had been told that I would see her again, soon.

And then when the stewardess came—I was an unaccompanied minor—my mother seemed to break. She held me tight, sobbing into my hair, unwilling to let go, while the young, confused woman stood by wringing her hands, saying over and over, 'Ma'am, we must go now, all the others are boarded,' until, finally, the man who had been my father for a year, pried her hands and arms from around me, and picked me up, and hugged and kissed me on both cheeks, and said, 'Be good, Ginny, okay? Be good.' I saw the tears in his eyes too, and a whisper of doubt and fear began to take hold of me. There was no time to ask any questions. He put my hand in the waiting girl's hand, and she walked me firmly toward the gate. I turned to look back, and saw them, my mother crushed in his arms with her back to me, and him looking helplessly at me. It was the last time he would see me as a child.

She must have known. She must have known that my father would not send me back. She had been married to him, she had had two children with him, she had left him, even at the price of losing one of those children. She must have known what he would do. And I was soon to find out.

At the end of that short flight that took me away from everything I had known till then, the stewardess put my hand in the hand of another stranger. I looked up into a bearded, long-haired, vaguely familiar face. I had a fleeting olfactory glimpse of a motorcycle, a feeling of grease, of going somewhere with this long hair brushing my face. He laughed, a rich and happy sound, and took my hand in his great hammy square one. My fears and uncertainty left me for the moment. He carried my suitcase easily in the other hand, and did not let go of my hand till we walked outside the airport into a city I have never liked, then, or since. There was a car in the small parking lot, a black hearse-like thing with a shark face, but welcoming. My stepmother sat in the driver's seat, and a little girl with a small round face and huge eyes looked out of the closed window of the back seat. She smiled as soon as she saw us, and made to open the door.

'Millie! Stop that at once,' I heard the shrill acid tone of that voice for the first time, and all my uncertainty and fear came rushing back into my heart, my brain, and my legs most of all, which went weak. I clutched the large hand a little tighter, but he took it away to open the car door for me. My sister Millie—Milan—slid over to the other side to make room for me. Then she smiled at me shyly, but said nothing.

Her eyes were wide and fearful, even though she smiled. I got in next to her and smiled back at her, but said nothing. She looked down at her lap then, and began to twist the edge of her dress into a little knot.

'We've been waiting nearly half an hour, what took so much time? Was the plane late? You should have come out and told us,' the woman said. My father said nothing. She had started the car angrily, and she was now driving angrily, it seemed to me. She took swift and hard turns so that my sister and I fell on one another. I fell on her extra hard one time, exaggerating, and we started giggling.

'Stop that noise, I am trying to drive,' came harshly from the front seat. We looked at each other. I expected her to giggle some more, but she was quiet, her eyes large and frightened again. I felt a sense of foreboding. I didn't know then that she was afraid of this woman, or that the big bear-like man that was our father was no bear at all, but a cowardly baboon, old before his time.

Two years we were together, the four of us and a cook called Mary, the dog Leica, for a little time, the dog Toro for a little time, two red-eyed white rats for three days. There was church every Sunday, oil painting lessons, another school where I made no friends and was often sent out of class by the nuns to stand in the corridor with other delinquents, or to the principal's office. The principal was a Belgian nun, stern and starched, with her cat's eye glasses, and wood and silver cross, and she had lost her patience with me.

'Once every few years we get one like you,' she would say to me. 'We try and try, but some of you are just made this way. What is wrong, child? Why can't you just behave?'

I had thrown up in the middle of the classroom floor this time, after requesting the teacher several times that I be allowed to go to the bathroom. Then I had refused to go and wash up, saying there was no need anymore.

I knew this meant I would receive punishment at home too, but I didn't really care. I wanted to tell Sister Mary Vaughn that day that I missed my mother. But the more I thought about it, the more I realised that I did not miss my mother. I missed someone else altogether, and I had never met that person. It was a longing, a yearning that was growing like a cancer, like a hole in my being, this missing, this want that I could not put a name or a face to. I thought it would never leave me, and I thought no one would ever understand it.

Years later, I was sitting on a porch with a man I loved. It was not a red sunset, and no solitary heron flew overhead. It was a Sunday morning, a clear blue American sky, and a lazy single-engine plane hummed happily above us. And that panicky yearning overcame me, and I looked into his eyes as he held my hands, and I said to him, without really knowing what it meant, 'I miss you.' His English wasn't like mine. But he said, 'I know. You'll always miss me, even if you are with me for the rest of your life. It's not me you miss, Ginny, it's something else. I think it's not even you that feels this missing-ness. It's older than you, and it's older than us, my little motorplane on a Sunday morning.' And though his words made no real sense, I knew that he understood what I felt, and what I missed, and that he had felt it too. And that did not make the feeling go away, but it was a relief to know that even if I was alone with my feeling, I was not the only one in the world who felt it. There was at least one other person who did, and we had, for one perfect moment, felt it together.

She was an odd person, this stepmother of mine. She was young, much younger than my father. And much taller. Her height made her powerful where Ami, though as tall, or taller, than her, seemed ethereal, floating. She had long thick hair that she wore in a braid down her back. She seemed angry at all times, there was a thin brittle skin covering her anger, and it burst through, and leaked through, and sometimes the skin disappeared altogether, for weeks at a time, and these times would be hard on me, and hard on my little sister. Millie was like a darling little puppy, she was willing to be happy, she was willing to play, given half a chance. I sometimes wished I was like her. She wanted to talk to me, to her father, Mary the cook, even her wicked stepmother. I didn't wish to talk to anyone. Before that first month was over, before I had given up the idea that I was only there for a short time, before that idea had been wrenched from me, I still wanted to talk to my mother. I figured out how to make long-distance calls, and would call her every day when we got home from school, before our parents got home from work. Millie would keep watch through the window for the car, we could see it as it turned into the street, and we lived at the very end of the street, so there was plenty of time for me to say goodbye and hang up the phone. The first call I made told me everything I needed to know, but I kept calling my mother for the few weeks they were still in the country. I held on to a hope that they would come and take me with them.

'Ginny!' she said when she heard my voice that first time, 'Ginny, are you okay? Are you well? Are you getting on with your sister?'

'They have put me in school here, Ami. Why have they put me in school? What's the point of that if I am coming back in a month?'

There was a long silence. 'Ami?' I thought I had lost the connection.

'Do you like the school?' she asked me.

'No, it's terrible. There are nuns, most of the teachers are nuns, and I have no uniform yet, but they are going to take me to the tailor to get some made. Ami, why are they doing all this?'

'You'll like it,' was all she said. 'Are you getting on with your sister?' she asked me again.

'She's okay. She's tiny and just afraid of everything. She jumps if a leaf falls.'

Again, there was silence. And Millie turned from the window and looked at me with her huge eyes grown huger from the terror of being found out, and signalled to me that she had spotted the car.

'I have to hang up the phone,' I said to my mother.

'Take care, Ginny, you'll be fine. And try to do well at school,' she said.

And I knew then that she would leave the country without me. But hope stayed to plague me with visions of her standing there at the doorstep waiting when we got home from school, waiting with my bag and ticket, ready to take me away before my father and his wife came home from work. I wondered whether I should include little Millie in my daydreams. And then at the end of that month of daily conversations with Ami, the phone bill came. I hadn't thought of the phone bill. It was a surprise to us all. I understood then, how odd this stepmother of mine really was.

She came in the front door with the mail in her hand and sat down at the dining table to read it. Mary the cook came out at once with her tea, and a large platter with green beans that she would string and chop for dinner. My father went into the bedroom, as he always did, to change out of his office pants and shirt, to take off his contact lenses, to brush his teeth for the third or fourth time that day, to wash his hands again. Indira began to go through the mail just as Millie and I began our homework. I looked up at her for some reason and saw her staring straight at me with her slightly bulging eyes, and the hair on my neck prickled. She said nothing. I forgot about it. The next day would be the last that I would be able to call my mother, and I ran all the way from the corner where the bus dropped us off so I could have a few more minutes.

My mother cried on the phone. She spoke to Millie, but there was not much between them to say. What, after all, could they find out about each other from one clandestine, hurried phone call, after so many years of separation? Millie was seven years old. She didn't know so very much about herself other than what she was told. Her stepmother of the past few years, I wasn't sure how many, told her what she looked good in and what she liked to eat. Her father told her what she liked to read. I thought I would make it my job to tell her what and whom she didn't like. I listened to her little mumbled answers to my mother's questions about her height and weight and length of her hair and the state of her happiness. Soon enough she handed the phone back to me and went to her post at the window to watch for the car. My mother knew, and I knew, this was the last time for a long time that we would talk to each other. Millie signalled that the car was at the corner. I had only a few minutes. I could think of nothing to say, and just listened to the sobbing breaths my mother took before she said, 'Ginny, I love you, I'll write to you every week, you take care, and be a good girl, okay?' Still, I said nothing.

'Ginny? Can you hear me?' she said, and there was a panicky edge to her voice. I waited just a few seconds more, and then said, 'Yes, I can hear you. I have to hang up now, Ami. Bye.'

And I put the receiver down and Millie and I sat down on the red Rexine sofa side by side looking at a magazine, and we looked up casually when our parents walked in the door.

'Ask her what she has been doing this whole month,' were the first words out of my stepmother's mouth.

'Let's talk about this later, after I have changed,' he said in a low voice that was meant to be soothing.

'No! I have waited for three days since that bill came. You said we would get it out once her mother was gone. Now I want to know what is going on here.'

Millie and I were frozen to the spot with the magazine spread on our laps. I had no idea what would happen next. I thought, the worst they could do was stop talking to me, and that might even be a relief in this circumstance. I leapt in with both feet.

'I have called my mother every day for the past three weeks.' I said. 'I missed her, and needed to talk to her, that's all.'

She stared at me almost without comprehension, and her eyes were bulging dangerously and turning red. Then she took two steps up to me and did something that I did not understand until much later. She pulled me up by a fistful of my hair with one hand, and hit me flat and hard across my face with her other hand. Her glass bangles shattered on my cheekbones. I fell back on the sofa. I had put my hand up to my cheek without realising I had done it, and I could feel heat, and the wetness of blood from the broken glass on my skin. I could taste blood in my mouth where I must have bitten myself. Rage began to pound in my ears, and I looked up from the floor to my father's face. He was looking at me, but turned away when we made eye contact. Millie just sat there next to me. I noticed she had moved a little closer to me so that her leg was in full contact with mine.

'You cost me almost two thousand rupees with your stupid phone calls to your stupid mother. This was the money for two months' rent. Where is it going to come from? Is she going to pay this bill? Your stupid mother?'

My father tried to stop her with some words I did not understand. She didn't stop.

'She could have told her daughter not to call. Why did she not tell her? Of course she is stupid. She answered her calls, didn't she? Did she tell you not to call?' she turned on me again. I was afraid. I said nothing. I had never been afraid that way before, and did not even understand it as fear for my physical safety. I was shaking, I was hurt, and I was angry, yes. But most of all I was afraid she would hit me again.

She didn't hit me again for a long time. It was enough to know that she would, that she could, that I could not stop her, that nobody else would. The knowledge kept me from doing anything I thought might be wrong, but there was nothing really to do, other than go to school, go to church, go to the classes that she signed us up for. And sometimes I would just go down the stairs and sit on the stoop, or hang on the gate and watch the world go by, like a dog, and wag my imaginary tail at strangers who smelled like they might be friendly. I didn't get to wag my tail too often, most people smelled unfriendly, most were in too much of a hurry to notice me. I felt alone in the world when I sat there, and it was a good feeling.

I sat on the doorstep of the downstairs neighbour's house when the scooter port was empty, when I knew there was no one in the house. One day I was there for two hours before Mary the cook called me from the balcony of our apartment to come up and eat something. I sat there looking up and down the street, drawing pictures in the dirt with a stick. There was a construction site some way down the road where people had taken to dumping their garbage. Dogs went to the garbage whenever they needed a scrap to eat. There would be dogs coming and going up and down the street all the time. A brown dog came into view as I sat there, a little bit in a hurry. 'Hey, do you want to play with me?' I asked him. He didn't break his stride, just said, 'No, I have to go now,' as he padded along on his busy paws. I talked to cats sometimes, but they never ever answered me. Not once. The dogs, though, often did. Sometimes in English, sometimes in Marathi.

Even so, I prefer cats. They seem self-contained, and yet quite willing to get into a meaningful relationship. They commit, and yet won't fall apart if you abandon them. I would like to be a cat, given the choice between the two. When we played the dog game, my mother and I, in which we discussed and argued and finally decided what breed of dog everyone we knew was, she said I was a mongrel. I was pleased to be thought of as one of those wonderful brown citizens of the world. But I knew it wasn't true. There are no people that are worthy of being called mongrels.

Very early on the morning of my first Christmas there, the unfortunately named Lhasa Apso Pixie came to live with us. She was brought by one of our wicked stepmother's several sisters, none of whom were wicked in the slightest. This was the oldest sister, our stepmother the youngest.

'You can keep her for a few days,' she said. 'She's not very young, and she's a very good-tempered bitch—unlike me.'

She smiled when her sister began to object. 'Oh, stop with your complaints, Indira,' she said. That was our stepmother's name, but it was hardly ever said in the house, because my father never called out to her, and when he talked about her he referred to her as 'she', with a capital 'S'.

'These girls need a dog. Pixie is no trouble, the girls can take her for a walk twice a day, and I'll come and see how they are doing in a week.'

My father refused to call her Pixie. He said we should call her nothing at all until he had assessed her and decided on an appropriate and not-so-silly name. Three days later he came up the stairs after work and announced that the dog's name was Leica. 'That was the first dog in space, you know,' he said. After that day, he never called her anything but 'dog' himself, though. She was a lovely dog, not bitchy at all, she was happy, and friendly, and delighted us all. Millie would open our bedroom door after everyone had gone to bed and call her into her bed, even though we had been told in no uncertain terms that the dog had to sleep in the passage outside the kitchen. Even though this was Millie's first pet, and she loved this dog unreasonably, I was surprised at this daily act of defiance on her part. I had never seen her being hit, but I was sure she had been. There was too much of the same fear in her that I had in me. I forgot it after Leica came to live with us. And was reminded of it the day she went away.

I had had pets before, and I had lost pets before. It is always painful, whether they die, or whether they disappear, which cats sometimes do. Fitzy, the pert little black cat who had been my first pet, had died a horrific death, she had been caught by a pack of neighbourhood strays, those fierce mongrels that roam all the neighbourhoods in most cities. She had been ripped to shreds, but hadn't died fast enough. My mother had found her at our doorstep, she had dragged herself home to die there. She was still alive, but barely, and lasted a few minutes. I curled up under my bed and cried. I thought about Fitzy with her green eyes and shiny black pelt, but mostly I thought about how the top of her head felt under my chin, how her rough pink tongue felt on the back of my hand when I slipped it in front of her as she cleaned herself. I would miss her little warm body, the sound of her purr-motor when she curled up at my head at night. I learned something about bodies from that cat, about the need to be touched and to touch, the feel of life that comes through skin and fur and tongues and breath and even her claws breaking through my clothes to my skin when she was kneading me before she went down for a nap. I began to feel that sense of senses. I may have mixed it up as time went by, or some of it was rubbed off when my mother would say to me when I went and sat next to her in the room, 'Go sit over there, this is a big room, don't stick to me so!' but I never quite lost it all, the importance of the body that I live in, that I am.

Millie and I took Leica for a walk every evening. The day we lost her, we couldn't find her leash. She was desperate to go, so we just went, thinking she would walk with us, she knew who we were, she wouldn't want to run away or get lost. It was fine, until a young man on a scooter screeched to a halt at a traffic light, and the sound startled her and she took off running into a building site that she was familiar with. We ran after her, but I had the sense she was gone. We looked and called, Millie yelling hoarsely through her flowing tears and me holding her hand and saying we would find her, but I knew we had to stop looking soon, and we had to go back home and face whatever was to happen. We walked home in silence, in dread.

It was not a long distance, but it was one of the longest walks of our life. I held Millie's sweaty hand in mine, and she cried and cried without stopping, nodding vigorously all the way at my soothing words, my lies that everything would be fine, that we would find Leica the next day, when it was morning, when it was light. But I knew that her fear, like mine, was bigger than her sorrow at losing the dog. I left that unsaid, I left it out of the conversation.

I, the taller of the two of us, took the first hit as soon as we stepped inside the door. I did not cry or make a sound as the full force of my stepmother's hand snapped my head back. Millie held my hand tight, she didn't let go, and she didn't run off and hide. She just stood there, right next to me, still sobbing, but still holding my hand like a broken lifeline. There was a lot of screaming going on, and none of it came from Millie or me.

'It is forty-five minutes past the time you should have been home. You will not behave this way. She was fine till you came along.'

Mary the cook had come running out of the kitchen and tried to hold her hand as she prepared for her third or fourth blow, I had lost count. I just stood there, not feeling anything but the pounding rage in my head.

My father came into the room and was saying something in a low uneven voice. She wouldn't stop. She must have seen Millie suddenly, holding my hand. She took hold of our wrists and began to pull them apart. Instead of letting go, we held each other harder. Maybe it was our only act of defiance, but we would not let go of each other's hands. Then she raised her hand to hit Millie, and my father took one step in and stopped her.

'You will not,' he said. He spoke quietly, but we knew it was over then. He picked up Millie and walked into the little bedroom we shared, and left her there with Mary the cook. Then he came out and noticed me still standing there, and said, 'Go and wash your face.' And then he followed his wife into their bedroom, to persuade her that she should stay, that I was only temporary, that he would not allow me to go and live in a foreign country with my mother and 'that man', that he would not allow his daughter to be brought up by a stranger, and that she, Indira, would have to put up with me, at least for now.

The missing dog never came up in their conversation. Mary the cook brought us hot aloo parathas and cool yogurt to soothe us. She combed my hair and stroked my face and arms and fed Millie bites of her food, and we talked about the dog, finally. We talked about her in mourning, as if she was gone and we would never see her again. We laughed about her unbridled hatred for the poor mailman and the nasty landlord, we laughed about her barking at our school bags one night thinking they were intruders, we laughed about how she was blinded by the light when we tied her hair off her eyes in a cherry rubber band one day, and she had hidden under the bed until Millie crawled in and took it off. And Millie, crying the whole time, finally smiled a little. Mary the cook suddenly became Mary the saviour to me. She touched me. She brushed my hair, which had grown since I had lived away from my mother, she washed it, she fed me, she buttoned my uniform and buckled my shoes, she reminded me of my body, she made me alive in my skin, at a time when I was faded, as a person, but also as a physical being, an animal. She gave me a little card with a picture of Mary and baby Jesus on it.

When, toward the end of my stay there, I came home from school one day in fear and horror because I was bleeding from between my legs and did not know from exactly where or why, she was the one who gave me a wad of white cloth to put in my panties and told me that it was normal, that we all bleed once a month. She couldn't give me a scientific explanation, but she reassured me. She hugged me. And gave me, as she always did, a nice meal to heal my pain and fear. That night I heard our stepmother screaming at my father about having an adolescent girl living with them, the responsibility, words I did not understand, but also somehow did, I felt that I was a threat to her, and it thrilled me.

I did not understand the fear that parents have of female children, of the great power of girl-children on the brink of turning into goddesses. I did not understand the power of forbidden things, because I never found out that they were forbidden. My mother did not tell me, either by her words or by her actions, that what I carried between my legs was anything more special or dangerous, to me or anyone else, than my arms or my belly. I had no direction, so I perhaps took some wrong turns. But there, in those years of abandonment, betrayal, disappointment, loneliness, I felt the awakening power of the cunt. I did not know what it was, that surge, that electric knowledge, that recognition that all the vague and gathering clouds and all the static in the air were harbingers of a hurricane. My hurricane. My father understood it the day he saw me in liplock with his wife's cousin's oldest son, Christopher. We were outside the bathrooms at church one Sunday. My father, unfortunately for us, felt the need to wash his hands after mass. We jumped apart, but found many occasions to revisit the feelings of that first communion. Our luck ran out, though, much to my father's relief. Christopher joined the merchant navy, and within two months, my father got a job in Bombay and decided to send Millie and me to boarding school. Indira never found out.

When I returned from Japan, Kamal was at the airport to pick me up. I was dismayed when I saw him standing there. I thought I would go home to my own place. I had fantasised about going home, to my city, to my apartment, to myself. I couldn't get any pleasure out of dreaming up a single life, so I fantasised about the people who had been, who still were, and most of all, who had possibilities in my life. That excited me most of all—possibilities. I thought about Avi. I thought about him on the flight back. I fought back thoughts of Simi, of the way it was between mother and daughter, of how it would get worse and worse. Every image I had of Ami, it suddenly struck me, was with a drink in her hand. I stopped myself from thinking about that, it was disturbing in a way I did not comprehend then. I stuck to Avi Suarez, with his dark slinky eyes, with his voice like caramel with a touch of grit. I decided, somewhere over China, that I would call Avi Suarez as soon as I got home, whatever time that was. He could always say no, if at all he answered the phone.

But when I got out with my bag, there was Kamal, waiting for me.

'What the hell? What the hell are you doing here?'

'I came to pick you up,' he said, and as if nothing was wrong, made to give me a hug. I pushed him away and said loudly enough to make people stare at us, 'Stop that, Kamal. I really hope you don't think you are going home with me. Because that is not going to happen. Really.'

'Well, let's work it out on the way home,' he said, picking up my bag.

I was appalled. I wondered if I should get into a taxi and

go to Bree's for the night. But he had my bag, and was walking toward the parking lot. I let it go. I was dead tired, and I figured we would work it out on the way home. For so many reasons, and no reason at all, I did not work it out on the way home. I did not work it out at home, in my apartment on the third floor, where Kamal's things sat where they had been when I left, in a comfortable takeover. I did not work it out for two more years. I lived there, and let Kamal live with me, in a distortion of life, of what my life could be, what I wanted it to be. I did not call Avi Suarez that night, but I did call him a few days later. And we met, in his one-room rental in Bombay where he lived when he was not in his hometown, Delhi, when he was in my city for a job. We met that first time, and there were no words between us, just sounds, just the doing of what we both knew had to be done as soon as possible, what we had both known we would do from the first moment we met, in that taxi at the photo lab. If Kamal knew, he made no reference to it.

Kamal, he came home with me that night, he cried and explained and threatened and cajoled, and it took all of two, almost three years before I came to my senses again. Or before I got angry enough and tired enough of him and he could no longer convince me that I needed him around. I finally found out that I did not need him to get me modelling work, to teach me the business of photography—I knew he could not teach me the art of it because he had none, to manage my money—I knew he had managed to take it all, to give me companionship, protection, a sense of home. I knew I needed this man for nothing, I knew that he needed me so much that he had convinced me that I was the one who needed him. I took all the money out of our joint bank account, I did not tell him anymore where I went or why or with whom, I hoped that he would leave, that he would find somewhere else to go. He did not.

My father called. They were finally moving to Canada, and he wanted to see me. I went to their apartment which was in the heart of downtown Bombay. I hesitated for a long time before I rang the doorbell. I almost did not recognise the young sweet-faced girl who answered the door. But I knew those frightened eyes. In spite of the huge smile on her face, I knew my little sister. Milan gasped and threw herself onto me. I hugged her back. I was overwhelmed by guilt. I could have come and seen her anytime in the last five years that we had left the boarding school and lived in this city. I could have taken her out to dinner, or shopping, or to a movie. I could have helped her with her homework. I could have got to know her better. I could have been a support to her as she struggled to survive her vicious stepmother and her spineless father. I found my eyes fill with tears, but I held them back. I had justified not having anything to do with her by telling myself, and anyone who asked, that it was a matter of self-preservation. 'If her own mother didn't make the effort,' I said once to Bree, 'why should I? I didn't give birth to her did I?' And Bree had said only, 'Ginny, she's your sister. She's your flesh and blood. God tells you what is right. You choose not to hear it.' I thought of Mary the cook.

As we went inside, Millie kept hold of my hand. She did not hold it against me that I had not seen her in those years. She understood, I told myself. Perhaps she might have done the same, in my place. My father sat on a large red sofa not unlike the one in that other house I had lived in with them. The smell of a good mutton curry drifted out from the kitchen, and the TV was tuned to the Wimbledon final. John McEnroe was testing Bjorn Borg. I sat down next to him to watch. He smiled slightly and said nothing until the ad break. Then he turned to me and said, 'I want you to have this place when we are gone.'

That made no sense to me, so I said nothing. I looked out of the huge windows at the railway clock. Indira came down the hallway toward us, I heard her before I saw her. The hackles rose on the back of my neck. She could not harm me now, I told myself. I am an adult. I can hit her back. I didn't stand up. She walked in, and I was surprised at how much she had aged. She was several tens of pounds heavier, her hair had overgrown what was probably a really bad cut to begin with, and she wore pants and a giant shirt to cover the great shelf that her breasts and stomach formed together. After almost seven years, her first words to me were, 'Oh, it's you. Do you want to stay for dinner?'

Before I could answer, Millie said, 'Oh, please stay!'

And I said, 'Yes.'

They left for Canada a few months after that meeting. But in those months, I went often to see them. I did take Millie out shopping. I found that she had a huge file full of all the magazine covers and print ads that I had ever been in, all the posters for beer and whiskey, half-dressed and undressed. She had every little quote and interview that I had ever done. She even had a snapshot of a giant hoarding that I had once been on, in an advertisement for men's clothing. Her admiration and devotion embarrassed me. I introduced her to Bree. My father loved Bree instantly. He asked her what church she went to, what her father did, how many brothers and sisters she had, everything, in fact, that I had not. Bree brought her mother's beef chilly for them one day, and that won them over for good.

When the time came for them to leave, Millie cried and cried, and made me promise I would visit them. I promised. And then I was handed the keys to the apartment, and they were gone.

Kamal was beside himself when he heard about the apartment.

'We can have a studio right in downtown Bombay,' he said. I let him move his stuff into the place so he would leave my apartment. It seemed like a good idea at the time, but it entrenched him in my life for a while longer. It got worse. He became crabbier and older and balder and less and less liked in the advertising community. I was beginning to get desperate, and more and more entrenched in the bog of his life. And I remembered Gabriel's words to me that had slipped my mind at the time: 'Ginny, Kamal is not your parent.'

I wondered if there were words of wisdom that he had

planted in my brain to spring out like weeds when I needed them. Like magic beans. I smiled at the thought. It would be time soon. He would be gone soon. I knew it in my heart and body as certainly as the blood flow of my period.

Veeru brought in the mail one Monday morning in December. It was an uncharacteristically cold day, and the air was smoky outside. I noticed a movement at his feet, and saw that a small tabby cat had come into the studio with him. The cat, obviously male, meowed at me and settled down to clean himself. He looked up at me for a moment, so I spoke to him.

'I think you will have to leave, sir,' I said to him. He said nothing. Kamal walked in at that moment too, and was shocked. 'What is a stray cat doing here?' he asked Veeru.

'I don't know, I didn't bring it,' Veeru said.

'Give him some milk, and then we can send him on his way,' I said. Kamal, to my surprise, didn't object, and started looking at the mail.

'There is a German guy who wants to come and be my assistant,' he said.

I thought, 'I hope you will be living and working somewhere else with your new assistant.'

At the beginning of the next year, we came to the studio to find that Veeru had run away with all the lighting equipment. He had left a note for me. I read it and smiled, and Kamal lost his temper with me.

'What exactly do you think is funny about this whole situation?'

And then, we got a job together in Sri Lanka. Sri Lanka, again. This time, I was there with the man that I spent close to five years of my life with, from age seventeen to almost twenty two. Everything that can be wrong with a relationship was wrong with this one. He was two decades older, controlling, of course, how else would he have held on to me, a woman twenty years younger than himself, he had managed to bring me, again and again, back to the belief that I could not make it in the world without him. I had started out as an assistant, an apprentice. I lugged his bags, I had cleaned his studio, processed his film, made his tea, even, on those rare but awful occasions, slept with him. At the beginning of the end, I got my revenge by getting almost catatonically stoned, by having my ongoing relationship with Avi Suarez that I not only did not bother to hide, but publicised. Nothing had worked. He would not leave me.

We were in a beautiful little hotel in Colombo, right on the beach. I had left our hotel room the night before and gone off with a German I had met, a young and clean John Walker Lindh, with a beautiful mouth just made for kissing. We had what I now think of as German sex, which meant we kissed a lot, and he didn't seem to want to do anything more. That was fine with me. So we watched the sunset through his hotel window, and kissed. Naked. The next day, the shooting job was done, and I wanted to spend the day at the beach. It was to be my last day in Sri Lanka, though I didn't know it then.

I couldn't swim. At least not in an ocean. I lay half naked on an Indonesian batik sarong. I was exotic, among all the white hippies, I was stoned, from the German's ganja. I ignored Kamal. He decided to go into the ocean for a swim. I was jerked awake from my sun and ganja-induced stupor as if I had been shaken. I looked around for Kamal. I saw him, very far from the shore, waving at me. I had not sat up then, just opened my eyes and looked. I knew immediately in my gut that he was in trouble, probably a cramp, I knew that he was too far out to make it back on his own. He was waving, but not at me. He was waving frantically for help. I knew if someone didn't go help him he would drown. I knew it without a doubt. I put my head back down, closed my eyes tight, and didn't open them. I wished with all I had that he would die in the water that day. I made all the plans in my head. My shock and horror would be genuine, and no one could accuse me of anything more than intoxication. My flight back, perhaps with a body, I wondered how that worked. My life, my career, my money, my body was suddenly my own. This man had a wife, child, siblings, parents. To me, all that didn't count. I just wanted him dead.

Someone saw him, started yelling, and four or five men swam to him and fished him out. On the flight home, listening to his version of the story one more time, how he was such a strong swimmer but the current was so strong, how his leg had begun to cramp at just the wrong moment, how he would have easily swum back if it hadn't been for the cramp, how in fact he was beginning to recover and would have made it without the help of all those men anyway. And I thought, you don't know anything about yourself, do you, until you're right there.

I never would have thought of myself as someone who would let a person die by my inaction. But I am. I am someone who would have let this man die by my inaction. That's as close to murder as you can get without actually doing it. I knew too, that given another chance, I would do it again.

This time, when I left to visit my mother at her farm, I told Kamal in no uncertain terms that he had to leave, and take all his belongings with him, by the time I got back. I said I would have him removed if he was still there when I got back. It did not work. He was still there when I got back.

I called Avi. He said, as I had known he would, 'Figure out your own shit, girl.' So I figured out my own shit.

I called Roy. I called Bree and asked her if Laz would help me. We all met at the Irani restaurant across the road from the studio for breakfast one Sunday morning. I had told

Kamal I had an early morning shoot, and left at 7 am. I knew
he would not come into town that day, he went to visit his
family on Sundays. We talked as we dipped chunks of fresh
white rolls into very sweet milky coffee. We had already
eaten four platefuls of very spicy greasy ground lamb and
several green chillies, and were, as Roy put it, 'fulfilled and
fed up'.

'Let's just throw his shit out on the street,' was Laz's way
of doing things.

'You're such an idiot,' Bree told him. 'There's no need to be
so violent at all times. We can just put his stuff in boxes all
ready for him to cart away.'

He sat quietly as we three talked and argued and laughed,
but in the end Roy had the best solution.

'Let's pack all his shit and take it to his house in a van.'

Laz agreed that it was a good idea. He went to the
restaurant phone and called up a friend with a van to be
there in a few hours. Then he went to the liquor store and
picked up twenty or so flattened cardboard boxes, and said,
'Okay, let's do this.' And I knew I had the right crew.

The band of us began to throw Kamal's things into boxes. As
we filled up boxes and taped them up, we got better and
faster at it, and did it with cheerful abandon. As each box left
the room in Laz and Roy's strong arms, I began to feel lighter
and younger and stronger. When we were about halfway
through, Laz went out and came back with bottles of cold
Rosy Pelican beer and a bag of spicy peanuts. Bree lit up a
cigarette and we shared it.

'I am so glad you are doing this,' she said, looking intently at me. 'I knew you would, you know. I knew you would come to your senses. He is a very bad person, Ginny. He should never have done what he did.'

'I let him, you know, so he is not entirely to blame, Bree,' I said. She laughed. 'You cannot be that stupid. I know you are not. Let me try to explain this to you as I would to any other person who is not as smart as you. This man is more than twenty years older than you. This man is married with a child—two children? This man sees a girl—and you were no more than a girl when we met him, and you are little more than a girl now—and sees that need that you wear on your forehead, the need to be loved, to be needed and wanted, to be a child, we all see it. The point is, do we all use this need? Would I be able to go to church on Sunday if I did what he did? We all have a conscience, we all know what is right and what is wrong. I know, I am rambling on. My point is,' and she paused to inhale on her cigarette and passed it to me, 'this man is an asshole, and he plain and simple took advantage of you. You are not to blame here, so don't start with that shit.'

Laz heard some of her lecture as he went in and out with the boxes.

'Let me just take care of him,' he said. 'A good beating will teach that motherfucker a lesson. I told you right when you first met him, Bree. You should have let me break a leg or an arm for him, all this would never have happened.'

Bree laughed and ignored her brother, for whom a whack in the head was the first response to most things. To me she said, 'You know, it's been a long time, but better late than later. I have been lighting a novena candle for you for so long, and Mary has answered my prayers now. She always does.' But Mary did not answer her prayers when Laz disappeared. He never came back, and they never knew where he went.

I knew that Kamal would come straight to the studio on Monday morning, and I told Bree and Laz to be there for me. They came home with me and stayed over. Roy had to be at class, and went home. In the morning, though, he just didn't want to miss the drama, and he came back. My posse and I were there at eight-thirty, and Kamal walked in just as we had settled ourselves down with cups of coffee and cigarettes. He walked in as usual, full of business-like hustle and bustle.

'We need to get the place cleaned up . . .' was as far as he got before he noticed the bare studio.

'What the hell? Where are my things?' he shouted.

Laz stood up towering over him, and just leaned against the wall. I wouldn't want to run into him on a sunny crowded street, let alone a dark alley. His silent intimidation worked in an insidious way. Kamal dropped his voice immediately.

'What is going on here?' he asked.

'I—we—have packed up your things and stored them. If there is somewhere particular you want them sent, let me know, and I will have them sent there. You need to give me the keys to my place now, and you need to find somewhere else to live and work.'

He stared at me. I was reminded of my stepmother's bulging eyes, moments before she hit me. Kamal did in fact take a step toward me, but I did not flinch. Laz was between us in a moment. 'You had better get out of here,' he said to Kamal in a reasonable sounding voice, but every one of us in the room felt the open threat this time.

'Ginny, I want to talk to you alone. Can you all leave for a few minutes? I just want to talk to her alone.'

'No,' Laz said, not waiting for me to answer. For some reason, that irked me. I just didn't want another man taking charge of me, even if he meant well. I am sure they all always mean well. But I had the distinct feeling that day that I needed to kill him myself.

'No,' I said, looking straight at Kamal. 'I don't want to talk to you alone. I just want you to go now. You can come to the flat and pick up your things from there tonight at about six. If you are not there by seven, I will put your stuff in a box and leave it downstairs in the parking lot. And give me the car keys too. I paid for that car, and you can't have it anymore.'

He stared at me some more, but I didn't feel afraid. He began to get teary-eyed. 'Why are you doing this?' he said. And Roy and Bree, oddly enough, in unison said, 'Oh, my God.'

I wondered about this man. It made no sense to me that he was still standing there. But he was. I turned to my friends and said, 'Would you guys give us a minute alone?'

Again, Bree and Roy said together, 'No.' They didn't even stand up to leave the room. Bree reached out and held my hand and said, 'I'll leave if you really want me to. But Ginny, listen to me.' She took a drag of her cigarette and spoke to me while looking at Kamal. 'He can't tell you what to do. He is not your father, Ginny.'

There was a silence in the room. I heard Gabriel speak through her, his magic beans had grown a beanstalk. I climbed.

'Laz, ask him to get the fuck out of here.'

Laz didn't ask. He just looked at Kamal, daring him to say

or do something. Kamal saw the pantheon around me and visibly accepted defeat, at least temporarily.

'I'll not let you people get away with this,' he said, and quickly turned and left, slamming the door behind him. 'I'll kill that motherfucker,' Laz said. I dissolved into unexpected tears, and Bree put her arms around me and said, 'He's gone, and he won't be back. He's a spineless bastard. He won't be back. Let's go eat some lunch.'

And we went to Excelsior café, and the waiter brought us the world's best mutton biryani, cold lime juice, and bread pudding, and we celebrated my freedom and independence. It was my twenty-third birthday.

When I answered the phone on a late Saturday night after a gruelling day photographing bad clothes on bad models, I was not expecting anything more than a wrong number. In fact I thought it was a wrong number for a minute after the woman spoke. It may have been a subconscious attempt at self-preservation.

'We are calling to contact members of a student's family who is a parent or guardian. May I speak to such a person please?'

I did not understand the question at all.

'Hello? Is this Simi's home number in Bombay?' Blood began to pound in my head. I was Simi's guardian, and this was the school calling. The school would only call if there was an emergency. An emergency could only be a very bad thing.

'Yes. This is Simi's older sister speaking. I am her guardian.'

'Okay, please hold on, I'll put Sister Joan on.'

Sister Joan was the principal of the school. I waited very long minutes for her to come on the line. It could not have been more than seven or eight minutes, but it was a lifetime of terror while my mind went through all the possibilities. In all of them, Simi was dead.

After my twenty-first birthday, my mother decided that since she was living in Japan most of the school year, Simi should have a guardian in India, someone who was close enough to the school to be able to make decisions quickly. I was delighted that I was her guardian. I thought, finally, that Simi's parents took me seriously, that they felt they could depend on me to do the right thing by them and by Simi, should the need arise. I did not think the need would arise, and everyone forgot that letter that was written to the school nominating me the guardian of the then eight-year-old Simi. School had been hard on her at first. I went to see her when I could. One of those years I went to a sports day. Simi was running in four races, and in the relay for her class, and a couple of other events during the day. In the evening, before the parents and guardians went back to their hotels, there was a dinner, and then a theatre presentation. It was at the moment when Simi came out in a cloak and tight pants under the balcony in reply to some long-haired Juliet that I realised Simi was a star. She was happy in this school. Everyone knew her, she was smart and sassy and popular. She did well at academics, she played the piano, she was athletic, she was everything. I was as happy as any of the parents around me. I wished our mother could have felt some of the pleasure I did, but even when she was in the country, she refused to come to any of the school events.

'If she's that good an actor, I'll see her on Broadway, and if she's that good a pianist, I'll see her in the London Philharmonic, or at least the Hong Kong Philharmonic. I hate children's plays, and you know it. No, I will not succumb, and no, I don't feel guilty, so don't bother with that.'

Whenever I went to visit, a gaggle of girls would come running up to talk to me, and then would send one of the younger ones to tell Simi that her sister was here.

'I saw you on TV!' they would say, or in a print ad, or on a magazine cover.

'You're so pretty! How does your hair look so shiny? Do you know . . .?' and they would ask me about all the other famous models in the city, and get giggly and happy when they found I knew everyone. By the time Simi was found and brought to see me, her ratings had soared too, and they all looked at her like she was the princess. She was certainly the 'it' girl. We would meet in a small room off the principal's office called the parlour, and she would always run in, use the door frame to stop herself and lean beaming into the room to savour the pleasure of seeing me, and then she would come in and give me a huge hug.

This time as I sat there in the parlour, there were no giggling gaggles of girls. Two went by the door, and when they saw me, they whispered to each other and walked on slowly. I waited, yet again, for Sister Joan to come out and talk to me.

I was exhausted after the five-hour-long ride in a private taxi. I dozed fitfully the whole way, a disturbed and ugly sleep full of broken anxious dreams. I was ready to scream at everyone and anyone, but there was no one there, I was alone in my suppressed fear and panic. I had phoned Ami before I left, and had promised her again and again, though she had not asked me for any such promise, that I would call her as soon as I had any news.

I just sat there in that parlour once full of happy memories, and stared at the pictures on the walls. Mary and Jesus caught my eye, and I looked back at them. She looked as if she knew something.

'What do you think is wrong?' I asked her. She said nothing. She was thinking about an answer. I waited till she had formulated one. Minutes went by, and still she said nothing.

'Well, is my baby sister okay or not? You know, right? You can tell me. A simple yes or no will do, I don't need too many details.' She kept looking at me without a word. I wondered about her. She must have been a child when she had her own child. I wondered if she had had the option to say no. The angel Gabriel himself stands before her with a flaming sword and says, 'You will bear the son of God.' Did she have the choice, really? Could she have said, to the angel Gabriel, 'No, thank you kindly, you shining being, with your eyes, dark windows to heaven, with the sparks from your hair, your breath, your sword,' she steps back to avoid the sparks that singe her skin, 'I will not bear the son of any man but my beloved Joseph, thank you kindly, but no.'

No, she could not have said that. For the love of God, and the love of the shining angel Gabriel, left hand of God, she could not have said no.

'Your baby sister is fine,' she finally said, in a disappointingly normal voice, 'and I was not as impressed with Gabriel as you obviously are, Virginia.'

'Virginia?' I looked at the door of the parlour when I heard the other voice, and got off the floor. It was a young nun, unsurprised to see me kneeling in front of the Virgin.

'Sister Joan will see you now,' she said.

I was somehow calmer, and I said thank you and followed the scurrying nun down the corridors of the school into the infirmary. At the far end of a very long row of hospital beds, close to the window, lay Simi. Sister Joan sat in an uncomfortable wooden chair by her side. I walked very slowly toward her, though I wanted to run. Sister Joan's eyes were on me, and they did not allow running in the halls.

'Ginny, I'm so sorry,' Simi said. The flood that descended from my head to my feet, I recognised as relief. She looked pale and small and very poor. I wanted to run to her and hug and kiss her and tell her that she was fine, that everything would be fine, that she was wonderful to be alive and speaking. But again, Sister Joan was there, and I just put my hand delicately on her head and stroked it.

'I'll leave you two alone for a little while. Come down to my office in fifteen minutes, Virginia, and ask Sister Leela to sit with her. The doctor said she must rest.'

She got up and signalled Sister Leela to leave with her. They went out, and I saw that Sister Leela went into an office across the hall from the infirmary with her back to us.

As soon as they were both out of sight and earshot, I lunged on my little girl and hugged and kissed her.

'What happened? What's going on?' I said, unable to take it any more.

She smiled at me and said, 'I fell off the jungle gym and landed on my head. I was unconscious for some time, it may have been a few hours, because I missed lunch and then it was dinner time, and the doctor says I have a bad concussion.' She put my hand to her head. There was a huge lump, and when I looked I could see bruising and abrasions there. I was even more relieved. She was not dead. She had not been run over by a car and found dead in the street. She had not been buying illicit drugs in the town market and found dead from an overdose. She had not been raped by the gardener and found dead in the rose bushes. She had not been poisoned by school food and found dead in the toilets. She was just Simi, the little girl who fell off the playground apparatus and injured her skull, and perhaps her brain a little. She was not dead. Mary looked down at me here too, and smiled. She was not impressed with the angel Gabriel, I thought. She could have said no if she wanted. I would remember that forever.

I, as Mary pointed out to me, was impressed with the angel Gabriel, whatever form he showed himself to me in, whether it was the head doctor Gabriel, my real life angel-to-be, a dark blue Sri Lankan god-to-be, a Croatian soldier-to-be, or a Nepali thief-to-be, or Bree, who I suppose was not really Gabriel, but a more mundane, daily guardian angel. They were all put here on earth, as far as I was concerned, to tell me which way to go, to save my life, which I thought for the longest time, did need saving. Or they are there to make me beautiful.

There are those I love for who they are—my child, a friend, the cat—any cat—Jeremy Piven. And then there are those I love for what I am around them, for what they make me. I love the mirror that reflects me back as beautiful. I will never see my own face after all, only see the eyes of those who do. The love for one who confirms me is almost impossible to let go of. It stays forever in some deep part of me, a source of will, a source of confidence, a source of self.

I never took the risk of showing myself. I never abandoned my self-made exterior, my projected self-image, and showed anyone all of myself. I don't think I ever really looked at it myself. There were few times when the armour slipped, unintentionally or inadvertently. Or someone I encountered just paid attention, or happened to see through it, who caught the whiff, of that scent once so strong, now muted, hidden under manufactured perfumes of politeness and confidence, who caught sight of the person behind the persona, saw the tears, the fear, the raw wants, the child inside the woman. Someone who saw, in the peace of post-fuck, who in fact brought on the peace of post-fuck, me stripped down to my essentials. If I looked into his eyes and saw a beautiful reflection, in spite of all those exposed truths, when I entrusted my beauty to this person, I did not know how to draw back, and let that person, and so the truth of myself, go.

I was at the top of a very long ladder holding a reflector for Kamal as he photographed a spread of food for the menu of a fancy, in fact very fancy, restaurant at the Oberoi hotel.

'Move it out more over the left side,' he yelled at me again, for the thousandth time. My arms hurt from being outstretched for ten minutes each time he thought he had it right. I asked several times that he clamp it to the ladder, but he refused.

'It's easier to move and control when you are holding it,' he said. I thought, 'Asshole, bastard, motherfucker,' several times, but stayed up there. At least I was up on this aerie and not having to do all the work on the ground, which poor Veeru was. He had not run away yet in those days. I was approaching my twenty-first birthday fast, and thought about going to driving school as I balanced precariously above the forest of lights and lightboxes. I could see the bald greasy top of Kamal's head clearly from up there, with dirty grey strands plastered across the bald patch. He was aging so gracelessly. There are men who bald beautifully, the tops of their heads becoming soft and vulnerable like newborn babies' heads. And there are those that go from black to grey to strands of shining silver. Kamal was getting uglier, greasier, more like a troll every day. I stopped hearing the talk and itchy bustle that he always created when he was shooting. There was an unnecessary feeling of his doing the most important thing in the world, and an expectation that all around him, his slaves, should be grateful to be allowed to assist in doing that most important thing in the world. And too many lights, I thought. I would have lit this with a single flat box, it would have been perfect. But he had spotlights and fibre-optic circles and had created complicated shadows that he was now trying to mute. It looked hideous, as usual. I was hungry too, and there was some very good food right there below me, being allowed to congeal into inedibility. I knew he would soon complain about that, and the chef would have to take everything back into the kitchen to re-heat, to restore the gloss of the spice-infused oils.

When I fell, I didn't really feel it, I must have dozed off. I didn't feel it till I found myself looking into an odd face, full of concern, and a voice I had never heard before, but was completely familiar anyway,

'Hey, are you okay?'

I didn't answer. I just assessed my situation. I was in the arms of a very tall, wild yellow-haired man, his eyes were a dark smoky colour that I thought might be navy blue, but could have been any shade of darkness, his mouth was full and large, and there were shiny golden points on his face where his beard was growing out. There was a deep cleft between his lips and his nose that I almost reached out to touch. I must have been getting heavy in his arms. I wasn't heavy by any standard, but he must have been holding me for a few minutes.

'Oh, put me down,' I said, and he did. Standing up, I was at least a foot shorter than him.

'You fell off the—that,' he said, pointing to the ladder.

'Ladder,' I said. 'And you are?'

Kamal was standing beside us suddenly with a scowl on his face.

'Was your flight late? I expected you here earlier.'

So that's who he was. The German guy. He didn't answer
Kamal. He just stood there, towering over me, and I saw the
acknowledgement of me fade from his eyes to be replaced by
confusion. The moment between us passed as if it had never
happened. Perhaps it never did happen, and I just projected
all my wants and needs and desires upon that first perfect
moment between us. Whatever it was, I didn't fall to the
marble floor and hit my head and end up with a concussion
like poor Simi. He was my angel Gabriel for that moment at
least. I would like to think I could have died from a contusion
and fluid on the brain, and that he had really saved my life.

He stayed in the studio for the time that he was in Bombay,
about six months. He suffered dysentery once and bouts of
diarrhoea from eating street food, he caught colds, he slept
among rolls of background paper and light stands, and he
spoke for six months in an unfamiliar and foreign language—
English. And through all that, he suffered Kamal's bullying,
bad temper and constant suspicion about his relationship
with me. But he was cheerful for the most part, and his
English, if not his photographic skills, improved as he steadily
lost weight. He went back to his country when his time was
done, and I didn't find out then how it would be if we lay in
a bed together and if he turned those smoky indigo eyes on
me and looked into my reality, or how it was to be with
someone from whom I would have to hide nothing, and to
whom I would never need to lie. I didn't fall to the ground
and injure my skull, but I did have one sort of concussion. I
collided with possibilities. With a future that I was convinced
was impossible, and so did not dare want, or even think

about. I said to Bree many times over the time he was there with us that he must have a woman back home, or, more likely, he was not interested in us muddy beings. I was almost used to getting lost in the hair on his arms, like gold wire growing out of what I thought must be a solid gold core.

'You're a magpie,' Bree said to me one day as I nudged and pointed out his flat belly covered in a lush pelt of gold. We were at the beach on some calendar shoot for Kamal, and he had, like the cliché goes, like they say in Harlequin romances, emerged like a god from the grimy foam of the Arabian Sea.

'You just love these shiny objects.'

When I brought Simi to Bombay to recover from her concussion and get her CT scans and have her looked at by a neurologist, she had terrible splitting headaches. I gave her the maximum dose of painkillers I was allowed to, and she lay in a small corner of the studio with a mask over her eyes, whimpering a little. The cat who had made his home with me curled up beside her. Bree came by every other day or so, to talk to her, to read to her, to bring her treats—Christmas cookies and fried fish, crayons and a colouring book that Simi laughed at because it was for babies, but coloured anyway, an obscene pink nail polish that Bree painted painstakingly on both their finger- and toenails. I worked hard in my studio. I did odd jobs, calendars for liquor companies, this time from behind the camera, pack shots for hair products, photographs of young girls who said they wanted modelling portfolios, but I found out they were used to pass around to prospective grooms. I was quite shocked at the idea, and refused to do any more. The mother accompanying the girl who told me the truth about it was as shocked as I was that I did not know.

'How will you get married?' she asked me.

'I guess I'll meet someone and fall in love. I doubt I want to get married. Anyway, I haven't thought about it.'

'And what do your mother and father have to say about it?' That question I had no answer to. I really didn't think they cared one way or the other.

I somehow became the unofficial photographer for the gay community of Bombay. The studio was the general hang-out spot on slow days. They would drift in and out, always with grass and hash, and chocolate cake from the bakery downstairs. To me, they were a different breed from the usual clients I had. Their relationships were different, with me, and with each other. They had screaming rages, jealous fits, giant pouts, tantrums, and I loved the sense of everything being expressed rather than held in, and expressed in ways other than quiet angry words or long silences. For me it was an endless source of curiosity.

They were each flamboyant in their own way, but one of them really caught my fancy. He had prominent cheekbones and collarbones and hipbones and long hair that flowed like black water as he moved. I was unable to stop looking at him when he was in the room, and my admiration embarrassed and then flattered and then annoyed him, as did my staring and constant remarks about his beauty and grace. He was a stylist and make-up artist, so our paths often crossed. He would do my hair and face and clothes, and I would bait him mercilessly. He would explain to me patiently that though he thought I looked gorgeous, mainly because he had taken pains to make it so, he did not want to go to bed with me. He explained that I did not interest him in that way. I didn't really hear him. I didn't really care. I just continued, perhaps because he was not interested, in my relentless persuasion. One evening he and I were the last ones in a fancy house on the beach, a set for a baby shampoo commercial. The house belonged to a gay couple who had made their fortune from exporting fine leather clothes to Italy. In the film I was a young mother in a bathtub with a baby. All day I had been stuck in a bathtub full of bubbles, and all day the object of my admiration had made me look dewy and clean and 'sexy-but-motherly' and had arranged bubbles carefully around my cleavage by blowing them into place with a drinking straw. After pack-up, the crew and the agency people left, and I was still in a terry robe in the bedroom we had used as a make-up room, smoking and drinking Dukes lemonades. He was meticulous about washing his brushes and wiping his boxes, so when we went out, everyone had left.

'Just us?' I asked him, unnecessarily. We were friends by then, and I did so want to push it.

'Yes,' he said, and then, 'don't start'.

'Start what?' I was smiling, I knew what he meant, and he knew I knew.

'Let's just stay for a while, have a drink or something.'

'We've had a drink,' he said.

He took a pack of cigarettes from the front pocket of his jeans. He had to lift his shirt to get them, exposing his hip bone slightly and for just a moment, but it was enough to set me off.

He looked at me with exasperation. 'Ginny, Ginny, Ginny. This is just so annoying of you.'

Before he could light up, I touched his mouth. He sat down heavily on the leather couch. I sat down next to him. Right next to him. He turned to me to say something, probably something more about his disinterest in me, but his mouth was so close to mine that the kiss was inevitable. We were involved in something very like a prelude to real actual sex when I felt something cold and wet on my naked skin that I knew was not the hands or mouth or any part of my poor friend. And then I heard, 'What the hell are you doing? Is that you, Ginny?' It was one of the owners of the house. He dropped his jaw in shock and surprise when I sat up and revealed my reluctant and, I have to say, unresponsive partner.

'You!' he said when he saw him, and began to laugh. My infatuation was well known and well ridiculed in the gay community. I also realised that what I had felt on me was the nose of a giant Doberman. I knew this dog well, he was blind. We called the two men who owned him the seeing-eye people. I pushed his wet nose away from me. Being blind, his sense of smell was even keener than other dogs', and he was rooting for what smelled most interesting. There we were, a gay man with his pants firmly where he wanted them, zipped and belted, me, in the lonely throes of an unsuccessful seduction, and another curious gay man and his curious dog. There was nothing to do but laugh. And we laughed. And though I never stopped chasing that elegant man, there was no sting left in it anymore. He and his friends would visit me at the studio, and we would smoke and eat and banter and create photographs that none but this group could have done.

They all took over Simi's convalescence too. They brought her treats and silly accessories—film star sunglasses and scarves and straw hats because the sunlight hurt her eyes, food treats that were absent of nutrition but full of sugar and made her happy—gulabjamuns and silvered kaju squares and huge soft boondi ladus. And Simi was entertained. She had begun to get better, and spent less and less time sleeping in the corner. She was with me for a month, and though I was concerned about her health, in the end it was a quiet gentle time we had together. It was the first time that we had spent any length of time without our mother. Ami called, once, to ask about her. I told her she was fine, and gave her all the details of what was going on. I explained that I would not send her back to school because a second concussion when the first was not fully healed could be fatal, and I wanted to watch her. I said I would send her back when the neurologist gave his okay.

'It's a good thing you dealt with this whole episode,' she said to me when I was about to hang up. I waited for the thanks, or perhaps, I thought, she would tell me that she was relieved that I had been available and responsible and cared about and loved Simi enough to rush there immediately, and to bring her back and take such good care of her.

'This will make you think twice about having children,' she said. I was quiet for a moment, and then said, 'I plan to have two children at least. I wanted three, and I already have Simi, so I'll have two. Girls.'

She laughed. 'Does this involve a man? Or are you at least smart enough to have learned that lesson?'

She sounded fuzzy. Her voice was clear, but her words were not. They tripped in slow motion over each other, making me complete her sentences in my head, usually incorrectly. I had rarely been able to predict my mother's actions or words, and this time was no different. It was normal in my conversations with her, so I didn't pay much attention to this part of our communication. I wondered about her speech. It was not yet noon in Kobe, I knew, and couldn't believe it was alcohol that was making her sound that way. I forgot about it, and all the indications of her alcohol use, or abuse, until I saw Gabriel again.

After Kamal left, or I threw him out, I did go and see Gabriel. I thought I would talk about me, about the men in my life, about where my children were going to come from. But we talked about my mother. It had been seven years since I first walked into his lovely, though green, office. The walls were no longer pale green as they had been when I first went there and complained about how awful that green made me look. He had laughed.

'No, really,' I said, 'it makes me look like I have liver disease. A warmer colour would be so much nicer.' Two years ago he had the place painted ivory. The furniture was still green, but I was pleased. I had asked him if he chose that colour for me.

'Of course, Ginny, who else would tell me that my taste in wall paint colour was unacceptable?'

I was never sure whether he was serious, and preferred not to ask him.

He was not in his office when I got there. I sat on the lime-green couch outside and looked at the paintings. They had been replaced too, the old mouldy landscapes were gone, and there were close-ups of flowers by Georgia O'Keefe instead. I missed the old ones. They had been much less demanding and, of course, much less cuntish.

'Are you well, Ginny?' he asked me when he came in.

'Would I be here if I was well?' and then, before he could answer, I said quickly, 'You know I would be here even if I was well, whatever that is. I do love you, and you do have a huge place in my life. You are like a deity that is always there. You are like a trust fund that will never run out. When I use myself up, I can always get some from you.'

'Some what?' he asked, laughing.

'You know. But that's not it either. I think about you, you know? What you do, what you are like outside this place. Who you love and what you eat. Can't we just be friends ever?'

'We are friends, Ginny,' he said.

'But you know, can't we ever just meet for lunch? Or a movie? Can't you come to my studio and see my work?'

'I can, and I will. But tell me, how is it all going? Work? Kamal?'

I grinned broadly. 'I threw him out. He's gone. End of story. I hope I never see him again.'

He smiled too. 'It was how long? Five years? My god, Ginny, I am glad. You can't imagine how glad. You seemed to fade through those years. I was honestly sorry that I could not have just prevented you from being with him. Like a parent. I often wished I could just say no.'

I was surprised at this declaration. 'You know, if you had said no, I would have listened to you.'

'I know, that's why I didn't say it. I have to let you follow your own path, Ginny. I am here if you need me, and I am here to support you and guide you. But I cannot tell you what to do, or what not to do in that way. And you will be better for it, the more you make your own choices. If I had told you not to be with Kamal, I would be no different from him.'

As always, he was right. 'I got your letter,' I said, and took it out of my bag and began to read it out loud. I had read that letter so many times that it was bare in parts, where the ink had been rubbed away by the sweat in the whorls of my fingerprints. Not fingerprints, I thought, I meant the grooves on the tips of my fingers that leave fingerprints. I asked him what they were called.

'Fingerprints,' he said firmly. I gave up and continued reading.

Ginny,

You are never going to find that kind of response. Never. That kind of emotional intelligence, complexity, and most of all the brutal honesty that you expect is unrealistic. Also, you give way too much. No one wants to see a person exposed to that degree. It is frightening to other people. It is akin to seeing a naked man in the street. I realise this would not turn you away, before you start another needless argument, I'm talking here about other people. You need to learn to hide more, and yet balance that with . . . I don't want you to suppress or repress. Just shade it. Look at who's standing in front of you. Carefully. You can't just . . . let me put it like this. You take your clothes off, get naked when you want to take a shower. Or have sex. Not when you have just met someone. No, not when you have just met someone, even if you know you will have sex with them. Well, treat your psyche the same way as you would your body. Oh dear, that doesn't work with you, does it! (I really have to talk to you about that too.) Okay, treat your psyche as you know someone else would treat their body. With care.

You are always going to have that feeling of trying to squeeze blood from a stone. You are going to have to get your love, and attention, and that exposure, that nakedness in small doses, from many different sources. No choice, darling, no choice. I have seen this a lot. I wish I could hook up all you poor creatures that are so needy, and yet so full of love and so open to giving away all you have!

—G

'So what don't you understand about this?' I was silent after I finished reading, and sat there expectantly. As usual, he turned the conversation over to me.

'Well, I don't think it's asking too much to find someone who is willing to just—be.'

'And why do you think it is asking too much?'

I laughed at how he had turned it around. 'Because every man I've been with has been afraid, or unwilling, to take everything I have to give. In fact, unwilling to take even a little of what I have to give.'

'You mean sexually?'

'What's the difference? It's all the same thing, isn't it?'

'The same as what?'

'Sex is the same as love, as companionship. I mean, it is an expression of everything. I can speak love, anger, frustration, sweetness, friendship, and of course just plain want, in the language of sex. But I feel I am speaking a language no one else speaks. It's ugly.'

He considered me. He picked up his letter and stared at it. Just when I thought he wasn't going to say anything at all, he did.

'It is frightening to other people, Ginny.'

'Yes, you said that in your letter.'

'And it is true. Answer me this. And you don't have to answer now, but think about it. In fact, don't answer now. Think about it and write down the answer. Because I want to talk to you about something else right now, and we will get back to this later. Think about why you have ever had sex with anyone. And I mean, go through every person and be honest each time.'

'Okay,' I said. 'What did you want to talk to me about?'

'Something that I feel is more urgent. I hope it is just urgent and not too late, I have a feeling about this, and it isn't good, Ginny. I want to ask you about your mother. We have fifteen minutes, but my next appointment isn't for an hour. I want to know how she is and what is going on with her.'

'What do you mean?' I asked him.

He sighed, and looked down at his hands, the fingers laced together as usual. He looked tired. Then he looked up at me. 'Her drinking,' he said.

Simi had told me a little about her drinking in the years before they sent her away to school, and I had a glimpse of it when I was there.

'We had been to a friend's place for dinner, they lived in the next street. Sonja and Peter, you remember them?' I did remember. They were Australian, in Japan for some years. I suppose all the expats got together, it was not that easy to make Japanese friends. They had two children around Simi's age, one younger, and one older. I remember the older daughter coming around to play when I was there. They would play with dolls, and the neighbour's dog, a perfect little Chiba with a curly tail, and they went out trick-or-treating for Halloween. Sonja had dressed up Simi in a witch costume, complete with scary teeth. I remembered the girl, whose name was Angie, being in Simi's room without coming through the front door, and finding out that they lived in the next street, but actually it was closer to come over the hill behind the house, which ended right behind their house.

'So we stayed till almost midnight, because Ami got into an argument with Peter about something, they were always arguing, every time they met, and they kept drinking the whole time, and then when the time came to go home, Ami says, "Let's go over the hill", and I thought it would be faster and closer because it was winter—this was after you had left—so off we went. And it was so pitch-dark I was terrified and tried to hold Ami's hand, but soon gave up, because she kept stumbling, and I was afraid she would fall and be unconscious.' Then Simi smiled and continued, 'Actually I thought she would die, and that didn't worry me as much as being alone on the hill.'

I laughed. 'You were just a little girl, that's normal. You're still a little girl.' She tucked her hand into mine, as she sometimes did. She went on with her story.

'Anyway, so we stumbled and tottered home, and came around to the front, and Ami couldn't find the key, and then when she found it, she couldn't get it in the keyhole because it was such a dark night and there was no streetlight, nor did we have a light on outside, and she kept saying, "Damned bastard kept re-filling my glass", which I didn't understand, and finally, she stopped trying and stumbled over the step and puked all over it. And then she sat down there, leaned her head against the door, and went to sleep! I didn't know what to do, so I tried to find the key, and I did, but it was all covered in puke . . .' I began to laugh, and so did she. We both knew how she felt about bodily secretions, and about nasty things in general. 'Ewwww, gross!' was heard thousands of times from Simi's mouth on any given day. So it was particularly ugly that she had to take the puke-soaked key and try to open the door. She managed to open the door, wake our semi-conscious mother enough to get her inside the house, and put herself to bed. When she woke up very early the next morning, she found Ami asleep, still in her soiled clothes, just inside the door where she had left her.

'I'm sure she had peed her pants too,' Simi said to me. I remember feeling sad most of all. Not about Ami, but about the way Simi saw her. I said as much to Gabriel.

'There was a callous contempt in her for our mother. I don't blame her. But my impression of my mother, apart from the way she felt about me, was one of a tall, long-limbed, pale, smart, very strong woman with fine, shiny brown hair, and who could swim, for god's sake, one whom everyone looked up to, whom everyone loved, whom I could never even aspire to be like, someone who I was simply not worthy of being loved by because I was short, dark, I had coarse curly hair and a fat mouth, and I could not swim or do well at school and not one of my parents wanted me.'

'Is this about you or your mother?' Gabriel interrupted me.

'My mother. Simi, actually. What I am saying is, Simi saw, still sees, this same woman as a drunk, a loser, someone who is fat and old, someone whom she does not respect, let alone love. And in the last few years that Simi has been in school, she asks to spend her holidays with me rather than go to Hong Kong, where they are now, and our mother is upset by it. She wants Simi so much, and Simi couldn't care less.'

Gabriel looked at me even more sadly. 'You knew her as a young woman, Ginny. Your mother was barely twenty when she had you. She was thirteen years older when she had Simi. And most of Simi's disrespect for her, most of her impressions come from the effect of the alcoholism.'

I was stunned. Alcoholism? Surely not. That was like saying I was a drug addict. 'I smoke hash or ganja regularly, that doesn't make me a drug addict, does it?' I asked him.

'And I have never called you a drug addict, have I? But I am saying your mother is an alcoholic, Ginny, and I am saying you need to do something about it.'

'I don't think she's an alcoholic, and even if she is, what on earth do you think I can do about it? Has she ever, ever, listened to anything I have ever said? I'm the liar, remember? I'm the one never to be trusted, never to be paid attention to. What am I going to do? Why doesn't Varun do something? It's his responsibility, not mine.'

He nodded.

'And,' I continued, though I knew that our time was up, 'she's published four books, and everyone thinks they are fabulous. She can't be that bad.'

'Just because she is productive does not mean she isn't ruining her health. But that is something she, and her family, and that includes you, Ginny, will have to help her figure out. But first you must confront it.'

He wrote a number on a piece of paper. 'This is the name and number of a friend of mine. Call her and see what she says. You can say I asked you to call, she'll see you once for free.'

'I don't have a money problem anymore, at least,' I said cheerfully. I got up to leave. We had talked almost two hours that day, and I was talked out. I wondered how he went from one of us crazies to the next without losing his own mind.

Simi had told me many accounts of instances when our mother had had too much to drink. But I had seen much more when I visited at the farm. I saw how much she drank, not by the quantity, because she hid that very well, but by her state of mind and body. She was really no different, I thought, than when I was seven or eight years old. She didn't look particularly bad, though a little overweight, and, as I had told Gabriel, she was productive, creative, much loved and admired in the literary world, she had adoring fans, both women and men, and to me, she was unfailingly sarcastic and sharp as always. She was sharp. She was sharp with her words, but mainly, her thinking, her thought processes, were sharp. I bled from the many cuts she inflicted on me, but I admired her even as I tried to staunch the bleeding. I lost the piece of paper that Gabriel had given me, but I knew the name of the woman. I would call her if I felt the time was right, or if I could somehow get my mother to talk about this, I thought. I knew she would be fine. She was too big and strong to let something like alcohol get the better of her.

Her face was a translucent yellow, the whites of her eyes were not whites, they were turmeric bright. I thought it must be the light, at first. But of course I knew it was not. She was in a small room, private only because of a curtain that separated her from a wrinkled old man who was surrounded by relatives, from tiny babies to some people that looked a hundred years older than him. I could not tell what country they came from, but they were dressed in some traditional dress that looked to me like Greek shepherds' clothes. I knew they could not be Greek shepherds, we were in South Korea, and Greece was a long way away.

'They are Uighurs,' she said. 'He has been dying for all the time I have been here, and the family has been waiting. There have been some false alarms, if you can say such a thing about dying, and then the whole family begins to wail, until the nurse comes in and tells them he is still alive. His life, at this point, is not distinguishable from death, but it stops them from wailing when the instruments make the distinction.'

She smiled as she said all this, she was not complaining about it, just observing the passage of time, the way of the world and the people in it.

We had gathered there from our corners of the world, Simi and Millie and I. Simi came from Berkeley, where our mother had been so many decades ago, where she had lost her virginity in the'60s in the back seat of a Beetle, where she had been exotic and lovely, heard Jerry Brown speak, and come home with a degree in philosophy and literature. Simi wasn't following her path. For one, she had no scrap of virginity left to lose. I had already seen her through two boyfriends, one stalker, one abortion and one Masters degree in psychology from Pune University that included an affair with a visiting professor from Berkeley, which is why she was where she was. Millie lived in Canada, close to the American border, close to the spray from Niagara Falls, but not close enough to escape the bitter Canadian cold, the lake effect, the sunless, endless white fields of those winter months that only paused, never stopped long enough for her to even take a breath. Indira had died three years before, of an ovarian cancer that spread fast and took her, and everyone, by surprise. Cancer always takes those who have it by surprise, but hers took her life before she was over the surprise. She left financial ruin in her wake, for her husband, our father, to sort out, and he almost didn't make it. We commented, out of his earshot, that she was the sort to have died of that disease. It was a terrible thing to say, as if she was to blame for her cancer, as if, had she been a different sort of person, she would have lived a long cancer-free life. Perhaps she would have. Her bitterness filled her ovaries to bursting, and consumed her. And perhaps it was not her that brought on the disease, but we, who wished it upon her, when we thought dark thoughts about her every time her hand touched us, never in love, never in friendship, but with the force of an anger and disgust that we had done nothing to deserve. If there was one thing Millie and I agreed on, it was that she brought her death upon herself.

This was a different time. This was our mother, the three of us. If there was anything that brought us together, this fact would be it. Not her, or her actions, just the fact that she was our mother.

There was no malice in her, just a despair about the world, just a feeling that no one would ever understand who she was or what she felt. It was arrogance, of a kind, that had brought her to this. As I looked at that familiar face, I saw none of the familiar contempt in it. The clenched jaw was unclenched from its impatient vice, the eyes were not narrowed in anticipation of my next lie, the mouth was not punished by the teeth into a line of disapproval, cancelling words that might come out of it, that might acknowledge me. Her face was soft from tiredness and acceptance. She had been in no pain, even that first moment when she knew something was wrong. I asked her again and again, if she was, or had been, in any pain.

'No,' she said. 'Not pain, not really.'

I thought about what Gabriel had said to me, not too many years ago. I suppose it was too many years—if I looked at it from where we were now. He had said she was an alcoholic, and here we were, probably, no, definitely, in the last days of her life. None of us sisters had ever felt in any way responsible, let alone guilty for her life, and now we did not feel responsible for her dying, which was surely near.

'I feel something ... I feel sick,' she said softly, gesturing nausea. She coughed a little. I looked at the spit that clung for a moment to her lip, and then began to form a thread as it descended to her white hospital gown.

Maybe sometimes my re-constructions from excavation are wrong, but there's something to be learned from it. Detritus—uneaten pickles in a hamburger wrapper, a torn condom, a broken plate, say the child hates pickles, the man cares little about the pain he causes, the woman is unable to speak or live her anger, and throws plates. Clichés, I know, but saying more than a fresh McDonald's paper bag, a couple walking through a park, a perfectly clean kitchen. Clichés, on both sides. But still. No, it is not the garbage or the secretions themselves that interest me, it is the stains they leave, the evidence. Not virginity but the loss of it. Not life, but the loss of it.

There was blood in that spit that hung suspended from her mouth. We had been—she had been awaiting, with dread, but also certainty, this stain for almost three months now. From that frozen, foreign place in Korea, I was back home with her to the place where it began, where I began. She had wanted to go home, and knowing they had done all they could for her, they had agreed to send her home to die. An ambulance, two planes, another ambulance, brought us back. I was back in Bombay for the first time in five years. The journey was long and exhausting for me, but she, she seemed to grow stronger and brighter as we got closer to home. She sat up from her ambulance bed on the final stretch to the hospital and said, 'I smell home. We are here, aren't we?'

And I said, though it was not my home anymore, 'Yes, we are home.'

They gave her a lovely room, large and airy, with a big picture window. The view outside the window was now familiar to her. She knew the names of the trees, the whisper-soft purple blooms that covered them like a shroud, she identified the birds by their mating calls, she knew the smell in the air meant it would rain that day. In Korea, outside the enormous teaching hospital, there was a river, and all day and all night people gathered at the promenade and walked and talked, and we could see the smoke from the chimneys on the other side, making sunrises sooty and sunsets dark and foreboding. The food there she would not eat without a fight, every day claiming that they had dredged the river and were feeding her the pickings. Some of the food did look like it should not be eaten, but I fed it to her anyway, with a spoon and the cold metal chopsticks Koreans ate with. I felt as if I was feeding a child, not from memory of being fed like that, because I did not remember her ever feeding me. I had fed children, and now she was one too. Not mine, but a child nevertheless. Now at home, she had meals of rice and mushy yellow lentils and vegetables and boiled potatoes with a sprinkling of salt and cumin. She ate happily the first few days, high from being there, delighted by all the visitors who came to see her—family, ex-students, friends, devotees, women who said she had changed their lives, their way of looking at the world, of living in it. One young girl said to me outside as she left my mother for what she knew would be the last time, that this woman, with her writing, and her life, had taught her how to make the world accept her on her terms. I did not understand.

Simi and I would sit in the room and listen to the people that came and we would turn to each other in amazement, we didn't understand who all these people were talking about. This was not the woman we knew, we had known all our lives, who told us every day that we were deficient in one way or another, who never knew, nor cared where we were or even who we were. And here were all these people, there was never a day when the visiting hours were not busy, who told us, and her, that she was their mother, their friend, their mentor, their saviour. I thought, often, that this would be my own archaeological site, the life and times of my mother, from where I would reconstruct a different life, a different person from the one I had known, who had made me, who had changed and formed me, who had rejected me in every way possible for a parent to reject a child, and yet, I felt, from looking at her through the eyes of everyone but her children, I would find her. I would find a woman that I could love, and respect, and look up to, who would be my model, my idol, my goddess. And like all idols and goddesses, she would be dead.

But I had something. I had had, however imperfect, all those years with her. I thought about Millie, what she had said in the taxi that took us to Incheon airport the day she had said goodbye to her mother to return to her frozen home. I went to see her off, to make sure she got on the plane okay, but really, because I knew, or thought I knew what this parting meant to her. I found out I did not. She didn't say anything most of the drive. We looked out the windows, and had no choice but to listen to the drone of the taxi driver on his cellphone, we understood neither his words nor his tone, he could have been buying sheep, breaking up with his boyfriend, or talking to his dispatcher. The landscape was expressionless too, grey without menace, industrial without aggression, and past the industrial stretch, natural without dignity. Korea just lay there along the highway. It did not speak to our hearts, or to our thoughts. There was old snow along the wall beside the road, but even that did not convey cold. I had never seen a country so bereft of being, or one I less understood, or less wanted to.

'I will never see her again,' she said suddenly.

I turned away from the window toward her and realised with some shock that she must have been crying silently the whole time. I put my hand on hers. I waited. I thought she would not say anything more. I knew she would not see her mother again. She felt the loss, I thought, of a parent, but one whom she didn't know, couldn't have cared about. She hadn't known her after all. Like I had never known our father. I wouldn't miss him if he died, after all.

'I will never see her again,' she said again, and looked at me with those eyes I had always thought of as happy, as willing to be happy, but had been robbed, again and again, of the opportunity, and over the years, of the trust. There was still something there, though. Something like hope, and a smile always lurking in the turn of her lovely mouth. Our mother would have told her to hold it firmly, to make it thin, she would have told her that mouth was too full and bee-stung-looking.

'I always thought I would get to know her one day, you know?'

I understood how little I understood. I had had this mother, day after day after day. She was there in my life. Millie did not miss my mother, she missed hers. She had missed her all her life. She would never see her again, she would never have the opportunity to see her be the grandmother to her children, she would never know if her mother shared her own hatred of the cold or her distaste for the smell of bananas or the feeling of emptiness on bright summer days. She would never argue with her about the meaning of Eliot's poems or the creamy certainty of Beethoven's symphonies. She would never again be able to tell herself anymore, or ever again, 'I will get to know her one day, my mother.'

When I walked into her room in the Korean hospital, Ami was weak, but clear and alert. The ruined condition of her liver meant that they could not give her drugs to help her pain or sleeplessness, or anything at all. It could not process anything anymore. I didn't ask, during that first long day, the one question that I wanted to: 'Why?'

She answered it anyway. 'I didn't think this would happen to me.'

She told me of the hallucinations she had during the week of forced withdrawal. The doctor had ordered x-rays, and she had to leave her room to go to the labs.

'I stood up, which was hard, after being horizontal for so long, and I thought I was stuck there, I could not take another step. I was standing at the edge of a crater on the surface of the moon, a jagged edge stretched into the distance, and moondust covered the ground all around me, I could feel it, like a dusty, filthy floor, making me want to curl my toes. I couldn't see the bottom of the crater, nor the other side, so dark and dusty it was.' Her refusal to move, and finally her screams, sent the nurses running for the doctor. He was a man with hardly any expression, when I met him I could barely discern a feeling of stern but real concern, and the lack of lines said that even a frown had rarely visited that face, let alone a smile. He convinced her that though there may or may not be a crater in the room, she would have to hold his hand and walk through it with him.

'I trusted him somehow,' she said, closing her eyes, back in that moment.

'The funny thing was, as soon as I took one step forward, the crater vanished.' She opened her eyes, there was some animation that came through the terrible yellow of bilirubin.

'Not really pink elephants, I might have preferred those!' she said, almost laughing.

'Dr Kim is my Heracles,' she said to me one morning when the grim doctor had come and gone. So, she thought of herself as Prometheus, chained to a rock, a crow ate her liver and it regenerated in the night so he could eat it again the next day. In reality, as did Prometheus' liver, it would have regenerated, if there was even the tiniest bit of it left. She had not the tiniest bit left. Heracles might unchain her from the rock, but we were in the long day of the crow, and the night would not come for her as it had for Prometheus. There was nothing left to regenerate.

She asked me again and again, in those two days before her youngest daughter arrived, 'When will Simi come?'

And now, after washing her and cleaning her, after feeding her and combing her fine fading hair, after stroking her yellow hands and feet, the waiting was over. There was that blood on her mouth. The stain spread like paint on watercolour paper as it touched the white of her hospital gown, and I tried to hide it from her.

Blood. It has always been there with me. I found its essence in the stain on the kitchen towel into which it had soaked from the gash I had made in my finger, while chopping onions, very fine, for what would become the best lamb curry anyone had ever experienced. In the rusty iron smell of it when I pushed the smeared white of my panties almost into my nose to know it better. In the slickness of the pinkish slime that I find when I touch myself after this man has left his spit and slime and exhaustion and elation in it. This was different. It was lifeblood, end-of-life blood, death blood. She understood what it meant when it came. We all did. She, closest to death, understood least what it meant — to not be in the world anymore. It was really the fear of the unknown, the final, ultimate unknown that I saw in her eyes each of those final days. It was what made her say to me again and again that she wanted her head stroked, her arms stroked, her back stroked, that she wanted to be touched at all times. This woman, my mother, who had always shrunk from touch, who had always refused me the gift of her touch, who, when I put my arms around her and my head on her belly, had pushed me away and said, 'It's really too hot for all this much affection', suddenly yearned for that affirmation of life—human contact. And now it was time to end all contact. To end all physical being. Life was suddenly just time gone by, it was her time to die, and she wanted to be reminded of her physical self, she wanted to live in her body now.

As Simi and I sat in that hospital stairwell waiting for the doctor to tell us our mother was dead, I wondered what her grandchild would remember of her, what my little fatherless, nine-year-old son would remember of his grandmother.

As a grandmother she had been nothing like she had been as a mother. When I called her that mid-summer's day to tell her that my pregnancy test was positive and that I would be pregnant for another seven months, she was silent. And then, into the dread that had built in me over those silent seconds, she laughed. It wasn't a sound I had heard from her before. It was more a girlish giggle than a laugh, a funny little tickle of sound that came dancing through the crackly phone line. I thought I was mistaken. But then she did it again.

'Ginny, I won't ask where this creature came from if you don't want to tell me. But I'll be a grandmother, and I have to thank you for that.'

I thought I was mistaken again. I didn't say anything more, I didn't want to believe in something that would probably last a few days, or weeks or months, and then disappear like it had been a figment of my imagination. But as the days of my pregnancy went by, I saw something I had never seen in all my life as a daughter. I knew it was some strange love for that unborn person, I knew that I was just a vessel for some unacknowledged dream that had somehow come to be. She admitted to herself that she was delighted, and treated me as well as she possibly could. She phoned me to beg me to come live at the farm.

'Bring Bree, or Roy, or anyone in the world that you want to be with,' she said. 'It has been raining, the lake is full to overflowing, there are birds visiting, and grass everywhere, and I will row you around on the lake, and we can tell Simi to come and stay and I will get to see you both. Your father will be home for a few weeks, and we can all be together for a while. It has been so long since we all did that.'

I was close to speechless. I called Simi.

'What's going on with her?' I asked her, thinking she might know better, she at least got to see her every other week when she came into town to teach at the university.

'Don't know,' Simi told me in her quick and direct way, 'but this baby of yours seems to have addled her brain.'

'Baby of mine? Simi, I haven't asked you how you feel about it, but surely you didn't expect me to ask your permission to have it?'

'No, no, no!' she said, 'it's nothing like that! I'm totally excited. Of course, you won't love me as much when you have your own little girl to love, but then I'm sure you will let me share her, won't you? And I won't love you as much either, when I have her to love!'

'Little *girl*? You realise, it might be a little girl with a penis?'

We were both silent at this idea. It seemed quite unlikely. We didn't mention it again.

'Will you tell me?' she asked me suddenly.

'Tell you what?' I said, knowing exactly what she wanted to know.

'Nothing,' she said, and I didn't push it. I would tell her,

I thought. I would tell her when the child was there with us, and she would know, when she saw her, who her father was.

Beloved. I had always wanted to be beloved, not just loved. I had this idea that the man who loved me would love everything about me. Not just the things that are easy to love, not just my breasts and my cunt and cooking that would someday be worthy of love. But he would love the things about me that I did not love, and the things about me I could not change. He would make me not want to change them anymore. He would make me love them. He would love my hair, my pregnant belly, my secretions, bloody and sticky. He would make everything ours, not just mine. And at fifteen, I had this idea that I wanted to leave a trail of broken hearts behind me, I didn't think then that a heart is a living bloody thing. When I had seen a single one broken, I realised, luckily early, that I was too squeamish to deal with the clean-up, with the sticky, gooey, oozy mess of heartbreak. And I was too squeamish to deal with the guilt. But I wanted to be beloved.

I wrapped up a single moment I had had with a stranger into a cocoon of titanium threads and stored it in some chamber of myself that I thought I would never need to open. But it was there, and it was heavy and sharp, and it hurt me when I breathed too deep, like shrapnel in the lung, shrapnel too close to my heart. It was a kind of unrealised, unconfessed yearning that had begun to ache by the time I had gotten over my delight at Kamal's enforced departure. Bree commented on it occasionally.

'Have you been to see Gabriel lately?' she said one Saturday afternoon, as we sat drinking beer and smoking and my two studio hands cleaned up after an assignment that had made me enough money to not have to work for the next three months.

'Why?' I asked her, though I knew why she had asked the question, I was aware that I spoke less and less to her, I knew I had withdrawn into some darkness that appealed to me in some fatal way.

'I'm fine,' I said to her, but I did promise I would call him and make an appointment.

'Do it now,' she said.

I did, because I saw no way out.

It was, as always, good to see Gabriel. Or to have him see me. As I waited, I was struck by my own familiarity with that room, where I had waited so often for this man, waited in the antechamber before going in to confession. He would listen, but he never gave me absolution, nor a way to earn the forgiveness of some heavenly judge. And he was the angel himself. Before I went too far with the analogy yet again, his office door opened, and he signalled me in, he had a phone to his ear, but was not saying anything. Someone was talking on the other end, and it sounded like a woman, a little hysterical. I sat across from his desk, and he sat down too. A few minutes later, he apologised to the person at the other end, promised he would be there, and hung up.

'Ginny, my dear, you look lovely.'

That was all he said, and then waited. It was up to me, as always, to confess, to unburden, or to just sit there and look at that beloved face, and of course it was, a beloved face.

'It's funny, I came because Bree said it had been a long time since I had been to see you. I figure maybe she didn't want to deal with whatever it was that she thought was troubling me.'

'Is something troubling you? Is it about your mother?'

I was annoyed. 'Why does it always have to do with my mother?' I asked him a bit roughly, and he only smiled. I ignored the smile, and in fact the whole mother issue.

'Actually, I'm here because I had a moment of weakness. Or perhaps it was a moment of clarity. And I can't make up my mind which it is.'

'Hmm. Elaborate, and maybe if you talk about it some more, you will know which it is. I think that's really interesting, Ginny, and important, that you at least know that these are your two options.'

I was puzzled. 'What do you mean, two options?'

'Clarity or weakness.'

'Oh. Yes. Well. I've been thinking about this man. Or boy. Whatever. He's probably a couple of years older than me, or the same age. So depending on whether I'm a girl or a woman, he's either a boy or a man. Anyway, to get right to the point, he's about my age.'

'That's not right to the point, but I'm sure you will get there soon enough.'

'Yes, I will, won't I? And if I stray too far you will bring me back to it. The point is, I find myself thinking about him more and more, and now pretty much all the time.'

'Is this someone I know? Or someone you know? Or at least someone you saw on the street? You didn't make him up, did you?'

I laughed. I felt silly suddenly, about Gabriel, about sitting in the office of a highly respected psychiatrist, someone who should be helping people more needy, or at least more crazy than I would ever be, people who were paranoid, schizophrenic, depressed, detached, about to kill themselves or someone else. Not me. I was perfectly well-adjusted, balanced, and nothing more than love-sick, about some shiny object that had caught the fancy of a basic part of my magpie brain. Or that part of my imagination that lived in my cunt, that brought this man to my bed every night, and now every day, where I would entwine my muddy self with his gold and silver skin and look into his smoke-blue eyes looking into my cinnamon ones. This was really not a topic of discussion with Gabriel, and I was embarrassed.

'You know, it's really not that important,' I said. He didn't even sigh.

'Ginny,' he said, and I did not detect restrained impatience, or feigned patience, and this was, after all why I trusted and loved this man, 'a single thing may or may not be important. The point is, you felt the need to be here, and you are. All of what you say and feel is a little glimpse of who and what you are—not just for me, but for you too. So there is really nothing you could say or feel that is not important in some way. We just have to figure out where it fits in, and why. Sometimes we won't, but it will all make sense somehow.'

'I think I really just want to have this man. Or I want him to have me,' I said.

'Who do you think he is?'

'I think he is someone who will know how to touch me. I think I have forgotten how it feels to be touched, or I am afraid I never knew how it feels to be touched. I know there is something out there, a way of being, a way of feeling, and

I am afraid I will never know it,' I said, and to my own surprise, my eyes and nose began to drain in rivulets down my face.

'Oh Ginny, you see, this is important. This is so very important. You did never know, my dear, how it is to be wanted for no reason at all. You just went along in this stream of other people's lives, your mother's, your stepfather's, even Simi's. This was not your own stream. If your want for this man feels unfamiliar, it is because you are unfamiliar with your own wants. You don't know what you are, and you are just waking up to it.'

I sobbed, and he, yet again, handed me his clean white handkerchief. The first time I had met him, he had given me one just like it, and I was relieved then that it was not starched. I took it, and blew my nose in it. He laughed, and said, 'You can keep that one, too.' He remembered.

I crumpled it up and clutched it with both hands in my lap.

'You said, that this could be a moment of clarity, or a moment of weakness. Do you know?'

'I think it is a bit of both. The weakness is in my attempt to find me in someone else's eyes. But I don't know where else to look. The clarity—I don't know about that, really.'

'Who is he then? No, not that I want to know, I just want to know if he is a real possibility, or . . .'

'Oh, he is not a figment, if that's what you mean. He is a man I met. He came to work with Kamal. I had very little time with him, and very very little time with him alone. But there was something, I felt it, and I felt that he felt it. If I make the slightest effort, I could see him again. Or at least find out if he will see me again. But I really think I would regret it if I let this go, if I second-guessed myself, if I made this smaller than it is. You know what I mean?'

'That you don't want to bury your instinct and intuition under good sense?'

'Yes, Gabriel, yes, that's exactly what I mean. I feel, and I mean feel, not think, that if I don't chase this into the ground, I'll hate myself when I am eighty years old.'

He smiled, perhaps imagining me at eighty.

'Where does he live?' he asked me.

'He's doing a teaching stint for a year, so he's not in his home town.'

'So where is he?' he asked me, impatiently this time.

'Tallahassee, Florida.'

He looked at me blankly for a moment, and then we both burst out laughing.

'All you need is an American visa, then?'

The pregnancy was easy. Every day I grew softer everywhere in my body, except my belly, which grew harder. I couldn't stand the smell of frying garlic, and the smell of a particular herbal soap that seemed to suddenly be everywhere. Otherwise, I was hungry all the time, I was happy most of the time. Simi, Ami, the boys that worked at the studio, all treated me normally, and allowed me to order them around as usual. Bree was more and more distant, and I wished there was something I could do to change that, because, if nothing more, I enjoyed her mother's beef chilly and fried fish, and even had terrible cravings for it in the middle of some rainy nights. Simi had summer holidays during my sixth and seventh months, and was disappointed that she would not be there when the baby came. I thought about asking her to take a term off from college, and stay with me in Bombay, but thought the better of it. She finally seemed to have found what she wanted to do, and I did not want to disturb this flow. My mother, uncharacteristic as my mother in her new role of grandmother-to-be, was doting, but not doting on me, somehow. She cooked and washed and looked after me, but I never got the feeling it was me she was looking after. I asked her to bring me some baby clothes, preferably pink and frilly, when she went on a trip to Hong Kong where Varun was working at the time.

'Don't be silly, Ginny, it could very well be a boy, and I know you, and I won't allow you to dress the poor thing in frilly pink and pretend he is a doll.'

I was puzzled again. She would have wanted a granddaughter, the mother I had known and loved before this. And, god forbid, if I had produced a male child, I would never have heard the end of it, how I had broken the line of women that went all the way back to her great-grandmother or some such. I thought she would assume the next female in line was on the way. She did not. She did not let me assume it either. And, she was, plain and simple, patient and kind. She was rarely sarcastic. She told me she would be back from her trip in good time for the baby. In fact, she timed it carefully, and left me with a thousand instructions on what to do and ten thousand on what not to do. She lectured Simi, and the neighbours, and anyone who came and went about what they should do in the event of any emergency. She made me make an appointment with my doctor who would deliver the baby so that she could know and make sure herself that it was really fine for her to go away.

The doctor was a family friend, she was recommended by Sanju's mother. My mother demanded that she do an ultrasound. I lay on the couch and watched hopelessly as my mother machine-gunned questions at her. Shama maasi was normally a daunting little woman, cheerful but strict. She went about her business, taking my pulse, blood pressure, palpating my hard belly.

'Can you feel any movement?' she asked me.

'No, not yet. But then, I don't really know what to look for. I feel like there's gas wandering around sometimes, like there are little bubbles in me, like I am a giant coke bottle.'

'That's probably the baby,' she said.

'Okay, my dear, put your knees up and apart for me, so I can use the vaginal probe,' she said. I was surprised, I thought the ultrasound was done on top of the belly, and said so.

'No, you're right, this is new, and early in the second trimester, it will give us a better picture,'

I got into position. It was a rather pleasant sensation as the slim plastic penis slid easily in.

Ami was watching the screen. It showed that familiar triangle of black and white, pulsing and moving. I could not see clearly. The glow of the monitor filled the room, and the whuff-whuff of a muffled heartbeat took us underwater, I was floating with the creature in my amniotic fluid.

And then there was a gasp from my mother.

'What?' I asked, but not with any alarm, because she did not seem alarmed.

'Just how beautiful this is,' she said. I was startled to see tears in her eyes. I don't think I had ever seen tears in her eyes. Not even when her beloved cat was brought to her in tatters, when it had bled to death in front of her. No, it was I who had cried when Fitzy died.

Ami's face looked a way I had seen it before. I could not remember when.

'Oh, I wish we had this stuff when I was pregnant with you girls. But this is really amazing. Look, Ginny, I can see fingers and toes. It's so tiny, but it has fingers and toes. I tell you, I can't wait to meet this little person.'

She was still wiping away tears when Shama maasi laughed and said, 'Oh, you! I've known you since we were in college, and I've never seen you like this! Wait till I tell everyone!'

They both laughed. Shama made little print-outs for me to take home to show Simi. I wished she had been there to see this. I promised myself I would take her to the next appointment, it would be a treat to see her reactions. She would probably be thrown out by Shama for squealing too loudly.

In the taxi home, Ami and I were silent at first. And then she began to tell me about her pregnancy, the second one, me.

'You would think,' she started suddenly, 'that all babies are ugly and prunish and hairy when they are born. That's what I thought anyway. My mother told me not to expect too much when you were born, she said you would be as ugly as a newborn puppy, because I had seen a litter of puppies when I was seven or eight, and I was appalled and disgusted. So I was expecting a hideous, hairless, mewling and puking blind little bint. But you, Ginny, you were beautiful from the moment you were born.'

I was speechless. My mother had never before or ever since called me beautiful. I was still glancing in the rearview mirror at my own face, thinking that it was a bit fat right then, when she said, 'Millie was not planned, you know, Millie, poor little thing,' and then she stopped, and put her head in her hands.

The taxi had brought us home, and I paid the driver. I was determined to continue that conversation. She went upstairs ahead of us, and it took me a while to climb up. I was tired for some reason. The troll heard me going upstairs and stuck his head around the door. I was alarmed at the thought that he was naked behind that door. I had just never wanted to think of him naked. I hoped fervently that he was not. And yet, I peeked through the crack in the hinge to see what I could see. My suspicions were confirmed. There was something shrivelled and something hairy. I stopped looking.

'When are you due?' he asked me, with a huge smile on his funny face. I was surprised again. He had been a different person to me from the one I had known all those years ago when Roy and I had lived there together. I had begun to understand that a baby on the way changed the way people treated me, even though there was no father in sight.

'In early October, probably.'

'Ah, maybe Gandhi Jayanti. A very Indian baby then.' I was startled by his words, not quite getting them.

'I could name her India?' I said, to be clever, just to end the conversation.

'Her? Are you sure?'

'In my heart, I am,' I said, clutching the banister. He noticed.

'Oh, you must be tired, and here I am prattling on. I'm getting very old, I'm sorry. You go on up, I'll come see you later. I want to see your mother, too.'

By the time I got upstairs, Ami had finished most of her drink and was getting ready to pour her second. I was glad, maybe she would be willing to talk about Millie then. I asked her where Simi was.

'She just called to say she went out to a movie, she'll be back for dinner. I'll just get started on dinner, you must be starving.' She got up and went into the kitchen, still talking.

'Was that Sarin you stopped to talk to?'

'Yes,' I said, feeling suddenly very tired and hungry.

She came out again with a glass of mosambi juice and a slice of bread thickly layered with butter and sugar. I choked up when I saw it, but ate it quickly without stopping till it was all gone. I could hear her in the kitchen, washing rice, then I heard the clack of the pressure cooker tins, and knew she was making rice and daal, and then I heard her open the door to the cupboard under the counter. She would take out potatoes, and she would cook a delicious bhaji, I knew, with mustard seeds and garlic. I braced myself for the wave of nausea that would hit me when the garlic released its wonderful, and now dreaded aroma. There was none.

The American visa was easy to get. I just walked back into Alex Hayes' life.

'Ginny, my God, it's been what, ten years almost? You look

great. I wasn't sure, when my secretary told me your name. But I don't know any other Virginias in this city. There aren't any other, are there?'

I laughed. 'Hello, Alex, yes, it has been almost ten years. How are you?' I asked him, sitting down across from him at the huge desk. There was a monstrous American flag taking up the entire wall behind him.

'I'm great, just great. I was back in DC for a few years, you know, and only just got back. You know I am married now, and have a four-year-old, and another one on the way.' He turned the photo frame on his desk to show me. A nice family portrait done in a studio. A woman, his wife, stood next to him, blonde and a bit plump. The child was gorgeous, all coffee and cream, with a mass of curly hair like a halo around her head. I was relieved, I could say honestly to him, 'What a beautiful child, Alex, what's her name?'

'Sarah,' he said, and I could see the love in his still stunning mahogany face, now with a little grey at the edges of his hairline.

'Well, anyway, let's get to it. I don't have very long right now, but it would be lovely if we meet up sometime. You know, come have dinner with us?'

'Yes, that would be nice,' I said, meaning it.

He went over my papers.

'Are you going to stay long?' he asked me.

'Well, I want to buy some equipment, visit a few friends, and, mainly, I've agreed to loan my collection of paintings to a museum, and they have agreed to pay for my ticket and stay in New York for a week. I thought it was a good opportunity to go.'

'You collect paintings?' he asked, puzzled. He was right, it wasn't something I would have done.

'I inherited them. Bijou.'

'Bijou? Really? How many?'

'Sixty.'

'You have sixty of his paintings? That's pretty awesome.'

He went through my papers.

'You know, Ginny, you could apply for a special type of visa, for artists and so on. An 'O' visa. Do you know what I mean? I know you've been a photographer for some time now, and you have published enough work to be eligible for it. Would you like some more information on that?'

I thought about it. Leaving home to visit was one thing. I had never considered that my life would be anywhere but right there in Bombay, among the smell of life and constant decay and traffic and brown dogs. Japan, China, Sri Lanka, I had been, and some places touched me. Even America. But I didn't know that I wanted to have my life there. In fact I knew that I did not. But his words intrigued me. I would have this option, with the visa he was offering me. I could change my mind, if I wanted to. I thought about Millie and my father, that other family in the great frozen north of Canada. I had been there too, and seen their life. Paper route at six every morning, including Sundays, breakfast of cereal and orange juice, layers upon layers of wool and fur and leather against the unrelenting cold, snow shovels and windshield scrapers. But there was also a kind of sweetness in the strangers I encountered on the streets. A willingness to talk kindly to everyone they met. Maybe it was the space between every individual that made everyone so easy.

Whatever it was, I remembered a sense of being allowed. Allowed in every way. Except in their house, where the sense of well-being disappeared with the cold, and a different sort of chill entered our bones, Millie's and mine, when we heard our stepmother's voice. She went to work, luckily for us, so there were times when we just sat at the windows and looked at the snow.

There was a huge field behind the house.

'It's a playground, for the elementary school,' Millie told me. 'It's full of screaming children in the spring months, and all day in the summer, when all the neighbourhood kids are there all the time.' I couldn't imagine it, but she described flowers and green grass in that whiteness. It was night, but it never really got dark. And as we sat there in the dark house in the winter snow glow, a large deer came up the path to the field and then into the field. He stood there a long moment, looking around at his world, his breath heating up the air around his head and face, and then, like animals do, when the moment was over, he turned and went away. We said nothing to each other, Millie and I. We just sat there in the semi-dark until our father and Indira fouled the air with their insistent presence.

'Why are you girls sitting in the dark? Are there no lights in the house?' and then they snapped on every switch. We didn't tell them about the deer.

'I didn't plan to have another child, after you,' my mother said to me that night before she left on her trip to Hong Kong, the last time I saw her before she became a grandmother.

'I knew I would not be with your father anymore, I knew I was going to leave him.'

It had taken more than two drinks. We had eaten her excellent rice and daal, and her expectedly delicious potatoes. I was full and happy and ready to go to bed. But she had been drinking steadily through cooking, through dinner, and after. She was maudlin and unwound and had started talking again about babies and childbirth.

'It won't hurt so much. It will, but it won't hurt too long, don't worry. I will be back anyway, and I'll be there with you.'

I had not thought about her being there with me. I had imagined I would be alone, and then I would be with the baby. I knew by then that I had no choice in this matter, that she had somehow appropriated this moment in my life too, like she had appropriated every other. I was tempted, often, to give in to this new her, to allow myself to be mothered. But I had no practice at it, and I was suspicious. I remembered too well the other children, the daughters of her friends whom she clearly preferred over me, whom she clearly would rather have had as her daughters, these girls with willowy long hair, with thin mouths and self-contained auras, with ambitions to go to ivy-league colleges, who knew Shaw and Eliot, who had read her writing and could discuss it with grace and intelligence, who were so many things I was not, that I had given up, a long time ago, trying to be even a bit of. These girls who never lied. These girls who had not claimed to have slept with her husband. These girls who could not make her a grandmother.

'The night Millie was conceived—he raped me, you know, he dragged me into our bedroom and had me on the floor there. He was angry when I told him I was leaving him. He was angry, and he was so much stronger than I was. Most men, even the small ones, are stronger than us. You know that, don't you? And then he left, on his motorcycle, that night, and didn't come home for three days.'

If there was something I was expecting from her, it was not this. It was not this. I wanted to put my arms around her and hold her. But I did not know how.

My father with his friendly face. His long hair blowing into my eyes when I sat behind him on his motorcycle, holding on tight. His huge strong hand grasping my tiny arm when he lifted me up easily from behind him and set me down on the ground outside my school every morning, so I could be on time for my before-school piano lessons. A baby sister, crying all night and looking at me with huge round eyes from a crib in my mother's room. And then they were both gone, and it was just my mother and I, in this same big city, looking for a life.

She left for Hong Kong the next day, and promised me again and again that she would be in time for the delivery, shouting instructions even as the taxi to the airport pulled away.

Simi and I settled into a routine. She had some time with me, but after that I would be on my own with my belly. I had stopped working, and spent my days hanging around, eating, going on long walks in the neighbourhood. Three days before Simi was to go back, and at the end of my seventh month almost to the day, I woke up very early in the morning with a bladder so full I thought I would explode. I got out of bed.

'What the hell are you doing, it's 6 am,' Simi said to me, groggy with sleep.

'I just have to pee, or I'll pee right here in bed,' I said. 'Go back to sleep, I'll make some coffee and then wake you.'

I sat heavily on the toilet. I heard the trickle of water, and felt the intense relief of release. I began to drift into sleep, listening to the sound of my water hitting the bowl. It was a while before I realised that my bladder was empty, and the trickle hadn't stopped.

'Simi!' I called. She came bouncing out of bed and stood in the door of the bathroom before I had even opened my mouth to call her again.

'What is it? Why are you taking so long?'

'I can't seem to stop peeing,' I said, and the trickle confirmed what I was saying.

She looked at me a moment and then turned and ran for the phone, yelling, 'My god, I think your water broke!'

I looked in the pot, and there was a something pink-looking floating in the piss.

It was eight weeks too early. Sarin called us a taxi. The neighbours helped me into it. Simi was deadly calm, she had a towel ready for me to sit on, and when she had made sure I was comfortable, she instructed the taxi driver, a very decrepit man who looked extremely uncomfortable and nervous, to drive like hell to the hospital. To me she said, 'Ginny, it's too early.'

It was Monday morning in Bombay, and the traffic snarled from one end of the city to the other, barely moving, but making a noise like all the world had come to a forced halt, and was squawking and screaming to be released.

Shama maasi was there, at the entrance, with a stretcher.

'I can walk,' I said to her.

'We have to try and stop this labour,' she said. 'It's too early.'

They had me upstairs in a beautiful room with a view of the Arabian Sea, and it was August the fourteenth, and I knew there was no stopping it. Tomorrow. Independence Day. Maybe I would name her India after all.

The drip they had put in my arm to stop the contractions had no effect. I began to really feel the contractions ten minutes after they had put it in. My heart was racing, and Simi was beginning to get nervous. She called Shama maasi in. She came in, took one look between my legs, and hurriedly took the IV out.

'Fully dilated,' she said, 'let's go'.

I walked into the labour room, and was helped up onto a high gurney. I found myself suddenly surrounded by a lot of faces. There was one in particular with a scar on his forehead, whose mouth I could not see because he wore a white face mask, who kept saying 'Breathe! Don't forget to breathe!' right into my ear.

The pain began to overwhelm me. It was shocking in its intensity, and I began to laugh.

Simi, standing right next to me, smiled and said, 'Hurts?'

'Yes, yes, yes, it hurts, and . . .'

They all waited for my next words, but I had none. I had an urge to squeeze and push and blow my insides out of me with all the strength in me, and I did just that, still laughing hysterically. I was truly stunned by the intensity and quality of the pain. It was brutal and exquisite at the same time, extreme arousal with a very rough lover. And then there was a feeling of emptiness, and I heard my own long, hoarse groan, 'Fuck, fuck, fuck, fuck, shut up all of you, I'm breathing, I'm done here . . .'

There was a narrow slice of silence before I heard the smallest mewl like a little lost cat. And Simi saying to me, quietly, in my ear, 'Ginny, Ginny, it's a little girl with a penis!' And then we both started laughing.

They took away my little boy after just a moment to kiss and touch, he was as tiny as a baby kitten, but he was perfect.

And then Simi watched as an intern stitched up the gash they had made between my legs from hole to hole to ease the way for the soft skull, I had not even noticed a scalpel on my flesh, so consuming was the other pain, and I instructed him to make sure he kept it all pretty down there. Simi and I were still giggly and hysterical, like we had run a marathon together. When they wheeled me back into my room there was a tray full of food waiting there, chicken soup, mutton biryani, hot chapattis and green beans, an enormous slice of chocolate cake. We ate every scrap together. When we were done, a man in a hospital gown walked in, and I recognised him as the breathe-man from the scar on his forehead.

'So, how is the new mother doing?' he said, a bit stiffly.

'Oh, I'm fine, and I want to say I am very sorry for having yelled at you, was I very rude?'

He smiled a more real-looking smile and said, 'You abused me, yes.'

'Oh, did I tell you to fuck off? I am sorry, I was lost in the moment. I'm so glad you didn't fuck off, and I am glad you are back now, so I can say I'm sorry.'

This time his smile was genuine and heartfelt. 'It's okay, Virginia. I must say, a lot of women have yelled at me, but none ever told me to fuck off, and for sure, none in all my years of medical practice began to laugh at the high end of labour.'

Simi smiled. 'My sister laughs at all the wrong times,' she said to him.

'Anyway, I came to tell you that your little boy is very little, he weighed in at just under three pounds, which is to be expected for someone who came into the world so early, but I also wanted to let you know that I have looked at him up and down, and he is just perfect. His lungs are fine, Dr

Shama was right to give you those steroid shots last week, that's what helped him be ready to breathe, and he doesn't even have any jaundice, which may develop later, but right now, nothing. When you feel like it, you can go visit him in the neo-natal ward, just ask the nurse to take you. And start to feed him as soon as you can.'

The intense relief was unexpected. I hadn't consciously thought there would be anything wrong with my baby, but then—I must have been worried somewhere inside. We went at once to see him.

The immigration lines were short at Atlanta airport, and the huge dark man looking over my papers was smiling and seemed just so happy to see me. The flight had left me looking dishevelled and dry, my hair was a single matted lump. I tried in the airplane toilet to run my hands through it, and then pat it down with a little water, to little effect. But this man treated me as if I was divine. He stamped my passport, he stapled a little white paper to it, said, 'Welcome to America,' and showed me his mouthful of perfect white teeth, like a toothpaste commercial. There was nothing fake about his welcome either. The flight to Tallahassee was so short as to make me wonder if we were landing in the wrong place. All I could see below was green. An endless sea of green. There was no city, no buildings were visible from the direction we were coming in, and I was filled with a sense of anticipation, and want, and dread. Should I have made a phone call, or sent a letter, or at least made sure that this man that I was making this trip for was actually where I thought he was, or that he was not newly in love and in bed, and wanted no interruption from a woman whose life he had once saved, but whom he did not remember at all?

There were no taxis at the airport, and I could not rent a car because I could not drive. All the whining in the world had not convinced Kamal that I should learn to drive, it was one of the ways, I suppose, he kept me from straying too far. Which was in a way ridiculous, because there was so much local public transport in Bombay, and, I strayed much farther by plane, to Sri Lanka, to Japan, and finally, out of his life. I wandered around feeling lost for a while. I went into the bathrooms and tried to look better by washing my face and putting on some mascara. I put on some perfume, but when I smelled my armpits, I knew it had not helped at all. I came out of the bathrooms and looked around. The whole world had changed while I was looking at myself in a mirror. It was raining, and dark. Massive sheets of lightning filled the air, and thunder rocked the building. I went outside with my bag to stand under the enormous concrete awning. The lightning made the hair on my neck stand up, and it terrified me. A slight red-haired man standing next to me wearing a blue shirt with a roman collar said, 'That's how it is in Tallahassee. We're in the swamp now.' He had a fine jawline, and twinkling eyes, and I began to talk to him like it was the most natural thing in the world.

'It's my first time here,' I said.

'Oh, really? Where are you from?'

'Bombay,' I said, and, taking the opportunity to find some help, asked him if he knew how I could get some transport.

'Where are you headed?' he asked.

I showed him the paper with the address on it.

'Oh, how excellent! That's a ways out, but not far from where I live. My student is coming to fetch me, we'll give you a ride. Are you visiting a friend?'

I didn't quite know what to say. If I said yes, then this friend should be here to pick me up. But he didn't know I was here to see him. He perhaps did not know I was even in the world anymore. I decided I would tell it as it was.

'I'm visiting a friend, but he doesn't know it,' I said, smiling. I held out my hand to him. 'I'm Ginny.'

'Joseph,' he said, and his hand was warm and firm.

We stood there almost an hour talking. By the time his student drove up and jumped out of his car apologising profusely, Joseph and I knew everything about each other. Or, he knew everything about me. I only knew he taught at the university, and that he was recovering from some deep heartbreak which hadn't dimmed his faith in people at all, which hadn't even stopped him from befriending a stranger fresh off a plane from a strange land, and listening with patience and almost love, while she unburdened her heart to him. His student, whose name I never caught, drove us through the city of Tallahassee to my destination. On the way, he pointed out the huge university football stadium, the Spanish moss on the trees that he told me were live oaks, a restaurant he said we should eat at the next day. I could see the obvious affection and respect his student had for him. He also reacted with very little surprise at the way Joseph had not just given me a ride, but taken me under his wings. Apparently the student himself lived under those same wings, and welcomed me into what I decided must be an ample space. As we got close to the address, Joseph reached out and put his hand on mine.

'I know we have just met, Ginny, but I know and you know that we will be friends. So if it doesn't work out with your friend, just call me, and I will come by and pick you up. I live close to here, and you can stay with me while you are here, I have a room for you, and my cat and I will be happy to have you.'

His friend laughed and said, 'He is serious, you know, I stayed with him three months before I found my own room, and his instincts about friends are balls-on accurate, if you will excuse the expression. He's not so good at picking his lovers, though.'

So there I was, standing in front of a house with a red door. Joseph and his student waited in the car. They insisted that they stay until I knew at least if anyone was home. I left my bag in the trunk. I stood at the door a long time before I finally rang the doorbell.

How long, after all, could I live life only thinking about the possibilities? Some of them have to come to fruition, some of them have to be real, to be eaten, to be consumed, and all will turn into excrement. Friendships, partnerships, parenthood and childhood. The difficult ones to accept are the ones that remain possibilities. The ones that you dream of, see not vague possibilities, but real ones: of love, of specific, exquisite details, of faces close to you, of eye colour and the smell of morning breath, the feel and colour of hair and eyelashes, the shine of tears, the exhalation of thrust and orgasm, the shared cup of coffee, the words, those all-important words of love and despair, truths that become lies because they are not lived, because they are not consummated. Truths of love and longing that become fiction because they are not performed.

I remember Ethan Hawke in *Gattaca*: He's a janitor cleaning an empty office. He sits down at one of the rows of computer terminals, he wants to feel like one of the people that work there in the day. He pretends to type. He turns and smiles at the person not sitting beside him. To me, this completes the fantasy. It seems to me a natural gesture, something he did while in the moment. One of those Ethan Hawke, actor, might have looked at later and thought, 'Damn, that was good.' One of those moments, words, actions you would not want cut out of the final work. Sometimes thoughts and words come together just so, and at that moment you know it's original, special, perfect. You will find out later, or someone will point out to you that it has been done, said, written before. And probably better than you did it. But that moment when you believe it is perfect—that's what I live for, and that, I think, is what we all do what we do for. To be perfect, for once, in the moment. Not in retrospect, like everything else. Like orgasms. Perfect right there, and all you remember later is the memory of a memory. And keep going back to find it. And it is perfect every single time.

And yet, at that moment of orgasm, I don't know who I am, what I was, where I am, or really with whom even. I deconstruct. I separate into molecules. It is a moment of loss so complete and so fine, a moment when I really cease to exist. It seems to me an opportunity, then, to reconstruct myself as—anything at all. Anything other than what I am, with all my imperfections, delusions, inadequacies. It is an opportunity to come back from that moment as anyone I choose—someone who can swim, drive, cook, ride a bike, who is thin and smart and beloved. But, every opportunity I had, and they are few and far between, I come back from that most perfect of moments exactly who I was before. Maybe in this moment of deconstruction, I didn't need an orgasm. Maybe I would be someone else, that me that I wanted to be, as soon as that door opened.

The door opened, and there he was, shiny and long-limbed, and his face, I loved it as I had the first time I saw it. The hair was shorter, he had stubble on his cheeks and chin that I had not seen before. I had stopped breathing, so there was no air in me when he lifted me off the ground in a hug that should have squeezed all the air out of me. It was a long time before he put me down again, but it wasn't long enough for me. I could have stayed there forever, I had nowhere else I had to be, and nowhere else I would rather have been. But he did put me down, and said, 'Ginny, my god, what are you doing here?'

I hadn't thought about how I would answer that question, so I said, simply, 'I came to see you.'

Then he put his huge hand on my face and kissed me, bending all the way down.

'Still fucking short!' he said, and we both laughed.

I remembered Joseph in the car at the same time he saw them.

'Friends of yours? Are you with them? Are they with you? Will you come in? Should I invite them in? Does all this matter at all, Ginny?'

We walked over to the car and made introductions. There was no awkwardness at all, thanks to Joseph, who said, 'Well? Will you keep her, or shall I take her?'

'I'll keep her,' he said, and took my bag from the trunk. We promised to meet up the next day, either at Joseph's place or his.

There was no woman in his life, and there was no other reason for me not to be there. I had acted on some feeling, some knowledge, some memory of something I had seen in his eyes, and something I had felt in my being. I knew there was something there for him and me. It was older than I, and it was older than us, the two of us. And I had let it take me from my safe life, from my city, from my friends, from my family, however dysfunctional, from my country, to this place, a mysterious swamp, to run this thing into the ground. To know, once and for all, who and what he and I were together, or apart. The weeks I was with him were of course magical, in the way new loves are. But I had never known a love, new or otherwise. All I knew, as Gabriel had told me, were ways to find a reflection of myself that I could live with. And sometimes the only way had been physical. I offered my cunt and all its accoutrements—my brain, my apartment, my cooking skills—to all who happened to glance at me, and hoped that what I offered was enough to make them love me. This was something else. I had seen recognition in this man's eyes for a moment, and I wanted to see if he had really seen me, and if he would tell me who I was.

I never wanted to turn the lights off, my desire to look into this man's eyes, for once, transcended my perceived, pervasive inadequacies. I wanted to see the dilation of his pupils, the breaths he drew into his perfect mouth, the fingers he put in my mouth, his glorious smile. I wanted to be with him, I felt no need to pretend I was anything other than what I was, I felt no need for him to be anyone but who he was. There was no guilt, no lie, no sadness. Every question was answered, every want fulfilled, every thought expressed. This was not sex. This was us talking to each other in a language we both understood every word of, that we knew the entire vocabulary of. There was no word for pain in it, only pleasure. Only sweetness.

'Hansi, come with me, I'll play Monopoly with you,' Simi said, and took him by the hand to the other room. There were so many people that had come to pay their respects, and though he understood that his Ami would not come back, he was confused by the dark heaviness in the house. Simi and I had sat outside the crematorium when they burned our mother's body, we had not wanted to watch when they put her fragile figure into the flames. We sat a while, and then smoke began to billow from the chimney. We held each other close. 'There she goes,' I said to my little sister, too young to lose a mother, and one she had never really had. She wanted to leave immediately and not wait for all the people to come out. She wanted to go back to the apartment and be with Hansi. I did too.

At nine, he looked only slightly Indian, with his odd navy blue eyes and shiny skin. He had his father's mouth, with the deep cleft below the nose, and would probably have his height too. He was already taller than most kids in his class. Everyone in Bombay had been stunned to see him again, and made much of him. He was undeniably pretty, and exotic to them all, and articulate, and full of stories of his life in Tallahassee. He talked about his kayaking trips, alligators, his uncle Joe, and more about his uncle Joe. Someone asked him about his daddy, and he said, 'Oh, I have Ginny and Simi and uncle Joe, who needs a dad?'

I knew it was time to take us home. Ami was gone, cutting the last threads that bound me to this country. I knew, finally, that it was not the country that was my home, it was she. It was she that I had tried to go to, tried to find shelter, comfort, safety in. And now she was gone, this was no longer home. I could take her with me now, wherever I went, and she would be with me, wherever I was, and I could make her, now, whatever I wanted. My goddess, my idol, my mentor. She was not here anymore, to taint my images with reality.

I had spent a little time with Varun. When I saw him at the airport in Korea, he seemed broken, and afraid, and smaller than I had ever seen him. It had shocked me. He knew he was about to lose the person in the world most precious to him, and all he could say to me was, 'I'm so sorry.' I understood. I understood that there was not a thing he could have done to change the course of events, after they had been set in motion. And neither he nor I knew when that was. All we knew was, here we were, at the end of that particular road. When he walked into the house after the cremation, long after Simi and I came home, he seemed to walk a little taller than we had seen him do in the months before. He must have had to meet every one of those many people who had gathered there, he must have had to keep his composure, calm his spirit, even comfort some of those who must have cried, grieving for their own loss. He came in and picked up Hansi and hugged him for a long time. And when he put him down his eyes shone, but he smiled at us.

'Let's have a drink to celebrate your mother,' he said. Simi and I looked at each other, and then all of us burst out laughing at the absurdity of it. But we had a drink to our mother, and after Hansi had gone to sleep we had a few more, and we talked, and we cried, and we let her go again, and we knew that we would be letting her go, together and alone the rest of our lives, and we would be learning about her the rest of our lives. Varun promised he would come to Tallahassee as soon as his current assignment was finished. He told us how hard it would be to go back to that empty house, the house where he had last seen his wife unconscious on the floor in a pool of her own bloody vomit.

'All we have now is each other,' he said. I thought, all he had now was us. The rest of us had always had each other.

His own daughter Simi, and, his other daughter and his grandchild, gifts from his beloved wife. Everything else did not matter anymore. And, I thought, it was surely time to go home.

Tallahassee was in hurricane season when I got back. Azaleas threatened my sanity with their blousy pink blooms. Pollen was everywhere, and I knew I would be sneezing and itchy in a day or two. Simi came with me, she had taken time off her classes to be with her dying mother, and the three months they had given her were not quite over yet. Home was heaven. I noticed mould on Bijou's *Blue*, which hung in the foyer. The paintings welcomed me. Yossarian came running up the stairs to rub against our legs. He looked thinner than he had been when I last saw him, he had shed his winter fat and fur. Joe clucked over us all like a mother hen, especially his precious Hansi, checking him to see that every hair was still unharmed. When everyone was showered and fed and Hansi was finally in his bed, we sat on the porch to talk and smoke and unwind.

'She's really gone now, Simi,' I said.

'Yes,' Simi said, and her eyes were bright with tears. Joe came out with wine and glasses for us, and set them down and went to hug her. I watched them, two of the three people I loved most in the world, and behind them a pulse of fireflies in the swamp gloom. I thought about the father of my son. It had been a strange long trip getting where we were, and we were a perfect family without him. Joe, with his infinite patience and wisdom and gentleness, Simi, not always with us, but there often enough that Hansi knew she was his family, and the cat and I, skulking around, always looking for someone to stroke us. I thought about my son's father often these last few days, about our short time together, about the year in Bombay during the pregnancy when I wondered whether to tell him he had a son, about the last eight years in Tallahassee with Joe, but without him. He had gone back home before I came back to live there with my son. I had found the house empty, and rented it. Though I knew he knew I was there, neither he nor I ever tried to find each other again. It was what it was, our love. We were in the world.

I had thought about him while washing dishes that night. I felt the heat coming off the stack of plates I had just rinsed, and I put my cheek against them. They were warm and smooth and hard, a ceramic fabric. And I thought how he would have said to me now, 'Hey, hey, you feel poor today? Come here, I'll kiss your poor.' It won't go away, the poor, but thus acknowledged, maybe it would settle down in the cushion of love, and curl up, and sleep. And leave me alone for a while.

Where is that voice, and where has it been all my life? Having heard it, I can't any more lift myself. Having been touched, I can't tell myself anymore that I can do without it. I am in a prison of language, of words. There are things I feel that are deeper and stronger and older than me. I love language above most things, if not people. But I do see its limits, and the limits it places upon me. We sometimes ignore or dismiss visceral, vital thoughts, ideas, feelings— only because they are not expressible in words. To dismiss them too long, too often, those fine and not so fine feelings, yearnings, to push them away from the reality of action, to drown them in words rather than act on them with spit and sweat, is to lose them forever. The moments of action will be gone, and the moments of talk will cover up nerves, wants, wounds, in layer upon layer of words that harden and form a kind of cement that can never be cracked open. It is a prison, yes, but one that becomes a part of you, a turtle shell, an exoskeleton, your armour against that which you want the most: Touch. Contact.

Words are lies. They are all lies.

I thought about the last time we talked, right here, in this house, when it was his, when he lived here with me. We had talked and talked. About love, and hope, and what life held for us. About diapers and college and repairs to garage doors and walking in grocery store aisles. About what I wanted, and what he did not want. 'The dirty socks on the floor can kill everything,' he said.

'But I don't care about that, if you will just get into bed with me anyway, and look into my eyes as you do.'

'It won't always be that way,' he said. 'The socks and diapers get in the way.'

I said nothing. 'See? You take that as a rejection of you. It is not. It's just the way life is. I don't want to worry about this. About your happiness.'

'But I want to worry about yours. No, I don't want to

worry about it, I just want you to be happy. And I will do what it takes to . . .'

'That is really nonsense, Ginny. We are all responsible for our own happiness, not anyone else's. I can try to make it possible to find yours. But it is not my responsibility. Neither is your unhappiness.'

I was crying by then, and I didn't know why.

He put his hand on my cheek, to calm me, perhaps. I brushed it off. He looked at the floor.

'Why won't you just take me on?' I asked him. 'Why can't you just own it? Why can't you just open your arms and your heart and tell me that you can do this—this—life with me? All of it?'

'I love you Ginny, I always have, and I always will. But you ask too much,' he said, so quietly I barely heard his words. I thought about what I had said to him, in answer to his question, asked with so much pain, so much honesty, so much anger, so much love, and most of all, it seemed to me, a demand for the truth: 'What the hell do you want?'

'I want to be with a man who will be my bra and tampon and credit card and cook and pedicurist and masseuse and driver and muse, vibrator, comb, gardener and pilot. And I will be everything for him.'

He listened, but without looking at me. When he did look up, there were tears in his eyes. They were brilliant, like sky the moment before rain. He considered me, in his calm considering way. And he held my face in his huge hands one last time, and kissed me in a final sort of way.

I had told the truth, for once.